FELICITY FOUND

A ROGUE SERIES EXTRA

LARA WARD COSIO

ROGUE PUBLICATIONS

PREFACE

rogue
pronunciation: / rōg/
noun
1. A dishonest or unprincipled man.
1.2 A person whose behavior one disapproves of but
one who is nonetheless likable or attractive
(often used as a playful term of reproof)

1

Felicity

I never in a million years imagined I'd end up here.

Here is Dublin, the city I once thought I'd left behind.

Here is an extraordinary house overlooking the Irish sea in exclusive Dalkey.

Here, at this exact moment, is bent over the kitchen sink, pulling clumps of mashed sweet potatoes out of my hair while I use one foot to keep the baby swing moving lest Ella wakes up. At the same time, I've got an eye on Romeo. He's in his high chair, a few feet away, squeezing fists full of sweet potato until the burnt-orange vegetable flesh squirts out between his fingers. Romeo squeals with delight at this bit of magic—much the same way he did when he smeared pieces of the potato in my hair moments ago as I was giving Ella an extra second of my attention.

Here is surprised by motherhood to two infants, one by birth and one by adoption, after years of living with the disappointment of "unexplained infertility."

Here is being married to one of the world's most famous rock guitarists, or as I once knew him, the boy who was my friends-with-benefits schoolmate.

Here is at my wits' end caring for these two precious babies—six-month-old Romeo and three-month-old Ella—while my husband is at the studio all hours finishing up his band's sixth album.

Here is at the crossroads of both loving and struggling with every minute of it.

I HAVE LIVED in a bubble of motherhood in these last few months, determined to experience all the good and messy moments this has to offer. That's meant that I've willingly hidden away with the babies in a cocoon of sleep deprivation, dirty nappies, rotating feedings and baths, angelic smiles and coos, and the sweetest cuddles ever created.

The isolation is self-created, because while I know I have my good friend Sophie for help and advice, I rarely bother her since she's got her hands full with her own two little ones. And my husband, Conor, is great support—when he's here. We could certainly afford to hire in help, but except for the first six weeks when we had a live-in baby nurse, I've opted to do everything on my own.

After living with the idea that I'd never be a mother, I've jumped into the deep end, and with Conor dedicated to the studio, I'm left with the babies and my thoughts. And I often think of the twists and turns my life has taken. I had such a sense of purpose as a girl. And that purpose was primarily to escape the oppressive pressure my mother put on me to be her emotional support as she bounced from one bad relationship to the next. As much as I loved her, I knew early on that the only way to escape that dynamic was to get far away.

I set my sights on Canada. I still remember the amusement in Conor's eyes when I told him my plan to attend university there. Besides being my occasional lover, he was my good friend, the one who knew all about my father being a non-presence, and my mother being too much of a presence. I thought he'd understand why I wanted to get away. Instead, he used my logic against me.

"You're running away, is that it?" he asked, eyebrows raised.

Though only fifteen, Conor Quinn was a looker. With black hair, bright blue eyes, and high cheekbones, he was destined to be handsome. Even before he really grew into those features, he was the one all the girls chased. On top of all that, he had an easy confidence about him that was magnetic. But he also had the most amazing ability to give me his focus when we were together. He could have been out with any number of girls, but for whatever reason, he was content to spend time with me —even if it involved some teasing, like with my big plan to leave.

"It's not running away, CQ. It's striking out on my own," I had replied with the confidence of youth.

"You could strike out here, you know? Get a flat, do your own thing."

"I'd still be at *her* beck and call, then," I moaned.

"Not if you get busy with having your own life."

"You don't know what it's like. Your parents are perfect."

Though Conor rolled his eyes at that, it was true. It's still true today. His parents are the loveliest couple. They had Conor late in life. Because they were older and only had one child, they were especially conscious of creating a stable and nourishing environment for Conor. The only pressure he ever felt was to pursue his exceptional abilities with classical music. When he turned away from that in favor of rock music, his mother was disappointed but it was his father who purchased his first guitar. His mother soon came around. Conor's always had their support. It was the right balance between parents and a child. They took care of him. Unlike my situation. I felt like the caretaker of my mother—if only her emotions—at too young an age.

"I just don't think the answer is to leave," Conor had told me. "I mean, won't you just be pretending to have left all your Ma's stuff behind, but really knowing it's all here just waiting on you?"

That bit of wisdom was not what I wanted to hear. I should have known better than to confide in Conor. See, even though he was gorgeous, he was also brilliant. Like, truly the cleverest boy I've ever known. He wasn't going to grant me my denial.

"Listen, I wasn't looking for an argument. I'm just telling you how it is," I said.

Again, he gave me the amused eyes. But, thankfully, he let it go. After that, he did me the favor of just listening and not dissecting as I made my complaints about my Ma and affirmed my plans to escape. He was a good friend in that way.

I'm lost in these memories and only pulled away by Romeo's squeals. They have a tenor different to the ones he made when playing with his food. These squeals are reserved for only one person —his daddy.

Conor is home unexpectedly. I usually make an effort to clean myself up a bit for him when I know he's coming, especially given the fact that when he comes home from the studio he's almost always ready to reconnect in an intimate way. It's only been a few weeks since I've been cleared to have sex again and Conor has been trying to make up for lost time ever since.

But I'm certain he'll have no interest in that at this moment. Half my head is wet from trying to get the sweet potatoes out, though I still feel bits here and there. My stretched out blue and white striped tee shirt is stained with breast milk. I didn't bother putting on trousers today, too busy taking care of the babies, and my burgundy cotton boy-short-style knickers are not remotely sexy.

By contrast, Conor is perfectly put together, wearing jeans with a fitted gray button-up shirt over a white tee shirt. His brown belt is secured low around his hips and matches his weathered lace-up boots. The silver pocket chain he's worn for years is his version of jewelry, and the only piece he wears besides his wedding ring. Though I love when he's got some scruff, he's clean-shaven. He's tall, with lean muscles, and I swear he got into even better shape when I was pregnant.

"There's my big man," he says. To Romeo, of course. He always greets the kids before me. I hate that it triggers a pang of jealousy in me. It must be that sense that I'm no longer his only priority. But still, I know it's not right. Sometimes, the feeling is so strong that I have to leave the room to get myself in order. I tell myself that he's doing the exact right thing, that I should, in fact, find it incredibly sexy because he is a wonderful father. I tell myself that it's only my out-of-control hormones that keep me from responding that way, and that I'll soon be over this irrational reaction.

I watch as he gives his son a few minutes of adoration before he then checks on Ella. His daughter is still sleeping, but that doesn't stop him from stroking the baby's cheek. Finally, he faces me, gives me a once over, and smiles his *Conor smile*. Like the pocket chain, the smile is one of his signatures. Only, this one has the power to make women melt. It's always worked on me. Except that at this moment, I'm too aware of how awful I look to fall for it.

He reaches out and touches my wet hair, retrieving a glob of orange sweet potato.

"You are a mess," he says, still smiling.

"Yes, I know that."

"Rough day with these two?"

"Normal day." I start to move away. I have things to do. I need to clean up Romeo's high chair, the floor under it, and get him into a bath. I need to prepare for Ella waking. She'll want her own feeding —after a diaper change. I also need to find the time to look over my emails because though I'm technically still employed as Rogue's Media Manager, I've done a piss poor job of it in these last few months. With the band almost done with the new album, I'll need to find a way to get some balance between family and work.

"I know that look," Conor says.

I stop and turn back to him. "What?"

He flicks the bit of food into the sink. "That little crinkle between your eyes. That's the look you get when you're worrying over a thousand things at once."

"As it happens, I do have a lot to sort out."

Again, I start to move away, but he grabs me around the waist and pulls me to him. Though I've lost a lot of the baby weight, mostly with the help of breastfeeding, I am still heavier than I'd like. Conor has never let that change the way he touches me, which is not only sweet but does wonders to make me forget about all the beautiful women with perfect bodies who throw themselves at him on a nearly constant basis. Such is the cost of being married to a rockstar. Though, he's not just your average grungy rockstar. He's currently being featured in an American magazine as "Sexiest Man Alive."

I've long agreed with that designation. The problem is, so has he. Yes, he's ridiculously handsome, but he also knows as much and doesn't bother to hide the fact that he enjoys the effect he has on women—and plenty of men.

He's using all his considerable charms at the moment by, not just holding me to him, but by sliding one hand down my back and letting his fingers trail over the generous curve of my backside. I should expect him to grab a handful next, but I know he won't. Not yet. This teasing technique is deliberate. He likes to build up the anticipation, wanting me to reach a degree of neediness before he will move to the next level. This technique always works on me.

At least it did. I lost my sex drive not long after I got pregnant, not long after our impromptu wedding. I thought I'd feel more myself after the morning sickness subsided, but it hung on well into my third trimester. By then, I was so fatigued and swollen that the very idea of sex, even with the sexiest man alive, held no appeal. Conor was patient and understanding. But I know it wasn't easy for him, especially once I had Ella and was cleared to be intimate and still my desire did not return.

The thing is, I know how his touch *should* be making me feel. I remember vividly how the slightest graze of his hand or a wayward glance would make me involuntarily bite my lip in anticipation that he'd do something more to titillate me. I should be silently urging him to do more than lightly trace the shape of my arse. I should adore a commanding squeeze or even a light spanking at the moment.

But I don't. I don't feel anything.

Dropping his voice an octave, he says, "How about I sort *you* out?"

"But I'm such a mess," I protest, hoping I won't have to resist him too hard before he understands—once again—that I can't find the desire.

"A *hot* mess."

He's giving me that *Conor smile* again. The one that is everything him: sexy, confident, and in control. It's the smile that has the power to seduce women in an instant. I used to be one of them.

When he covers my mouth with his, drawing me into a kiss, I think he hasn't really registered just how grubby I am.

"I need a shower, sweetheart," I say, breaking away. "Maybe you can watch the kids while I clean up?"

After a moment of consideration, he says, "I have a better idea. Let's get Romeo set up in that jumpy thing so I can get you clean and dirty all at once in the shower."

I've put him off so many times that I know I need to find a way to get back to the intimacy we once enjoyed so effortlessly. I conjure up a vision of us naked and wet, his hands cupping my still larger than normal breasts as he presses up against me, and it's all I need to nod my agreement. He is extremely talented in a lot of ways, one of those being this kind of thing where he reminds me that he still desires me, that I am still a woman and not only a mother.

Then again, he's always been good at separating things— including once we went from being pals to being friends with benefits when we were in school. Though I tried to project indifference about it all, it wasn't easy to resist falling for him.

2

Felicity

I still remember the shock on my friend Sophie's face when I told her Conor and I had this arrangement. She had made a splash showing up to school that year as a sixteen-year-old golden girl from America. We got on like a house on fire right away. There was a kind of vulnerability she projected that made me want to protect her. Who knows, maybe it was something similar to the way I cared for my mother? In any case, she was a great mate right away, even though we had very little in common.

I had already begun my thing with Conor by then and it seemed normal, but in telling Sophie about it, I realized it wasn't what a lot of other girls would do. Sophie looked at me with something like pity, thinking I was doing this at Conor's behest and settling for less than I should. But it was my plan all along. I had it firmly stuck in my mind that even if I was attracted to Conor, he and I could have no future. Not with me planning on going to Canada and him planning on being a rockstar. I was very pragmatic that way—likely in reaction against my mother's fanciful thinking that the *next* fella she met would finally be her Prince Charming. That, combined with the sporadic presence of my own father, led me to be much more protec-

9

tive of my heart than I should have been at that age. Conor tells me I have an old soul, as if it's this grand thing to admire but I've come to see that it was all the result of fighting to protect myself against the kind of disappointment that my father invariably left me with and my mother modeled after each man left her. Not exactly as romantic as Conor would like to see it.

Still, he never made me feel that disappointment—jealousy, maybe, but not disappointment. I had suggested our arrangement, so how could I be disappointed if he stuck to it? He'd go seamlessly from tenderly holding me in his arms in his bedroom, to roughly nudging me to get me in on a joke when we were with our group of friends. His ability to draw a distinct line between our intimate times and our friendship could be jarring. But the worst of it was when I saw how he fancied Sophie.

It was clear as day he was interested in her. It was also clear that Gavin wasn't going to let the fact that he had a girlfriend at the time stop him from laying his claim on Sophie. I was witness to this little bit of a mating ritual when Conor attempted to charm the newly arrived Sophie with promises of showing her around as a personal tour guide. My heart sank as I watched this interaction—not just because I felt discarded, but because I was sure Sophie would fall for him. He was the one all the girls wanted, after all.

Turned out she had already set her sights on Gavin, though. And so, I breathed a little easier. But it was a wakeup call. It made me realize I had to steel myself harder against developing feelings for Conor. Either that or stop sleeping with him.

I wasn't prepared to do that, though, even if it meant I was opening myself up to possible heartache.

Luckily, there was only one other time I felt that pang of jealousy. It was Sophie, then, too.

We were all at a club, having one-by-one climbed in through the toilets window—the only access we had since we were underage. Once inside, it was so crowded that most of us lost track of each other. But Conor grabbed my hand to keep me from being swallowed up by the masses of bodies writhing to the techno beat. It felt good to have the extra bit of connection. He was usually so disciplined that he never touched me with any kind of intimacy if we weren't in his bedroom. But this was a sweet gesture, not just him being protective, because when we were in a safe spot together, free from any worry of being split up, he kept holding my hand.

It was only when Sophie found us a minute later that he let go of me. Soon, Gavin showed up with four pints in his fists. God only knows how he made that happen, but we were all only too happy to indulge. We spent the next half hour letting the music wash over us, not bothering to try to talk. Gavin came and went as he saw people he knew. The drink went to my head, and even more so to Sophie's. I could tell by the way she wavered on her feet and tried to cover it up as a dance move. I saw Conor approach her. He bent at the knees to get eye contact with her and asked her something. She responded with a dizzy smile and by throwing her arm around his neck.

I think it was more to steady herself, but given what happened between them years later, who knows? She could have been attracted to Conor even then and just buried it until it could no longer stay that way.

What I do know is that I was once again relieved when Gavin swooped in to pull Conor away from Sophie just as it looked like he was ready to lean in to kiss her. That was the last time I saw them in a situation like that in our year at school together. Maybe me confessing to Sophie about my arrangement with Conor helped to put an end such moments. At the time, I hadn't consciously thought how this might be a strategic way to keep them apart. But now I can see that I was doing my own bit of laying a claim. That was about the same time that she and Gavin became an official couple, anyway. Conor completely backed off in deference to his friend.

Those episodes likely account for how quickly I was able to guess years later that Conor had had an affair with Sophie. I could spot it clear as day. He hadn't just slept with his best friend's wife—he had fallen irretrievably in love.

So much time had passed when I learned this, though, that the same feelings of jealousy and insecurity hadn't occurred to me. I was more interested in being the one to display the discipline of separating feelings from friendship. And it worked. For a while.

Now, we've come full circle and I'm with Conor again. Though, I don't know if he ever imagined us in this situation.

Our shower starts the way I had envisioned, us naked with all four showerheads pouring down on us as he holds my body against his, his mouth taking mine greedily. Even now, when I'm mostly numb, his kisses are one of my favorite things in the world. But instead of making me melt like they usually do, his kisses and the way he holds me as if he's trying to find refuge in me, surprises me. There's no passion in his kisses, just need.

It's not like him. Most of the time, he makes love to me with the kind of toe-curling, high-heat that's all about satisfying the deep ache he's so good at generating. Other times, it's less personal, more of a release that's built up when we've been separated for a while. That's what I expected it might be today since we haven't spent a lot of meaningful time together with him in the studio so often. Instead, his hands and body seem to be seeking some kind of solace in our physical connection. I feel it in the way he clings to me, cradling me in his arms as if in doing so he will somehow feel the security of that embrace in return.

I pull away and try to look into his eyes, but he goes in for another kiss instead.

"Wait," I say, breaking away. "What is going on? What's wrong?"

"What do you mean? Nothing. I thought we—you're not into this, are you?"

The word he could have added—*again*—goes unsaid. And I don't explain that it's *his* mood this time that has put me off.

Instead, we shower together in an almost perfunctory way. I step out before him, thinking he might take care of himself if I give him the chance, but he shuts off the water only a couple of minutes later.

Like most men, he isn't big on discussing his feelings. But when he goes straight from the shower to getting dressed while I sit on the side of the bed in a robe, I can't stop from trying again.

"What is it, sweetheart?" I ask softly.

"Hmm?" he murmurs, not looking at me as he buttons his shirt.

I hesitate, not sure I really want to press him for answers on why we just gave up on having sex. I decide to pursue a different line of questioning. "It's very nice to have you pop round during the day, but why did you?"

Glancing at me, he shrugs noncommittally.

"What have you been recording today?"

That gets a reaction out of him. He meets my eyes and stays fixed there for several long seconds. There's a mixture of surprise and wariness in his gaze. Even now, after we've been together for almost three years, he's still thrown when I can decipher the reason behind his moods. He spent so many years nurturing his love-from-a-distance for Sophie that he never experienced the intimacy of a real relationship. It's still dawning on him that that's what we've had almost from the minute we rekindled our friendship upon my return to Dublin to care for my dying mother.

"'The Point of No Return,'" he says at length.

Ah. Now it all makes sense. That song is about his and Gavin's good friend Christian Hale. It's about the heartbreak and anger of Christian having committed suicide last year. Now I understand what it was Conor was seeking with this unexpected visit.

"Come here," I tell him and extend my hand.

Hesitating for just a moment, he soon joins me, sitting by my side on the bed. When I wrap my arm around his and rest my head on his shoulder, I feel him waver. It's barely perceptible and he rights himself quickly. He's always been the strong one, the one in control. He's never fallen to pieces like Gavin has. It would be inconceivable to him to do so. But in that brief flash of emotion just now, I realize he hasn't truly grieved for Christian. Everyone was so concerned with Gavin's response that it left little room for anyone else to express their own pain. The song Gavin and Conor wrote for Christian is a step in that direction, but with Gavin wailing out the vocals, he gets all the catharsis from it.

"You know, I still get these pangs," I say. "It's moments where I'm going along like normal and then suddenly it hits me that my Ma is gone. Even now, though it's been a few years."

Conor pulls away from me to meet my eyes. He's not always the most emotionally intelligent man, but he's a smart man. I can see he knows why I've brought this up. But yet, when he speaks, he chooses to deflect from my point.

"Especially so now, I'd suppose," he says, nodding to Ella. She's stirring in her swing, sleepily opening and closing her eyes. Romeo is busy in his exersaucer, pulling on tabs and pushing buttons for the reward of the click and bell noises.

"Conor, you can lean on me. I *want* you to lean on me."

"I don't need—" He stops abruptly as Ella cries out. She's wide awake now and has heard her father's voice. She can't ever get enough of him. I was never a daddy's girl, but it's already clear at this tender age that Ella is one through and through.

Standing, he goes to her and pulls her free from the loose restraints of the swing and into his arms.

"There's my girl," he coos.

I watch as he lavishes his attention on our daughter, wondering whether I should pursue my entreaty for him to open up to me.

In the end, he makes my decision by handing Ella off to me with apologies for having to return to the studio.

"Do you think you'll be late?" I ask.

"Yeah, I think so. We need to push through on this one. No more delays."

He's talking about the song "The Point of No Return." The song that sent him home from the studio in search of some kind of comfort. I feel like I've failed him in that regard.

"I'll wait up for you."

When he smiles, it's the smile that makes you feel every heartbeat in your chest. He's done allowing me to see any of his sadness over Christian.

"You'll be fast asleep when I get home and we both know it," he says. He leans down and kisses me on the forehead. "And that's okay, honey."

"Wake me, then."

"It's fine," he says dismissively.

He's gone in a flash after that and I've got Ella leaning into me, looking to nurse.

3

_____

Felicity

Two hours later, I've got some semblance of calm. I've fed Ella, cleaned up the kitchen, bathed Romeo and gotten him down for a nap. I skip eating lunch. I'm rarely hungry, though I do try to keep hydrated if only to ensure that I can keep nursing. I've just sat down in the living area with my laptop when the doorbell sounds. Ella is occupying herself nearby, lying on her music-themed play mat and gazing up at the black and white piano keys that will make a sound when she's old enough to stretch up and reach them.

The ultra-modern home Conor purchased and furnished in his preferred minimalist style has been overrun by baby things. He cringed when I started bringing them in before the babies were here, but quickly accepted the new norm. Having two infants under the age of six months, there was no choice but to give in. Life is no longer about us. I wonder sometimes if he regrets how forcefully we jumped into the married-with-kids thing.

The doorbell rings again, forcing me from my thoughts. I've found that I tend to do that quite often—get lost in my thoughts. The time will slide by in a blur and I'll have nothing to show for it. Just like now, when I've opened my laptop but not even gotten as far as logging on.

Standing, I smooth down my clothes—comfortable Lucy brand trousers and a fresh top—and head to the door. I assume it's the grocery delivery service. Even though I want to be the mother that does it all, I won't reject these kinds of conveniences.

But when I open the door, I'm surprised to find Sophie there along with her little ones, Daisy and Hale. Daisy is two years old, the image of her mother, and holds a stuffed pink bear in her hands. Sophie is holding Hale in his car seat. He's close in age to Ella, having been born just one month before her.

Sophie is the kind of woman you want to hate because she's so perfect—a literal supermodel whose body has bounced back after two children—but you just can't. She's sweet and caring and genuine. Though it may seem weird to some given her history with my husband, we are good friends. That's not to say it was always easy, but we've put the past behind us.

"We were just at the Farmers Market," Sophie says cheerily, "and thought we'd stop by on our way home to share some of our goodies."

Her hazel eyes are bright, her skin is clear, and her long blond hair is clean and subtly styled. She looks well rested but I know that's not the case because we texted each other in the middle of the night while each of us was up with the babies. Still, she somehow manages to look amazing.

"Is it Farmers Market day?" I ask with distraction, watching as she ushers Daisy inside the house familiarly. I realize I have no idea what day of the week it is and vow—once again—to get my act together.

Following them into the living area, I see Daisy has joined her cousin on the play mat. They're not cousins by blood, of course, but that's how everyone refers to them. Conor and Gavin might as well be brothers, anyway. Sophie's sitting on the sofa, leaning over the car seat as she loosens Hale's straps, careful not to wake him.

"Yes, it's Thursday," Sophie replies. She pulls a container of freshly squeezed carrot juice and some sort of granola bar crumble from her tote bag. "Here, have some of this. This will give you a natural boost."

Eyeing the unappetizing orange liquid, I say, "I'll be just like the energizer bunny after this, will I?"

Sophie laughs. "Just try it. I've never steered you wrong, have I?"

She's right about that. Sophie has been a huge help to me in making the adjustment to motherhood. And even before then, she was the one who encouraged me to give Conor a real chance. She's even been my go-to stylist, helping me to navigate the rockstar world I naively joined, first by working for Rogue, and then when I became part of the band's "family" by being with Conor.

I brace myself as I take a swallow of the juice but find that it goes down easy. It's surprisingly refreshing, and I drink several gulps more.

"How are you doing today?" Sophie asks. She looks me over and then glances around the house.

It's not in shambles, thankfully. And neither am I, though Sophie seems to have come with the idea that there's something to be concerned about. And then it dawns on me what inspired this impromptu visit of hers.

"Conor called you?"

She starts to shake her head but thinks better of it. "He just mentioned you might be having a rough day."

"Me? He's the one—" I stop myself before revealing Conor's struggle.

"He meant well. And you have to admit that you've had trouble . . . focusing lately."

"Of course, I have. I don't get more than two and a half hours of sleep at a stretch. I'm always exhausted. But I'm fine. This is just how it is right now. Soon enough, the little ones will fall into routines. We all will."

I know I sound defensive. Defensive and annoyed. But don't I have that right? My husband has conspired with my best friend to check up on me. He has confided in his *ex*, for want of a better term, that his wife is somehow deficient in how she is managing his children. All because I'm a little *unfocused*?

Sighing, I say, "If he wanted to help, he didn't have to send you. He could have stayed here so I could nap."

"Gavin says they're at a critical moment in the studio right now."

Not so critical that he wasn't able to come home for sex in the shower, I think but don't say. Sophie's the first one to support Gavin and the band's efforts. She's always seen and validated the art in what they do, especially in Gavin's lyrics—even when those lyrics were aimed at hurting her.

"I know," I say. "Conor says they're working on 'The Point of No Return.'"

As if he heard this, baby Hale fusses in his sleep. We both look at him. He's a sweet baby with a mellow temperament. But he was named to honor the man who had taken his own life. I wonder if Gavin sees his friend in his son, if he now thinks it was a mistake to have this constant reminder.

"Anyway, I hope you're not mad at Conor."

I look up, oddly surprised by the fact that Sophie is here. My mind has been fuzzy lately, I do have to admit that. This has all been harder than I thought it would be. I honestly love every minute of it, but at the same time, I feel like I'm teetering on the edge all too often. I think about my mother a lot, wondering what kind of grandmother she'd have made. I imagine she'd be tickled by the double-dose of grandbabies. I also miss having her to just speak with. She and I always had a good rapport, one where we were both quick to laugh. I miss her laugh.

"They'll be fine. You just go now."

I know it's Sophie who has said this, but I have no idea what she's talking about. I've gotten lost in my thoughts again. "What?"

She stands and takes my arm, pulling me up with her.

"I will watch the kids," she says and leads me toward the frosted glass staircase. "I want you to sleep as long as you need. Don't worry about a thing."

Now she's pushing my lower back, forcing me to take a step. "Wait. What about you?"

"I told you, I'll watch—"

"No," I say. I stop and catch my breath as tears fill my eyes. I'm embarrassed and frustrated to be taken care of like this. "Why is it so easy for *you*?"

Sophie smiles. It's a smile of warmth and understanding. "I'm just pushing through a bit better right now, Felicity. It's not easy for me. But if you and I take turns, we can help each other through, okay?"

It's a very generous answer because I don't believe her. For whatever reason, it *is* easier for her. She's able to handle her two small children while I struggle with physical and emotional exhaustion and self-doubt.

I'm in no shape to argue however. Instead, I wave my hand as thanks and head upstairs.

4

Felicity

As soon as I'm in bed, curled onto my side and looking out at the gorgeous sea view, I'm wide awake. My body is depleted, but my mind is wired.

I fear that I've done something to worry Conor. Is he disappointed in the kind of mother I am? He has to be, what with Sophie being, yet again, the shining example of what he could have had. She's the ideal woman—beautiful, effortlessly stylish, well-spoken (she came from money), a natural mother. She's even told me how she makes sure to keep things unexpected and sexy in the bedroom for Gavin. I can't remember the last time I made the first move with Conor.

I turn onto my other side, away from the mesmerizing green water in hope that I can still my thoughts by staring at the wall. Instead, I fixate on the large abstract piece of artwork hanging there. It's a splatter-style painting that forms a loose figure of a woman. If you study it, you can just make out that it's a woman staring out into the distance, her back to you. Conor got it when we were still doing our flirty friends dance and not yet together and told me it reminded him of me. I hadn't taken that as a compliment at the time. There's something forlorn about the woman to me. He assured me that wasn't what he saw. Instead, he said he saw a vibrancy that drew him in. In any case, I'm captivated now, looking at the way the artist was able to direct his gold, sienna, and orange splatters. There are the tiniest hints of royal blue in the mix and I find myself trying to spot them all. It's an optical trick, compelling you to examine the piece. This is the thing that drew Conor in, I realize, not some feeling that it is reminiscent of me.

Turning on my back, I stare up at the ceiling.

Just close your eyes and sleep, I tell myself.

But it's no good. I'm unsettled, and I can't shake it.

It's this feeling of failure. I was fine until Conor came home. Sure, I was tired and a little frazzled by Romeo's one-man food fight with me. But at the time, I had laughed it off. The two of us shared this amazing moment of prolonged eye contact as we laughed over it. I felt so connected to him that it seemed our bond had been cemented by that silly act. I even thought at the time that I couldn't wait to tell Conor about it.

But then he came home, and he obviously needed something from me that I couldn't give him. It wasn't sex. It was some kind of relief from the burden of his grief. I failed my husband at that.

And then Sophie came swanning in with her good intentions that only made me feel like more of a failure with my kids. Why can't I shake the fatigue and just push through like she can? I love her dearly, but sometimes being the contrast to her seeming perfection is too much. I mean, really, she's watching four children under the age of three years old downstairs while I've run away to my bed?

This sense of failure feels all too familiar. It's exactly what I felt with Richard, my ex-husband. I didn't just feel it when we split, but for years before that when it was becoming increasingly clear that I was not measuring up to be the kind of wife he expected and required.

That's probably what's got me in this funk. I'm worried I'll fail as a wife to Conor like I did with Richard.

A self-pitying tear starts to escape my eye and I sit up quickly, swiping at it.

No. I won't do this. I won't sink into this self-destructive trap.

I did not fail as a wife to Richard. He's the one who changed all the rules so that in the end we weren't even playing the same game.

My mobile chimes. It's a text from Conor.

I changed my mind.

I furrow my brow at the short message. But he soon sends a rapid succession of clarifying texts.

Wait up for me.

Or wake up for me when I get home.

I want to see your beautiful face.

I want you to tell me about your day with the little ones.

I want to hear your laugh.

I want you.

And just like that, I feel a million times better. That's the thing about my husband—he knows exactly how to reach me when I need it. I know that the love we have isn't anything like what I had with my ex-husband. Conor has never made me feel like I'm not enough or that he wants me to be something else. He's always made it clear that whatever I am is exactly what he wants.

Smiling, I text him back. *I am yours, every hot mess bit of me.*

His reply is quick. *You better believe it.*

Cradling my phone to my chest like a love-struck teenage girl, I settle back into bed. Within minutes, my eyelids grow heavy and I fall into a deep sleep.

ALMOST THREE HOURS LATER, I wake with thoughts of Richard in my head. Though I feel well rested, I have a sour taste in my mouth. Stretching in bed, I realize it's not because I was thinking of the bitter end to our marriage, but the sweet beginning of our relationship. Even though I've completely moved on from him, I still have good memories and I don't quite know what to do with them. When a relationship as significant as a decade-long marriage collapses, it's tempting to view the whole thing by the negative light in which it ended. But I never did that. I always granted myself the right to remember the good times with fondness, believing it was only fair to accept that even if it all ended terribly, there had been a genuine, beautiful beginning.

That beginning took place when I was in my third year at the University of Toronto, well in toward my Management and Marketing degree. I had decided on the area of study as a purely practical matter, believing it opened up a wide range of career opportunities. I could go in any number of directions after graduation. At the same time, I was immersed in a culture that spoke French as easily as they did English and that bolstered my high school-level French to a new level. I fell in love with the French language and extended my course load so I could indulge in exploring French literature as well. I first saw Richard when he was assisting the professor in one of those classes.

When I laid eyes on him that autumn morning, I felt a rush of heat fill my body. He wasn't a stunner like Conor, but he was definitely handsome, with sandy hair and a body so fit that his clothes couldn't hide that he was some kind of athlete. It was clichéd, but I knew in that instant that I not only wanted that man, but I'd have him. That feeling was confirmed when he glanced up from the materials he was sorting through and looked directly at me. I don't know if he had already seen me and so this wasn't as fated as it felt, but it didn't matter. He didn't scan the room. He didn't look to the professor. He looked directly at me. He would later tell our friends that the smile I gave him in return was what made him instantly fall for me.

"It was a mixture of sweetness and sex. I simply *had* to know who this girl was after that. I had to know what that smile was all about," he'd say, and I'd hit him playfully for sharing something like that. But, really, I loved it. I loved that he was possessive with me.

My experience with boys before Toronto was limited to Conor. He had been good to me when it was just the two of us. But the line he was able to draw when we were with other people always reminded me of the limitations of the deal I had negotiated with him. And I was left feeling like he could take me or leave me.

The boys I dated in those first few years after moving to Toronto were immature and only out for a good time. I didn't mind that as I was busy trying to build a life for myself in a new country. I fell in with a group of Irish girls who had had similar plans of escape and we looked after each other.

That scant relationship experience, along with my own father's indifference, meant I was a sucker for Richard right from the start. Our first date lasted three days because he said he couldn't bear for it to end. He couldn't get enough of me and being wanted like that was intoxicating. My Irish girlfriends thought it was too much too soon, but I quickly left them behind when I got lost in Richard and his world. And I did get lost. The essential *me* was lost to him for so many years.

I shake my head to rid myself of these memories and jokingly make a mental note to research what "maudlin musings about your ex" indicate. I know it doesn't make any sense, but it's the best explanation I can come up with. I have no reason to revisit the past like this. Not when my present is so good.

DOWNSTAIRS, I find Sophie in the living area with the kids. She's made a picnic, of sorts, on the floor, having spread out a throw blanket to sit on. Daisy is her main co-conspirator as they snack on Cheerios and sip juice out of the mismatched bone China teacups that were my mother's. They are one of the few things of hers that I've kept. It instantly annoys me that she's used them, even though she would have no idea of my sentimental attachment to them. They sit in the glass-door cabinets with all our other cups.

Hale and Romeo (will our boys ever forgive us for those names?) are both asleep.

Ella was too, but must have sensed my presence, because she has started her usual build-up to a full-on cry. It's her hungry cry and I know it well. I can feel my milk ready itself for her.

Sophie looks up with a smile. "Did you get some rest?"

"I slept like the dead," I reply gratefully. "Thank you."

"I'm so glad to hear it."

"Be sure to let Conor know his plan worked out." There's an edge in my voice. I hadn't any intention of making a dig at her like that. It slipped from my mouth so quickly and easily that it didn't feel connected to my rational thoughts. But there it was.

Sophie's caught off guard and hesitates to respond. Poor thing. She's only trying to help and what do I do to repay that? Snide remarks and inexplicable mood swings.

I should say something. Apologize. Or give an explanation. For some reason, I can't. My throat suddenly feels thick and I can barely swallow. Instead of speaking, I take up Ella and get comfortable on the sofa. She quiets and quickly finds what she's after to nurse.

"Well, we're going to head out," Sophie says.

I nod, still unable to spit out the right words, to do the right thing. As I focus on Ella, Sophie gathers her things and her children. She gets halfway toward the front door before stopping and turning back to me.

"I know you're dealing with a lot," she says, "but I hope you will remember that I'm your friend."

"I don't need pity, thanks." Again, the words fly without my consent. What is my problem? I'm filled with regret and about to beg for her forgiveness when she responds.

"The thing is, there's only so many times I can let you take things out on me. I've had more than my fair share of that in the last few years from Gavin. I just . . . can't do that anymore." She squeezes Daisy's hand and adjusts the hold she has on Hale's car seat. "Call me when you're ready, okay?"

Tears pool in my eyes in an instant but all I'm capable of doing is watching her go.

5

Felicity

I've never seriously thought I could have postpartum depression. Instead, I simply dismiss the behavior and unbalanced responses I have a hard time explaining as a result of simple fatigue. I rationalize that my lack of focus, mood swings, and anxiety can't be postpartum because I've never once doubted my love and connection with Ella. I assumed that postpartum meant a disconnect with your child, or worse yet, wanting to harm the child or yourself, and there is none of that. Also, no one else—not my doctor, not Conor, not even Sophie who was just here to witness my troubling behavior— has suggested I might suffer from any kind of depression, let alone the kind that comes after having a baby. Maybe I've dismissed the idea out of denial. Or maybe it's because I have good days. *Truly* good days where I feel like I've got it all under control.

Today has not been one of those good days.

I vow to reach out to Sophie to properly apologize and get things back on track with her. I also intend to eat a healthy dinner and look at some work emails. I'm convinced that if only I can get into a normal routine, everything will fall into place. But before I get a chance to attempt any of that, I receive a phone call that becomes my undoing.

My father's name flashes on my mobile and I debate answering it. I've avoided his calls the last few times, though, and decide to answer it if only to get him to stop calling again for a while. I expect he'll do a perfunctory check-in, as is his standard way of communicating, and then we can both feel we've done our part. It's our normal pattern, but things soon deviate toward something much more discomforting.

"Ah, there you are," he says. His tone is, as usual, breezy. No matter how long it's been since we've spoken, he always acts as if it's been mere days. I once went seventeen months without speaking to him and it was the same *Ah, there you are* from him when we finally connected.

Our relationship is complicated but mostly boils down to him being a non-presence. He made it clear very early in my adolescence that he didn't have a lot of interest in knowing the highs and lows of my life. When he left my mother, it was a package deal of leaving me, too. He treated my mother and me as if we were just an error he moved on from. The new family he had after us was the one that "stuck." We were the ones he discarded. In response, I tried to mirror his remote attitude as much as I could, though inside, of course, I always hoped he'd realize the error of his ways and dote on me as I fantasized a father should. That never happened. And neither did my mother ever get over him choosing another over her. After years of living with both her and my disappointment, I decided it was better to just accept that he would never be the father I wanted. That freed me to simply take what he was willing to offer me on those rare occasions when he reached out without being devastated by all the many more times he gave me nothing.

"Yes, here I am," I say. I try to remember how long it's been since we've spoken. I know he called after Ella was born. I was just home from the hospital and don't remember the conversation well. There was too much going on with Romeo to care for, too.

"You're well?"

"Yes, fine. And you?"

This is how our conversations usually go. Very impersonal, as if we're the sort of long-term neighbors who will go as far as greeting each other but nothing more.

"Your husband away, then?"

"He's working, but not on tour, if that's what you mean."

My father had an odd reaction when he found out Conor and I got married. We basically eloped, with a simple ceremony in the back garden of the rental house we'd been to once before on Formentera, one of Spain's Balearic Islands. Conor had set it all up as a surprise to me and it was the most romantic, perfect moment of my life. It was just about the two of us, which was exactly what I wanted. I later learned my father was upset that he hadn't been there to be a part of it. The sudden claim of familial concern was disconcerting. It seems that whenever I've discounted him from my life, he finds inopportune ways to reassert himself.

"When will I get to meet my grandchild?" he asks.

"You mean your grandchildren?" He hasn't met either of my children yet.

"No, I mean the girl. Not the dark one."

"What did you say?" I ask, incredulous.

"I'm just wanting to meet my natural grandchild, that's all."

"Wait a second." Heat rises to my cheeks as I try to process what he's said. I've never known him to be racist. But then again, I've never really known him. "You're saying you don't want to meet Romeo? But you do want to meet Ella?"

"Listen, Felicity, you needn't get into a strop over it."

My voice has risen but I only realize it now that he's reacting to my response in such a condescending way.

"I don't know who you think you are—"

"I'm your father. And that little girl's grandfather. *Family.* I'm getting on and I may be coming late to the realization of its preciousness, but doesn't family count for something?"

His tone has softened. There's almost a plea in it, and I second-guess my reaction. I'm confused about what's even happening. The lack of clarity I've been fighting these past few months has returned in full force.

"I, eh, yes, it counts," I mumble.

"That's right. I might not have been as . . . involved as you'd have liked when you were growing up," he says, "but this is an opportunity to change that. I want to be there for my granddaughter."

It's not an apology to me, but it is a partial acknowledgement of his mistakes and a step toward a course correction. Except, that is, for the glaring omission of Romeo.

"Yes, but I have a son, too. You have a grandson. You must include him."

"I'm not interested," he says firmly, cutting off any other argument I might want to make.

"Then, I have to end this call," I say, my voice shaking.

"Felicity—"

I disconnect the line and stare at nothing, my eyes glassy. I can't handle this in addition to everything else that has been overwhelming me lately. I don't want my father to be in my head. I don't need that struggle piling on top of my other insecurities and fears.

But there's no stopping the flood of tears that streams down my face. They're tears of anger and frustration and disappointment. They're an attempt to release the confusion and disbelief at what my father was asking of me, that I grant his claim that only one of my children is legitimate enough to be considered family. But the release doesn't work. I'm weighed down by the oppressive feeling that I can't cope anymore. That everything is *too much*.

All this goes on while the babies are lying on the floor nearby, somehow sleeping through my breakdown. I feel incredibly alone.

Forcing myself to focus on something other than self-pity, I open the laptop I've had every intention of using all day. My chest aches from the crying bout that is only just now starting to subside. I take in ragged breaths as I try to focus on the screen. Without consciously thinking of it, I type "postpartum depression" into the search engine. The symptoms match what I'd recognized in myself earlier: lack of focus, mood swings, and anxiety. Other symptoms like feeling overwhelmed, being quick to cry, and withdrawing are also dead on. The more I read, the sadder I feel. I finally stop reading, as tears cloud my vision. Yet, nothing can pull my eyes away from the glow of the laptop. I fall into something like a dissociative state, blocking out everything, trying to escape my worries.

And this is how Conor finds me when he returns home at close to midnight. The concern on his face as he sees me sitting in the dark, with only the light from my computer screen illuminating the room, both babies nearby and fussy in diapers that I can suddenly tell need changing by the smell wafting in the air, splits my heart in two. There's no doubt that he's horrified by the picture of neglect I've created.

The fact that he goes first to Ella and not me sends me into another full-blown crying jag. I wanted his attention. And the fact that I wanted it over my own daughter is so guilt-inducing that I want to vomit. Only, I have nothing in my stomach to come up. Another sign of postpartum is a loss of appetite.

"Honey, shh," Conor says and reaches for me. He holds me in one arm and Ella in the other as I cry.

"Don't call Sophie. Please don't call her," I say, crumbling into him.

"I won't."

"I'm so *sorry*, Conor."

"For what? No need to be sorry." He kisses my forehead and instead of soothing me, it makes me want to disappear. He's *too* good of a man. He's too perfect for a broken person like me.

"Shh, now," he says.

"I don't want to be put on medication. I don't want any drugs in my system."

Now he pulls away from me, his eyebrows raised. "What are you talking about, Fee?"

"I can't take depression medicine. I can't have it in my body because then it'll transfer through when I nurse."

He stiffens the moment I say *depression*. That I'm bringing him my problems is one thing, but for it to be depression, for it to be the one affliction that he's had to deal with for years with his best friend Gavin, *and* for it to have taken the life of his friend Christian, well, it must make my weakness even more unbearable. What more is he supposed to take? I wonder. When does he get to have a break from being the strong one?

I collapse onto the sofa and sob again, my cries suddenly encouraging both Ella and Romeo to match me. I don't look at Conor because I can't bear to, but I'm sure he's ready to run. From me. From this insta-family I've forced on him.

And I wouldn't blame him.

6

Conor

My wife is lying in a heap on the sofa and my two children are both crying. I don't have the luxury of waiting to see if she will snap out of it and attend to the babies. I scoop up both Ella and Romeo and take them to their room.

"Hey, hey, it's okay. Hey, hey, it's okay," I sing softly as I change first Romeo, then Ella. "You're my baby and it's gonna be all right."

I'll admit that I don't change them very often, but when I do I've made a habit of singing to them as we go, and it always seems to delight them. Luckily, it's worked this time as well. Once I've got them each wrapped snugly in a thin blanket, I carry them to the rocking chair in the corner and we get comfortable.

I'm not sure if either is hungry, but I plan on trying to rock them to sleep before worrying about how to feed them. Felicity switched from giving Romeo formula to breastfeeding once her milk came in after Ella was born. The baby nurse cautioned that this might be too much to ask of her body, but Felicity was keen on establishing that connection. It seemed to work but has left us without any backup formula in the house as far as I know. So, if the babies are hungry now, I'm not confident I can get Felicity to handle that.

"Sleep now, my precious girl," I murmur to Ella. "Sleep now, my big man," I whisper to Romeo.

I count myself lucky when they each settle, closing their eyes. Leaning my head back against the chair, I release a sigh.

Jesus.

What had I walked in on with Felicity? She's falling apart.

When I left her earlier, she'd seemed fine. Well, not fine exactly. She was a little overwhelmed. That's why I called Sophie. I thought it might be a help for her. Sophie always seems to have a handle on things. I just asked her to pop round to see if she could lend a hand. Now, I'll have to find out from her what's going on. Only, Felicity was adamant that I not call her.

Fuck's sake.

What a mind fuck. I'm sitting here, still half in recording mode— wearing a leather jacket, smelling faintly of beer and weed, with my mind on the song we're struggling to complete. But I've got to switch that off and get into caretaker mode. It's jarring.

When I hear a sniffle, my eyes dart toward the open door. Felicity is standing there, her head hanging as she stares at the floor.

"Come here," I tell her, keeping my voice low so as not to disturb the delicate balance I've achieved with the babies.

She moves toward me reluctantly, as if each step takes monumental effort. When she reaches me, I have no way to touch her. Both my arms are wrapped around the babies. After a moment's hesitation, she sits down at my feet and leans into me the way I've seen Roscoe, Danny Boy's dog, lean into him. There's so much more than exhaustion going on here.

"What can I do, Fee? Tell me how I can help."

She stays mute.

"Let's bring Lizzy back on, yeah?"

Lizzy was our baby nurse. She was wonderful support. I still don't know why we let her go.

"I can do this. I promise," Felicity says. But her voice is hoarse and unconvincing.

"What happened today?" When she doesn't answer, I ask again.

"I don't know."

"Did Sophie come by? Was she any help?"

She nods against my knee. "She was phenomenal. She's like super-mum, the way she watched over all the babies so I could nap."

I furrow my brow because her declaration is at odds with the way her body is trembling and fresh tears stream down her face.

"I need to know what's going on, honey."

"I'll be fine."

The words come out forced, though it's what she knows I want to hear. But I don't want to be fed bullshit. I want the truth, even if it's ugly.

"Let me put them down," I say and ease up from the rocking chair.

I carefully put the babies into their own cribs and lead Felicity out of the room. I wrap my arm around her shoulders and she feels frail to me. She has no perception of how she really looks. She's lost the baby weight and more but keeps complaining about her figure.

In our bedroom, I turn on a bedside lamp and take off my jacket as she curls up into a ball on the bed. I have been accused by almost everyone I know—including Felicity—of wanting to be in control. They're not wrong. This situation, whatever it is, is entirely out of my control, though, and the anxiety of that helplessness shows itself in the tightness in my chest.

Felicity has always been made of tough stuff. I never expected to see her fall into depression. But it's got to be related to all the pregnancy hormones. It's only temporary. I just need to figure out the way to get her to cope.

I sit on the end of the bed, near her feet. Her demeanor is pure shame. I know that she will see herself as a failure because of this, even though the thought has never crossed my mind.

"What do we do? How do we get you feeling better?" I ask gently.

Again, she's silent, though her eyes are open. She's staring at the artwork on the wall. It's the piece that had reminded me of her when I got it. At the time, it was that thing that I couldn't define about her. It was the thing that kept drawing me to her and away from my fiancée. Now, I look at the outline of a woman in a different way. I see the woman as something elusive. Like I'll never be able to grasp more than the mere hint of her. That thought scares me. I've been surrounded by people suffering from darkness and depression for too long. I won't let Felicity slip away from me.

"There's nothing wrong with formula," I tell her. "We'll get you to the doctor in the morning, get some sort of antidepressant in you, and this will be behind us. That's it. That's the answer, since you're not willing to speak up."

It seems all I had to do was take control for her to snap out of her melancholy. She sits up and swipes at the tears wetting her cheeks. "I said no to that. I won't be medicated."

"Then tell me what we're to do, Fee. Because I won't go on this way. I know you don't want this either. So, tell me—"

"Maybe I can speak with someone?"

"What? With who?"

"I don't know."

"Talk to me. Can't you talk to me?"

Her bottom lip quivers but she still doesn't look at me.

"Okay, not me. Then who?"

It takes a long moment, but then she says, "I was reading that talk therapy is a good alternative to medicine."

"So, a therapist of some sort? A stranger?" I should have kept that last part to myself. She doesn't need me to guilt her. Jesus, that's no help at all.

She looks at me, pained. "I don't know how to say what I'm feeling, Conor. I don't know how to express what this is. I just know that I was barely holding it together before and then it all burst out of control earlier this evening. And I'm *so sorry*."

In response, I crawl onto the bed so that I can hold her from behind. I wrap my arm around her waist and pull her into me.

"Don't apologize. You have no reason to apologize. There's no harm in needing help. We'll bring Lizzy back. We'll get you to the doctor for a recommendation for someone to talk to. We'll figure this out."

"I don't want anyone to know," she whispers, sounding like a little girl.

"Not even your doctor?"

"His office will leak my troubles to the tabloids, just like they must have done about every bit of weight I gained along the way and how long the delivery took and—"

"Okay, we won't go to them. I'll find you a therapist who will be completely confidential."

"How?"

"Don't worry about that. Let me sort it."

I can feel a burden being lifted from her as her shoulders relax. She's asleep within minutes.

Carefully, I ease my mobile out of my pocket and type a text.

I've got a question.

I wait less than two minutes before I get a reply.

I've got an answer.

7

Conor

I knew Gavin would be the one to help me sort out a solution. I knew it because he's the type of friend who will do anything he can to help—and because he knows all of Dublin. He's got more people who count themselves as his friend than can fit into the O2 Arena. Sounds outlandish when you know that the capacity of that venue is 13,000, but I swear it's true. Gavin has spent the last dozen years being an inclusive bastard—unlike me. I've never shaken my loner tendencies, which accounts for why it makes perfect sense to me that Gavin will be able to scour his enormous list of friends to find what I need for Felicity.

Turns out that he doesn't have to reach very far. After some brief back and forth texting on the subject, he calls me. It doesn't matter that it's close to two in the morning and that he's likely knackered from our draining studio session, he's ready to help.

"I think we have someone in our midst who will do quite nicely," Gavin tells me.

I had extricated myself from the bed with Felicity and now stand on the balcony overlooking Dalkey Bay. The air is bitterly cold, but I barely feel it. I'm too focused on finding a way to help my wife.

"Really?" Even for Gavin, this is quick work.

"As long as she doesn't need a psychiatrist? Someone who can prescribe meds?"

"No, I told you. She's adamantly against any kind of drugs. Just wants someone to talk to." *About things she can't admit to me.*

"Okay, then this person will work."

"Someone local?"

"Very."

"Spit it out, then." I know Gavin isn't trying to play coy, but that's how it comes off in my haste to find some concrete action.

"Just take down this address and have her there at ten tomorrow morning."

I do as he says. Because even though I hate to feel out of control like this, I'm desperate.

I'M up with the babies at half past eight the next morning when Lizzy arrives. I'd texted her at seven and was surprised to get a reply right away. She said she hadn't committed to any other family yet and was happy to return.

She's done herself up more than I remembered. Then again, when she was first here, the babies were so small, and I was so sleep deprived, that I don't think I noticed much about her other than I was grateful for her extra set of hands.

Now, I can't help but see that she's a stunner. She's got long brown hair that is straight and shiny and a nice figure that suggests she exercises. A runner, by the look of her toned thighs in her leggings. Her eyelashes are dark and frame pale blue eyes. Her lips are tinted red, but she's taken pains to make it look natural. She's taken pains. For me. I don't suppose that's surprising. I've had a lifetime of women eager to get my attention.

"I'll take him," she says and leans in to relieve me of Romeo.

She's wearing a hint of perfume. It's something expensive. Maybe a gift from her boyfriend? Does she have a boyfriend?

What the fuck am I doing?

Falling back on my old ways, maybe? Which means looking for the easy distraction of a woman other than the one I'm with.

"Thanks for coming, Lizzy."

She looks up at me, and there's a flicker of something in her eyes. Some playfulness. Or sensuality. Then she bites her bottom lip slowly, making it clear why she was so quick to return my text earlier. My eyes drop to her chest. She's wearing a clingy tee shirt that scoops low at the neckline and I can see the outline of a lace bra over her c-cup breasts. I wonder what her nipples are like.

A few years ago, I wouldn't hesitate to accept what she's so obviously ready to give me. I can practically feel the heat of her body from our short distance. I wonder if she waxed before she came over, in the off chance that we could do the daddy-nanny thing. I could ask her, and I bet she would offer to show me. She'd settle the babies and have me meet her in the laundry room where I'd find her completely nude and waiting. Maybe she'd be up on the washer, spread and on display. Wet and eager. I bet she's a moaner. I'd have to cover her mouth while I pushed deep inside her, watching as her breasts swayed.

"I'm always happy to come. For you," she says.

I smile. God, she'd be fun. I can see that.

With a sigh, I shake my head a little. "I'll let Felicity know you're here."

She doesn't hide her disappointment, but soon focuses on the babies and I head down the hall. Before going upstairs, I duck into one of the guest toilets and ease the door shut. Leaning over the counter, I try to relax. I'm rock hard, my cock pulsing with a life of its own. Should I take care of it? Let the fantasy of Lizzy continue? Maybe she follows me here and silently drops to her knees in front of me? And I watch as she peels off her shirt and bra and reveals small rose-colored nipples. Then she slowly—so slowly—pulls opens my jeans and releases my aching, dripping cock. She teases the tip with her tongue, gathering my juices in her mouth like she can't get enough. Pulling away, she directs my cock to her tits, rubbing her hardened nipples against the swollen tip and shaft.

"Fuck my mouth," she says.

And in my mind, I do just that. She's exceptional at this. Taking me in deep and sucking like her life depends on it. All too quickly, I've come into the sink and feel both spent and guilty.

Amn't I husband of the fucking year?

I clean up quickly, all the while rationalizing that fantasies are harmless, and I was only relieving the stress I've been under for the last week. I just needed something to free me of my worries for a moment. It changes nothing about how I feel for Felicity. It changes nothing about the fact that I'd never cheat on her.

When I glance up and at the mirror I see my father's face. Not that he's actually in the room with me, of course, but I've begun to see so much of myself in him. Or him in me, I suppose. Especially since I learned of his diagnosis.

I haven't told Felicity yet. Not with her being so off. She thinks I'm mourning Christian. And I am, but that's not the totality of what's been weighing on me. No, I've got a lot more than that going on. But for a few minutes just now, I got an escape. I don't know if I should apologize to Lizzy or thank her when I see her next.

Looking at myself once more, I run my hand through my black hair and raise my eyebrows at the image there. I look calm, in control, and devastatingly handsome. If only the first two were actually true.

8

Felicity

I'm agitated and there's no use hiding it. I suppose this is a "safe" space to let all my troubles out into the open anyway.

I scan the room, trying to find comfort in the décor, but the green walls are off-putting. When I rest my eyes upon the woman sitting opposite me, I'm unnerved. She's lovely, but I can't remember her name, despite her warm welcome of me just moments ago. I'm sure she introduced herself. But I was too preoccupied with other things. Things like the fact that Conor brought Lizzy back into our house this morning. Things like Lizzy, while being wonderful with the babies, has never made a secret of how she lusts after my husband. Things like, wouldn't Conor rather be with an uncomplicated young thing like Lizzy, anyway?

"I would love to learn a little about you."

Startled from my thoughts, I shift in the soft chair. "I'm terribly sorry, but I've completely forgotten your name."

The woman smiles at me, her patience clearly a virtue. As it should be with her profession. She's my brand-new therapist. I know that much. Conor pulled me from bed, supervised me while I brushed my teeth, forced me to have tea and toast, and then drove me here.

"I'm Ms. Patterson. But you can call me Amelia, if you like," she says.

Now that rings a bell. Amelia. I like that name. I like her. I can tell that already. With some people you just know whether they've got a kind spirit, and that's what she has. She's got thick brown hair, a heart-shaped face, and beautiful legs. Her navy pencil skirt and striped blouse make her look put together and make me feel all the more undone. I don't remember if I dragged a brush through my hair or not, and the clothes I'm wearing are the same ones I slept in.

"I must look like a crazy person," I blurt out and paw at my hair.

"Not at all," she assures me. "Now, I know very little about you other than you're a new mum, yes?"

I slowly nod and let my nervous hands fall to my lap. I lace my fingers together to stop the compulsion to play more with my hair.

"Tell me about being a mum."

Her voice is soothing, coaxing, calming. Whether it's warranted or not, I'm lulled into feeling she's someone I can trust, someone who will help guide me out of this dark period. The relief I feel is so intense that I burst into tears.

"Now, now," she murmurs and holds out a tissue. "Whatever it is, we'll work on it together. You're not alone."

What a wonderful thing to hear at this moment. She must be about my age, but she's got a motherly way that I realize I've been longing for. I might be a mother myself, but I need to be cared for, too. I'm still crying, but it's through a smile now.

When I've managed to collect myself a few minutes later, I tell Amelia everything. I pour my heart out to this woman, desperate to believe that she'll be careful with all I'm entrusting her with.

I don't know how long I've gone on when the words finally stop falling out of my mouth, but I suspect we've gone well over our allotted fifty minutes. Falling back into my chair, I take in a deep breath and on the exhale, I feel the most peaceful I have in a long time.

Amelia, on the other hand, looks a little concerned. She's tapping her pen against her notepad, thoughtful.

After a silent minute, she looks up at me. "So, to sum up what you've told me," she says, "in the last couple years, you returned home after living abroad for more than a decade so you could see your mother through the end of her life, you got married again after a rough divorce, become pregnant when you never thought you could, adopted a baby, and shortly thereafter gave birth?"

I tick through all those things in my head before nodding.

"And," Amelia continues, "you've been feeling something you think might be postpartum depression, but you haven't been able to share this with anyone. Not your husband. And not your best friend, who, if I have this right, had a years-long love affair with your husband while she was married to another?"

Again, I mentally check off the list she's offered and nod. "Right. Oh, and my estranged father has just contacted me, too."

"Oh?" She flips to a new sheet in her notepad. "You haven't mentioned him."

She's right, but it's only because I've had so much else to tell her. But now I relay to her a brief history of the shaky relationship I have with my father, including how I had to end our call when he denied the legitimacy of one of my children.

Afterward, I'm exhausted, but the good kind of exhausted. The kind that feels well earned. I'm also amazed that we're still going.

"Don't you have another client? I don't want to keep you," I say and glance at my mobile for the time. It's been ninety-four minutes since we started.

"Oh, thank you for thinking of that, but I've held this time slot open for a while now. There's no one waiting."

It suddenly occurs to me that there *is* someone waiting: Conor. He insisted on staying close by while I had this session. I'm sure he didn't expect it to take this long.

"I shouldn't take any more of your time." I stand and wipe at my eyes.

Amelia puts aside her notepad and stands. She offers me her hand. "It was a pleasure to meet you, Felicity."

Though it's the proper thing to say, it sounds so final and I nearly panic. "Will I see you again?"

"Would you like to?"

"I would like it very much." In fact, I feel that I *need* to see her again.

"Does this time work for you? Shall we schedule again for Thursday?"

She wants to see me twice a week. I really am a mess. But I'm ready to try to get a handle on things and quickly agree.

When she walks me halfway toward the door to the outer office and stops there, letting me take the rest of the steps on my own, I hesitate. Oddly, I want to hug her. Or do something to thank her for letting me unburden myself. But when she just smiles at me and waits for me to find my way to the door, I remember that this is a business relationship, and our time is up.

CONOR IS STANDING in anticipation when I step out into the waiting area. He smiles, and I feel that familiar tingle. He's far too good looking. And he knows it, which has always driven me crazy. But right now, I don't care. I just care that he's here.

I go to him, and he envelopes me into his embrace. I lean into him but he doesn't falter. He works out religiously and his body is all defined muscle. But it's his inner strength that I love so much. When we became friends again after I came home to Dublin, I thought I had him figured out. I thought he was this immature playboy who was content to chase girls and live on the surface of things. I thought I'd have things to teach him about love and commitment. But he's been proving me wrong over and over. He's wiser and more stable than I ever thought he was capable of being. To my surprise, I've been the one who has learned from him.

"Ready to go?" he asks and presses a kiss into my hair.

"We should get back. I—" I stop and pull away from him as a realization hits me. "I've never been away from them like this. I've never *not* been there."

Conor takes my face into his hands and bends his knees so he can look me in the eye. "You are an amazing mother, honey. And you deserve to take the time you need to get back on track. Don't start guilting yourself over this."

Reaching up, I place my hands over his, squeezing. With a hard swallow and a nod, I do my best to consciously let go of the fear that was threatening to overtake me.

"We'll make one quick stop on the way home, okay?"

"Where will that be?"

"You'll see," he says with a smile.

9

Felicity

As Conor leads me through a maze of alleyways and side streets, I have no idea where we're walking. It doesn't matter, though. I'm content to feel the warmth of his hand on mine as he tugs me along. Speaking with Amelia, unloading the burden of things I hadn't even known I was harboring, had an instant effect. My steps feel easier, my eyes less heavy. A lightness has returned to my being. If this is how I walk away from every session with my therapist, I'd be glad to go every day, just so I can get through this thing that has been dragging me down.

"Here we are," Conor says and gestures to the royal-blue door in front of us.

I recognize the café as the place where Conor and I first met upon my return to Dublin.

"Feeling nostalgic?" I ask with a smile.

"A bit. Anyway, you need to eat something."

We go inside, and I take in the familiar black and white checkered flooring, clean white walls, and mismatched kitschy floral-patterned vinyl tablecloths. It all adds up to make a cozy spot for a quick meal.

We even claim the same table we had that first time, the one right in front of the window.

As is commonly the case, the female waitstaff fight among themselves to determine who will be the lucky one to serve Conor Quinn, rock god. Though I'm virtually invisible when I'm at his side, he causes a stir wherever he goes, and I know he gets a thrill out of it. But he's also deft at minimizing the intrusion it causes, including now when he charms the young woman who won the battle to be our server with his sexy smile while ordering more food than either of us can eat, along with a pot of tea.

"So, why here?" I ask when we're left alone.

"I dunno. I suppose I was thinking of simpler times, back when we first found that spark."

"Then? We were just friends then."

He raises his eyebrows. "You wanted to tear the very clothes off me on that day."

I laugh, remembering how he had caught me looking at him with lust in my eyes. Though he was game to flirt, he wasn't really interested in me on that day and I remind him of that.

"How do you know that?"

"Because you were engaged to another woman at the time," I say simply.

He leans back in his chair and studies me. "Fee, the minute we sat down here together—no, the minute I saw you shaking the rainwater off yourself just outside that door," he says and gestures to the front of the café, "was when it all started."

"That's sweet of you to say, but it's just not true. You were only playing games for the longest time."

He smiles, conceding the point—at least partially.

"Okay, maybe I didn't know that day that you'd be the one I'd marry. But I knew without a doubt that I needed you in my life. I *knew* it. And that's why I say it all started here."

My chin trembles as I fight back tears. I didn't know I had any more tears to give at this point.

"Unless, actually, we want to go further back and count that confession you made to me. You know, the one where you said you *still think of me?*"

Here I am again, smiling through tears. And laughing. Conor's always been good at knowing when to lighten the mood.

"I can only imagine," I say. "I mean, you were with one of the most beautiful supermodels in the world, but here I was—plain old me—mentioning that you cross my mind on occasion. Must have created quite the temptation for you."

My effort to downplay things goes nowhere.

"It was everything, Fee. Honestly, it was the thing that started me on questioning if I could keep going with Colette."

I nod and sniffle.

"So, really, I thank God that you never stopped lusting after me."

"You'll never stop being led around by your ego, will you?"

"Better than being led around by other things, isn't it?"

Before I can respond, our tea and food arrives in the shaking hands of our waitress. Her cheeks are bright red as she hurries to settle everything. Conor notices her nerves and helps her place the teapot in the middle of the table before she dumps it all over us. Then he takes the girl's hand and gives it a squeeze.

"You all right, love?" he asks.

She squeaks and nods. Literally, *squeaks.* Just like a mouse.

I cover my mouth, so she doesn't see me smiling.

Like the proverbial lion with a mouse, Conor licks his lips and fixes the poor thing in his hungry gaze. "We'll take a photo before we go, yeah?"

She manages another squeak and scampers off.

"You know, it might be better for you to *not* acknowledge some of these girls," I tell him.

"Why would that be better?"

"The ones like this girl, they're petrified of your attention. They want to be near you but can't handle what it means to actually interact with you."

"Meaning they might want to just admire me from afar?"

I smile because he sounds disappointed by the idea of not being able to solicit a reaction from the girls who drool over him. "That wouldn't be as much fun for you, would it?"

"No, it wouldn't," he admits, and I shake my head.

Conor is a flirt, but it's harmless. As wildly as my emotions and insecurities have swung lately, I do believe he's committed to me. Just look what he did today. He skipped going into the studio, took the initiative to bring back Lizzy (whether she's my first choice or not, she's dependable), and is spending the day looking after me.

I lean forward and offer him my open hand. He takes it in both of his and smiles at me.

"I love you so much, Conor," I tell him. Before he can return the sentiment, I continue. "And I'm so sorry that I've fallen . . . down." I'd rather think of last night as falling down than falling apart, because the recovery of the former seems so much easier than the latter. "I'm so ashamed of the fact that I've let you down. I've let the babies down. I want to be a better wife and a better mother."

Now he takes my hand and presses his lips to my skin for a long moment. "You have nothing to be sorry for. Nothing to be ashamed of. *Please* let that go. You have to know that I don't expect perfection. There's no need to try to be this—this *ideal* wife and mother you seem to have in mind."

"You mean I don't have to be like Sophie?"

"What's that mean?"

He's looking at me with curiosity, as if the idea had never occurred to him that in contrast, I am a very pale shade of the vibrant portrait of a wife and mother that Sophie presents.

"Just that she's basically Mary bloody Poppins, isn't she?"

"Mary *who?*"

"She's practically perfect in every way, is what I mean."

Conor rolls his eyes. "I thought you two were friends?"

"Yes, we are friends. It's just so hard to live up to her standards."

His brows crease as he considers this. I can see why. I've made it seem like she's been judging me, and I've fallen short in her eyes. And we both know that isn't Sophie's style.

"She just sets a very high bar, is all," I say. "Everything's so easy for her."

"You know how you get around feeling like that?"

"How?"

"Stop comparing yourself to her."

"Yes, well, it's hard not to when I see how well she manages everything."

"She's *not* actually perfect, you know?"

I give him a dubious smirk. "She's a tall, blonde, supermodel who looks like she never had one baby, let alone two."

"That doesn't make her perfect. It makes her genetically lucky."

"She cares for her two children—mostly on her own—like it's nothing."

"More likely she keeps her hardships to herself, is all."

"She makes her own organic baby food."

"Waste. Of. Time." He scoffs. "You can buy the same thing, just as natural and healthy."

Since he's countering everything so well, I up my game, saying, "She makes sure she never goes more than a couple days without giving Gavin an orgasm, no matter what."

"Well—" Conor stops himself, and I can see that this revelation flusters him. It's not only unusual for me to share Sophie's confidence in this way, but it's also a sharp contrast to our own sex life, as I admit next.

"I haven't made the first move with you since before I was pregnant."

"I know being pregnant wasn't always easy."

He's regained control of himself and so I move on. "She's never had to see a therapist because she couldn't manage the very good fortune of having two small children at once."

"Everyone's got their issues."

"What is hers, then? Honestly, I can't begin to imagine—"

"Jesus, she *cheated* on her husband. How's that for not perfect?"

"With *you*! She cheated with you."

"Even worse, isn't it? Her own husband's best friend." He tsks disapprovingly.

This forced incredulity he's adopted purely to make me feel better is so ridiculous that it actually works. I smile, shake my head, and then laugh.

"It's nice to see your smile," he says.

This sweet sentiment is eerily reminiscent of what he told me a few years back when we were right here in this same spot, and I was having it rough with my mother. It meant more then than I was ready to admit. It reminds me of the unexpected sequence of events that led me to becoming friends with him again, of how he forced me to let down the protective walls around my heart, and how he's always tried his best to care for me. I know that I have so much good fortune, but that has just made admitting to my struggles all that much harder. I just hope he keeps holding on.

10

Conor

I had decided to let Felicity take the lead in talking to me about what was going on with her. But our conversation after her therapy appointment was incongruously light and devoid of answers. It was clear there was no use in trying to coax details from her. So, I let our conversation flow without applying any pressure on her.

That didn't mean I wasn't frustrated by it, though. Once home, Felicity went straight for the babies, eager to nurse them and relieve the swelling in her breasts. I need some kind of release, too. Conscious of pursuing the *right* kind of release, I ignore Lizzy's lingering gaze and go upstairs to change into workout gear.

My mobile buzzes as I'm lacing up my trainers. It's Gavin, so I answer without delay.

"Hey, Gav."

"How's things?" he asks.

"Fine, good."

I hear him laugh. "Glad all is fixed."

"I didn't say that, did I?" I snap. Jesus, Felicity's mood swings have rubbed off on me.

"Have time to make it to the studio today?"

He's ignoring my rude reply and I'm glad for it. "No, my head's not there. I need to go for a run."

"It's lashing down."

"I don't care. I just need to go."

"Come by and I'll go with you."

The offer is Gavin's subtle way of showing his support. He'll employ my technique and will wait for me to offer up my thoughts rather than push. That and a good, hard run sounds exactly like what I need, and I agree before ending the call.

Back downstairs, Felicity looks like her normal self. She's on the sofa, holding Ella as she nurses. I stop and watch her for a moment from a discreet distance. She looks so natural, so at ease and content. But that's not the whole story. There's something churning inside of her that led to me coming home last night to find her disconnected and neglecting our children. What if I hadn't come home at that time? How long would those fussing babies have gone without proper care?

"Going out? In this rain?" Lizzie asks.

She's come from the kitchen and has Romeo over one shoulder as she taps him firmly on the back, eliciting a burp out of him.

"Well done," I tell him with a smile.

"You'll catch your death."

"Ah, I'll be fine. I can handle myself." I give her a wink to make the comment suggestive. Old habits die hard, don't they?

She leans toward me ever so slightly. "I'd love to see that. Next time."

I can't quite make out whether she knows what happened in the bathroom earlier today or if her not-so-veiled offer to watch me wank is spontaneous. Either way, I again, can't help myself. I raise my eyebrows and smile at her. These little flirts—*flirt* might be too innocent of a word, actually—are a fun distraction, but I need to get my head straight. Which was the point of going for a run.

"Thanks for your help, Lizzy. I know Felicity appreciates it a lot."

I give Romeo a kiss on his plump cheek and move past her to the living area to let Felicity know I'll be stepping away. But she's nodded off, exhaustion having taken over. I imagine her chat with Ms. Patterson is partly to blame. It can't have been easy to bare her soul to a complete stranger. A quick, soft kiss to her forehead and I'm off.

"I'D INVITE YOU IN, but you'll bring all the rain in the sky with you," Sophie says when she sees me at her doorstep.

The rain is coming down in thick blankets and I am completely soaked even though Gavin's house isn't far from mine. I'm shaking slightly, too, which Sophie soon notices. It changes her playful attitude right back to her usual caretaker mode.

"Oh my goodness," she says and takes my bicep. "Come in and dry off."

I step inside but wait in the foyer while Sophie goes for a towel. Her house is one of those places that offers instant comfort. Unlike mine. Whereas my house is all modern cool ceramic tiles, polished concrete, and dark Calamander wood flooring with lighter striations, Sophie's house is light and airy with purposeful supple accents, including a soft wool rug layered over the hardwood floor and cashmere throw blankets always within reach. I wonder how our clashing styles would have worked had we ended up together.

When Sophie returns with a towel and wraps it around me, she rubs my shoulders vigorously to warm me up. And I know then that I would have let her do whatever she wanted with the design of the home we might have had together. As was always the case with her, it's my heart that leads and longs to give her free reign to do as she pleases.

"Gavin told me you two were headed out for a run, but I thought he was joking," she says with a small smile.

"Where is the bastard?"

"The 'bastard' is getting Daisy to nap. He sings to her until she falls asleep."

I nod and follow her into the living area. Though she would

never stop me from sitting on her sofa, wet as I am, I sit on the floor near the heat of the gas fireplace. She joins me, folding her legs into some sort of yoga position she makes look easy.

It's quiet in the house. Quiet between us as we sit and look at the flames. It's peaceful in this home, with no undercurrent of impending chaos like in mine. Hale must be sleeping. There's a video monitor on the coffee table that is dark, but I know that the second the slightest noise emanates from it, we'll both snap to attention and spring into action.

"Look what's become of us," I say with a rueful laugh.

"What do you mean?"

"So utterly . . . *domestic.*"

Sophie smiles. "Don't tell me you miss your single days."

"They weren't bad."

"Don't romanticize it. Those were lonely times."

"I was never lonely," I say. "In fact, sometimes I *almost* had more than I could handle when it came to the threesomes."

When Sophie rolls her eyes, it's a weak attempt to hide the blush coming to her cheeks. It amazes me that she can still be shocked. That we can still play this game where I say things to get a rise out of her and it works. It makes me long for that connection. Again, I want to retreat to what felt like simpler times. Just like when I thought to take Felicity back to the same café where we reconnected upon her return to Dublin. But if I'm honest, I know those days weren't all that simple. Just different.

"You're in a funny mood," Sophie tells me. "Tell me what's going on."

I look away from her. Those hazel-green eyes of hers have the ability to see too deeply into me and I don't want that right now.

"I'm guessing Gav told you."

"Not everything."

"Well, I'm sure you can tell for yourself that Felicity's having some trouble right now. That she needs some extra support." *That I can't give her.*

"Yes, I know she does. I'm really glad she's seeing a therapist. I want to help her, but she clearly doesn't want to take it from me. Anyway, I wasn't talking about her. What's going on with *you*?"

I turn back to her in surprise. Then again, it should come as no surprise that Sophie still knows me. A love like ours never had a chance. But that doesn't mean it wasn't real.

"I'm fine, Soph."

She nods without conviction. And then she laughs quietly.

"What?"

"I was going to say something that, on second thought, is really inappropriate."

I smile, intrigued. "Have you met me? I *like* inappropriate."

That gets another laugh out of her. "I was going to say that I understand—all too well, in fact—that it can sometimes be hardest to talk to the person you're closest with. But you can always talk to me."

She's right. It is inappropriate given that's how our relationship developed. When she couldn't talk to her own husband, she turned to me. It went on for years like that, with us having an emotional intimacy we shouldn't. We staved off the physical intimacy for as long as we could, and then, when we gave into it, it was the thing that broke everything. It broke our friendship. It broke her marriage. It broke my friendship with Gavin. It's taken a long time to get all of those things mended. It would be beyond inappropriate to go down that path again. It would be stupid self-destruction.

But, god how I want to. I want to give in to those old feelings and find my comfort in Sophie McManus all over again. I want to refuse all rational thought and succumb to the temptation to follow my reckless heart. Because that pure emotion for her is familiar and feels so damn good.

The screen of the baby monitor lights up in response to Hale starting to fuss and we both look at it. It's just the intervention I needed.

"Thanks, honey. I appreciate that," I tell her. "But what would help me most is if you keep trying with Felicity. I know she's been hard to handle with the mood swings, but don't give up on her."

Sophie watches me for a minute and a silent understanding of my deflection passes between us. "Of course, I'll keep reaching out to her," she says. "Besides, you know that I am not one to give up easily,"

I smile my thanks. I want to say so much more. I want to tell her how fucking special she is. How, I hope Gavin understands—*truly* understands—how lucky he is to have her. How I'll always savor that brief, perfect, time when we let nothing hold us back from loving each other. But I don't say any of that. Because it would be *inappropriate*. And I'm not that guy anymore. At least, that's what I keep telling myself.

11

Conor

By the time Gavin and I head out, the rain has lightened to a drizzle and makes for a good run. I push hard, running at a pace that I know isn't easy for him, but he keeps up. Just having him by my side as we wordlessly move through the deserted streets of Dalkey provides the comfort I know he intended. Focusing on my breathing means I can remove everything from my thoughts. I don't think about my wife's troubles. I don't think about whether the babies sense that something is amiss. I don't think about my father and what will become of him in the coming months, or years, if he's lucky. And I definitely don't think about how much I want to fuck Lizzy.

There are patches of sunshine when we finish. Gavin directs me to follow him along the side of the house and has me sit at a small table overlooking the sea while he goes inside for water. It's summertime, but the Irish sun is typically weak. I'll take it over the downpour from earlier, though.

I've got my feet up on the chair opposite mine and my head tilted to the sky, eyes closed, when Gavin returns. I hear him sit down with me, open a bottle of water, and gulp it down. I could sit quietly like this indefinitely, but I know it's only a matter of seconds before Gavin needs to say something.

My count is at thirteen seconds when he speaks.

"This therapist seem like a good fit, then?"

I look at him and nod. "First round seemed helpful, anyway. Where'd you come by her?"

"Shay."

"Shay?" The idea that our drummer Shay is seeing a therapist is bizarre. He's the ultimate stoic male. Never wants to trouble anyone with his issues. I always knew his brother, Danny Boy, was a pain in the arse, but I learned only recently that they had a truly shite childhood that would have fucked up anyone. Danny Boy turned to heroin to escape it. Thankfully, Shay turned to drumming.

"She's Danny Boy's therapist. That's the connection."

"Oh." That makes more sense. I laugh, thinking of Danny Boy lying on a sofa and spilling his guts. Pity the woman who has to try to set him straight.

"I know," Gavin says, seeming to agree with my thoughts. "Danny fucking Boy. But I figure she must be good because he's taken it down a notch, don't you think?"

Danny Boy's been hanging out in the studio with us. And Gavin's right that he's become a tamer version of himself. He's still visibly restless, with a perpetually bouncing leg and ceaselessly picking at his cuticles, but he hasn't had any major fuck ups since Julia O'Flaherty showed up to the studio last fall. She was primed to make trouble, that was all too clear. Danny Boy froze, so I shut it down. Never did tell Gavin about that one. Didn't see any reason to stir up the past. Because that's what Julia is—history.

It's no secret that Danny Boy and I have a rocky history of our own. But I am glad to see him stabilize himself. I've even come to like the guy a bit. We've got motorbikes in common. And Shay. We both want what's best for him. I'm sure Shay is relieved by the truce we've built. That poor guy has had to deal with more than his fair share from Danny Boy over the years.

But it seems that Danny Boy's therapist has played a part in setting him on the right path. That's not an easy feat. It gives me more confidence that Felicity is with the right person and will soon be back to her old self.

"Yeah, he has. Hard to trust that it'll last, though," I say.

"Time will tell."

Picking up the water Gavin had brought out for me, I down the bottle. The run was good but hasn't really given me the release I felt I needed after understanding that I'd get no answers from my wife about what was wrong. Before I realize I'm doing it, I've squeezed the water bottle nearly flat in my fist.

"Con?"

I look up to see Gavin watching me, his face a mask of concern. "Yeah?"

I expect him to give me some kind of encouragement or get philosophical maybe. Instead, he does something better. He offers a concrete way to exorcise some of the things plaguing me.

"Let's get into the studio early tomorrow," he says. "Meet me at nine, yeah? I think if it's just you and me, we can finish off Christian's song."

"Grand, yeah. We're so close, anyway."

"It's a fucker of a song, isn't it?" He laughs, knowing the stress and frustration has been self-inflicted.

"That it is. I mean, does it do him justice? That's what's stopping us, right?"

Gavin rubs his face with both hands, presses them there for a moment, and then nods. "You know what I keep worrying about?"

"What?"

"Patsy listening to it. I need for *her* to think it does justice for her man, you know?"

Patsy is Christian's widow. For a renowned band like ours to put out a song about Christian Hale's suicide is guaranteed to be big news in the music world. We don't want to come off looking like we're exploiting his death. And we don't want to reopen wounds for Patsy.

"Yeah, I know what you mean." I haven't been able to find a way to push through to get the guitar I want on this song. Being blocked like this is new and unwelcome.

Seems Gavin is ready to be the one to push us both through on this one because there's resolve in his eyes when he looks at me. "We'll figure it out. Just like we always have."

I have the feeling he's not speaking about just the song anymore. He tilts his head, imploring me to accept this offer of partnership. He knows I need it, but not *why* I need it. The fact that he still hasn't asked me to share more with him is not lost on me. My nostalgia earlier when speaking with Sophie dissipates as I remember why I chose this man's friendship over her. He's my brother, after all. If not by blood, then by deed.

Nodding, I agree, "We'll get it."

Gavin stands and before I can join him, he squeezes my shoulder. "Us together? Nothing can stop us."

"You got that right, Gav." I let him go inside without me, wanting a minute to sit and absorb his words.

There was something in his voice that implied a kind of permanence, as if he was saying he's got my back for the long haul. Looking at all we've been through, there's no doubt in my mind that that's true. And that I would do anything for him in return.

AFTER A SHOWER and a quick bite to eat back at the house, I head out again. I'm hoping a visit with my parents might help ease my free-floating anxiety. They've always been my anchors, after all.

Knocking twice, I let myself into my parents' home. This is the house I grew up in, with the back garden where Rogue made its first stabs at creating something meaningful as a band. Tidy and middle-class, the home has been well-maintained over the years. The improvements my parents have only recently grudgingly allowed me to pay for include new furniture and a kitchen renovation, along with fresh paint and carpeting to bring the space into modernity. Despite the passage of time and the changes, I always feel a sense of comfort and ease when I walk in the front door.

I hear the television coming from the living area and my mother and father bickering in their familiar, playful way about whose turn it was to make the next cup of tea.

"Your favorite son is here," I call out.

The fact that I'm their only child doesn't stop me from making this declaration. After years of trying, my parents had given up hope of conceiving and I was a "surprise" to them in their late thirties. Now they've just crossed into their seventies.

"How do you like these, Ma?" I ask, holding up the bouquet of fragrant tuberose flowers I brought with me. I started years ago bringing my mother flowers whenever I visited. At first it was as an apology for not visiting often enough, then it became a habit.

"They're lovely, sweetheart," my mother says accepting both the flowers and a kiss on her cheek.

"I'll get a vase," my father says, clicking off the TV. He pushes out of his easy chair with a spring in his step I know is owed to my visit.

It is such a simple thing to make my parents happy. A quick visit or even a call. Every time I see them I vow to visit more often. But then I let life and my own interests take hold, and before I know it, a month has gone by without seeing them.

"Sit with me," Ma urges, and I join her on the floral-patterned sofa. "So, how's my boy?" Her smile is eager as she pushes her reading glasses into her mostly gray hair and examines me.

"Fine, good."

"Here we are," Da says as he returns to the room with the vase. He hands it to my mother and then squeezes my shoulder warmly. "Nice of you to pop by, Son."

"I know I should stop in more often."

"Ah, we understand. Lord knows you've got your obligations."

"We're always happy when you can make it," Ma says.

"The tour is over, then?" Da asks as he eases back into his chair.

I exchange a look with my mother. "Eh, yeah, Da. It's been over."

"Ah, yes. I was only joking you."

"Cuppa, sweetheart?" My mother rises to her feet and heads to the kitchen before I can even answer whether I want a cup of tea.

She's trying to diffuse the situation of my father pretending his memory lapse was in jest. It pains me to realize that this is the same routine they've done for the last couple years, with him either forgetting something or getting the details oddly wrong and her covering for him. It was easy to laugh it off when they were both in on it. But despite my mother's attempt to carry on with this charade, it's no longer funny.

"Da, how are things with you?" I ask.

"The same as always. I do my walks and read my spy novels."

"What about your crosswords?" Doing the daily crossword has been part of his routine for as long as I can remember. I figure it has to be a good intellectual exercise.

"Oh, and of course your mother has me taking her out dancing, which you know I don't mind. It's good fun with the ladies there." He gives me a conspiratorial wink.

I notice he's ignored my question about crosswords in favor of trying to suggest he's a player down at the dancehall.

"Let me check on Ma with the tea."

I get up and find my mother has everything ready on a tray but is struggling to pick it up.

"I'll get it," I tell her. But before I do, I ask whether my father has been doing his crosswords.

"No, he stopped some time ago. It was getting to be nothing but frustration. The words are so often on the tip of his tongue, you see."

I nod and try to ignore the pang of sadness this brings.

"What can I do, Ma? How can I help?"

She smiles at me, touches my cheek, and sighs. "Bringing the tea out will be fantastic help, love."

We share a lengthy moment of eye contact, and I understand that her focus on the tea is her way of saying being present in the here and now is the only thing I can do. She's right, but it does nothing to soothe my worries.

12

Felicity

When I see Amelia for our second appointment, I've come to realize that my bad moment when Conor came home to find me non-functional was just that—a *moment*. Since then, I unburdened myself with that very long talk with Amelia and gotten a lot of rest. I feel so improved, in fact, that I tell Amelia we don't even need to keep meeting.

"Well, that's wonderful news," she replies.

I examine her for sarcasm but find none. She's smiling pleasantly, her notepad and pen untouched in her lap.

"Yes, I think it is. I mean, after our session I felt like the weight of the world had been lifted from me. And between Lizzy and Conor, I ended up getting a lot of rest. Which, is really all I think I needed."

"I'm happy to hear that, Felicity."

After a moment of silence, I realize I'm waiting for her to validate my self-diagnosis. But she doesn't.

"So, really, I came today to say thank you."

"You're very welcome."

Again, I'm left waiting. I want her to say something to make me feel like I'm doing the right thing. I want her to say, "Of course, you can handle things from here on out. I could see straight-away that you just needed to unburden yourself. You've clearly got it all sorted now."

But she doesn't say that. She doesn't say anything, just watches me.

"I wondered whether you might let me buy you a cup of tea," I say for want of anything else to break the silence. In thinking about it after the fact, I feel it might be a nice gesture—especially since I'm telling her I won't be back and am therefore depriving her of my business.

"Could we make it coffee?" she asks.

"Em, yes, absolutely."

She rises from her chair and sets the notepad and pen on a side table. I take her lead and we both gather our purses to leave the office.

ONCE ON THE STREET, I confess that I don't have a place in mind for coffee. Amelia assures me she knows where we can go, and we walk in companionable silence until we come upon a donut shop not far from Trinity College, making it a popular spot for uni students. Still, we manage to snag the only remaining table. Amelia recommends the lemon meringue and I go to the counter to place an order for two coffees and one hipster donut.

When I sit across from Amelia with our order, I realize this should feel awkward. Having coffee with my erstwhile therapist is an odd way to end the relationship. But, I don't feel uncomfortable. Amelia has a manner that makes me feel like we've been friends for ages.

"We'll split this, then?" she asks, ready to tear the gooey donut in half.

"No, I'm not hungry. It's all yours."

"Oh, thanks."

She seems delighted for the treat and it's refreshing to see a woman eat unapologetically.

I look around at the busy shop, eyeing the college students who seem to be spending freely on the designer donuts.

"I know what you're thinking," Amelia says.

Startled, I turn my focus back to her.

"How can they afford two or three euros on a single donut?"

I laugh. "You did read my mind. When I was at university, I had three roommates and worked two part-time jobs at pubs. I ate best when the kitchen made a mistake and couldn't serve the food."

Amelia nods in agreement. "I had three roommates, too. We lived in a squalid little place. It wasn't far from Trinity, but the landlord was pulling one over on us with the cost, given the sad shape of it. Still, we got to live close to the school and had the best time, even if the lot of us together couldn't afford something like this." She holds up a piece of the donut and the lemon glistens under the sunlight filtering through the window.

"I went away to Toronto for school. Had to get away from here as soon as I could. I was determined to find some independence from my Ma."

"She leaned a bit on you, yeah?"

"Thinking back on it now, it's hard to hold on to the anger and resentment I had at her over it. But back then, it was a real thing. I just felt such pressure to put my life on hold to be her everything, you know?"

She nods. "It can be draining. My sister was like that for a long time until she sorted things."

"Really?"

"She had been in an abusive relationship with a fella who really did a number on her. It was mostly psychological, but sometimes it was physical, too. I'd get the calls at all hours. She'd never let our parents think she was anything but perfect, which to be honest, is a condition we both suffer from. Such people pleasers," she says, and I smile. "Anyway, it meant she'd never go to them. And I certainly wouldn't tell them the state she was in, so we went through it together. I'd patch her up—literally and figuratively—and she'd swear she was done with him." She sighs sadly. "Then the cycle would continue."

"Oh, I'm sorry to hear that."

"She was young. It all started in school. Thankfully, she pulled herself out of it once she agreed to see a therapist—not me, of course. It's been years now that she's been with a wonderful, stable, man. They even have a baby boy."

I'm relieved at the happy ending to that tale. I ask to see a picture of her nephew and we end up exchanging phones to scroll through the dozens of photos we each have. We coo and give out compliments on the beauty of the children. I notice she doesn't miss a beat when she sees that Romeo is of African descent. Though, she shouldn't have that reaction given that I told her about him in our first session. Still, I'm sensitive to it given the talk I had with my father.

We went through a private adoption service and could certainly have chosen a white baby, but we wanted to make the biggest impact we could and asked for the child who would have the most difficulty being placed. We were told that this boy, the child of a young Nigerian immigrant, had been passed over more times than they could count. That made our decision easy. We offered an open adoption but we were told the mother was very young and wanted it closed. We will, obviously, always be open with Romeo about how he came to be our son and brace ourselves for him wanting to find his birth mother one day. For now, though, he is entirely ours, and anyone who can't accept and understand that—including my father—has no place in our lives.

"May I ask a personal question?"

I groan inwardly. Perhaps I was too quick to give Amelia credit for her color-blind reaction. I nod but my body goes tense.

"Did you name your daughter Ella after Ella Fitzgerald?"

The relief I feel that she's more interested in my daughter's name than the color of my son's skin is huge. I laugh.

"Yes, we did, actually. Conor, he's in love with Ella's voice."

"I love jazz, myself. I'm tickled that you named your daughter after one of the greats."

"Turns out it was apt since she's got an amazing vocal range," I say with a laugh. "Her cries can be epic."

"Maybe she'll be a musician like your husband."

"I don't know that I'd wish that for her."

"No?"

"Well, at least not a rock musician. He's had amazing success, but it's a very transient life. The traveling is grueling. Setting down roots takes monumental effort."

"The exact opposite of what you had with your first marriage, I think you said?"

"Yes, true. Richard was stability personified. He had his life all planned out and I went along for the ride. Until he told me to get off," I say.

"It wasn't that abrupt, was it?"

"Indeed, it was." I tell her then the whole story of how my marriage ended, how blindsided I was by Richard's rejection of me when he thought I was infertile.

"What lovely revenge you've had, though," Amelia says.

"How so?"

"You turned around and married a rockstar who was actually capable of getting you pregnant. And now you have two beautiful children."

I'm about to reply when the phone in front of me vibrates. It's Amelia's, not mine. She still has my phone sitting on the table in front of her from when we were sharing photos. The speed with which she grabs her phone is impressive. I hadn't seen who was calling, and it's clear she doesn't want me to.

The interruption is a good reminder that I should be going. I can feel the need to nurse my babies. As with the last time I saw Amelia, I feel lighter. But this wasn't a therapy session, so why does her simple company give me the same effect?

"Well, thanks for indulging me with having a cup of coffee," I tell her.

"Ah, no. Thank you for the coffee and the donut. You really should get one for yourself on the way out."

We stand, and I realize the good feeling our conversation gave me is threatening to slip away. It felt so nice to have a chat with a friend. Could we be friends? Is that possible after the circumstances we met in?

"Listen, I have to say, this was lovely. Would you want to meet again for a coffee sometime?" I say in a rush.

"Oh, sure, why not?" she says breezily. "In fact, we could get together again at this time next Monday since I have the slot open? It would give me an excuse to have another lemon meringue donut."

I laugh. I'm looking forward to it already.

13

Felicity

Once I get to my car I realize that I'm very close to the studio where Conor and the lads are working on the album. I've never visited there and think it might be nice to pop in. But I haven't brought a pump and I'm desperate to feed the babies, so I ring Lizzy and ask her to bring the kids with her to meet me at the studio.

I make a slight detour on the way to stop at Marks & Spencer, thinking it would be nice to show up with some food. Once inside, I end up wandering and feeling that lack of focus once more. It takes me far too long to decide on an assortment of tea sandwiches and a random sampling of crisp packets.

By the time I get to the studio, I find a dozen or so fans loitering outside and Lizzy and the babies already inside. She's surrounded by the members of Rogue, and though they could certainly be captivated by Romeo and Ella's presence, her clingy, low-cut top leads me to think otherwise.

"Hello," I say, feeling invisible. All the good effects of my chat with Amelia have disappeared. I fight the tears rushing to my eyes.

Conor is the first to look up. I see him quickly assess me in the way that he's always done. It used to be that he'd add a sexy smile.

Now, his smile is one of concern. I shake my head to tell him not to worry. I didn't come here to make a scene. I didn't come here to fall apart in front of everyone.

"Good to see you, Felicity," Gavin says and leans in to kiss me on the cheek. "Your little ones are a gorgeous interruption. We needed this."

His generosity makes me smile. He and Sophie are alike in that way. They can be incredibly supportive.

"That's nice to hear. I brought some food in case you're hungry."

"Always," Martin says and relieves me of the bags in my hands. "Thanks."

His insatiable appetite has long been legendary, but now it's the sort that comes from his workouts. He's become a gym rat like the others and claimed his place as scream-worthy in their fans' eyes.

Shay and Danny Boy say their hellos and I greet the band's producers and sound engineers. All before Conor makes his way to me.

"Hey, you," he says, and kisses me gently.

"Good surprise?" I ask.

"*Good* surprise," he confirms.

My relief is interrupted by the sharp wail of first Ella, and then Romeo.

"The babies have been so good, really, I swear," Lizzy says with an apologetic smile.

"It's okay, I'm ready to take them." I look around at the small room. It's overwhelmed by a large, complex sound console, but there is a sofa behind me. "I'll nurse them here, if that's okay?"

All the men immediately look uncomfortable and my cheeks redden at the spot I've put them in.

"Lads, let's take the food to the kitchen for a break," Gavin says, coming to my rescue.

They all eagerly file out and I'm left with Conor and Lizzy. She helps me get set up on the sofa. I have no inhibition about exposing myself in order to feed the babies and Lizzy has no qualms either as she helps me make the proper adjustments. I glance up and catch Conor watching us. His eyes are on Lizzy's hand as she adjusts my breast into better position. When he turns away abruptly and starts fiddling with the sound board switches, I worry again about how I haven't been satisfying his needs.

We didn't have that much time together before the babies came along. He was on tour for long stretches right after we became a real couple. Our reunions were frenzied and highly satisfying, but in thinking about it, carefree time to focus only on ourselves and indulge the purely sexual part of our connection was short-lived. I imagine his patience is wearing thin.

"Conor, can you show me where the toilets are? I want to wash my hands," Lizzy says.

I watch as he turns to look at her, at the way his eyes drop down the length of her body before he can stop himself. She's young and fit and I have no doubt that at any other point in his life he'd show her to the restroom and then show her a whole lot more. Maybe he's even fantasizing about that in the second it takes him to respond. But then he does speak, and I relax.

"It's just down the end of the hall there," he says.

Once she's gone, he settles in beside me. He takes a moment to stroke each baby's cheek. The way he clearly adores his children has made me fall more deeply in love with him. It really is the sexiest thing a man can do, even if I don't feel that sensation deep in me the way I once did.

"How was your session?" he asks.

"Oh, I didn't have it."

He raises his eyebrows in surprise. "What do you mean?"

"I'm just feeling so much more myself that I really only went to thank Amelia for that one time."

"I see." The skepticism on his face reveals he doesn't trust my decision.

"I do really like her, though," I say. "I ended up buying her a coffee and a donut and we had a lovely chat."

"Okay."

"And we're going to meet up again on Monday for another coffee and chat."

"Like an appointment?" he asks.

I laugh. "I guess. A friendship appointment. I really get on with her. I think we'll be great friends, actually."

"Friends?"

"Eh, yes." I'm not sure what he's driving at and his questioning is beginning to irritate me.

"With the person who was meant to treat you for your issues?"

"With the person who is just nice to talk to."

"You have me for that. I hope you haven't forgotten that."

"No, of course not. It's just easy with her. We had a nice give and take earlier. It's just a relief to not feel . . . judged."

"Who judges you, Fee?" he asks in a rush, clearly exasperated. "Honestly, tell me *who*?"

"I don't know. I mean, I didn't really mean it like that. I just—I just can't speak with Sophie right now, not the way I can with Amelia. This is the friendship I need."

He considers this for a moment and I can see he's struggling to accept my logic. I know he wants to be able to fix me—and that, in fact, he does view me as needing to be fixed—but he will have to learn that some things are not in his control. I need to navigate this, whatever it is, myself.

Finally, he releases a sigh, relenting. "If that's what you need, then I'm all for it, honey. I want you to have everything you need."

"I'm going to get there, really I will. You'll be patient with me for a little while longer while I get steady?"

"Of course. I'm not going anywhere. You know that, right?"

"I do. But . . ."

"But?"

"I have moments where I wouldn't blame you for wanting your freedom back. We got together and your whole life was upturned—"

"For the *better*, Fee."

"I just know that it's a lot. I'm admitting it for you so you don't have to feel guilty for it."

"Please don't do that."

"I mean, I understand that you're probably feeling a little trapped by all this—"

"Don't do that," he repeats, his voice raised, and it stops me cold. He isn't someone who raises his voice unless there's a damn good reason. I watch him silently. "What you're doing is pushing me away. Just like you did when I was trying to leave Colette. You pushed me away when you thought you couldn't possibly be enough for me. You did that instead of *believing* me when I told you you were the one I wanted. Stop pushing me away. Believe me when I tell you that you and the babies are all I want."

I'm set to explain I had no intention of doing that, and that I'm sorry if that's how I've made him feel, but before I can get a word out, Lizzy returns. She's applied fresh lipstick and perfume and looks carefree and ready for anything—the opposite of what I feel.

"So, this is where it all happens?" she asks, eyeing one of the isolation booths that can be seen behind the glass wall above the sound board. She's oblivious to the tension she walked in on. Either that or has chosen to break it up. I'm still wavering on whether she's a godsend to help me or if she's the kind of temptation I don't want in such close proximity to my husband.

Conor, clearly ready to take the out she's offered, stands and begins to give her the rundown on the studio and how each space works. She affects fascination when he tells her how one room is carpeted and another isn't, each producing a different sound because of the flooring.

He's in his element, enjoying the rapt audience. And I'm here nursing two babies and thinking he's right. I have a habit of pushing him away. And if I don't put an end to it, it may just work.

14

———

Conor

I'm a dick.

I'm a dick because I know I have unfinished business with my wife, but here I am lavishing my attention on Lizzy.

Right in front of her.

It's childish, but still, a part of me thinks if Felicity wants to push me away, then I'll go ahead and give her a taste of what that feels like. It would be easy to slip my arm around Lizzy's shoulders, or better yet, her slim waist, and steer her through a personal tour of the studio. I imagine I could find many ways to let my hand "accidentally" brush against her high tits and tight ass. Lizzy has already made it clear she'd be open to that and more.

I'm only halfway entertaining these thoughts when I glance over and meet Felicity's eyes. She gives me a smirk and an eye roll. As usual, she on to me. She's always been able to read me, to call me out when I resort to bullshit like this. I can see in her expression that my minute of being a dick hasn't shaken her, though. This isn't the proof to her earlier declaration that she thinks I want my so-called freedom back. Instead, she's likely thinking of our time together early on when I was playing games, stubbornly unwilling to trust what I was feeling and what I wanted.

The thing is, that's not who I am now.

I lean down to murmur into Lizzy's ear and she shifts her body closer to mine. But her posture sags with my words. Still, she nods and sets about gathering the myriad of paraphernalia that goes everywhere with us and the kids these days.

"Shall we leave you?" Felicity asks. The babies are both fed and she's getting them burped and settled.

"Lizzy's going to take Romeo and Ella home. But you're going to stay for a bit. I want to give you a tour, play some stuff for you."

The smile she gives me is open and pure and real—it's the essential *her*. It's beautiful, and I know I'd do anything to get her to smile a million times more.

ONCE LIZZY HAS LEFT with the children and with the guys still lingering in the kitchen, Felicity and I have the studio to ourselves. I pull her by the hand and give her the tour and treatment I had thought about giving Lizzy. My not-so-subtle brushes against Felicity's body are ignored, however, and I'm quickly reminded of how numb she's become to my touch.

I've been patient with her lack of desire. I understand that the pregnancy was harder than she had expected. She had debilitating morning sickness for much of it. Her fatigue was so great that she pestered her doctor until it was discovered she had anemia. She felt she was gaining too much weight, though she always looked beautiful to me. And her sex drive dropped to zero. The point is, it never felt easy to her. She had waited all her life for this moment and was disappointed in herself that when it finally did come, she wasn't responding the way she thought she should. So, besides trying to be supportive, I just waited it all out, thinking once the baby came she would be back to herself.

That didn't happen. Instead, she veered into these mood swings that would send her from a lovely, competent mother, to someone unable to dress herself in fresh clothes or bathe. And the odd, antagonistic relationship with her best friend, Sophie, reared up again. That spell of jealousy and competitiveness had been squashed well before she even became pregnant and I have no idea what's changed. All I know is that my wife is having issues coping—with motherhood, with her friendships, with me. And just when I thought that a therapist might be the thing to help, she's cut that off.

"What were you all working on when Lizzy showed up?" Felicity asks, pulling me from my thoughts.

"I, em, a tune about memory," I say.

"Memories?"

"Well, sort of." I don't explain that the song is one that I've written, with only minor help from Gavin. I don't want to go into it. If I do, it will only add to her burden.

"Can I hear some?"

"Yeah, sure. Let's go to the Wood Room."

This larger space is where we have a full setup of all our instruments and is where we had been working out the kinks on the song I mentioned. My Telecaster is resting in its stand. The sound isn't routed into the room, but rather through the headphones we each have. I place Gavin's on Felicity, then put the guitar strap over my head and slip on my headphones.

Strumming the guitar, I settle into a place of comfort with it before starting the right rhythm. It's a rich, lazy tone that fills our ears. I watch Felicity rather than look down at the strings. I've always been able to feel my way on the chords, which helps when I want to project a little extra swagger on stage. But it also helps when, like now, I want to see what effect the music has on those listening. I see Felicity's face softening as the music washes over her. She closes her eyes and moves ever so slightly with the progression.

I lean into the microphone and sing the first few lines:

When it's all said and done

Will you remember your son?

Opening her eyes with a start, she examines me. The reaction could be because I'm not a singer. Gavin is the singer in our band, of course. I've spent all of our career backing him up or doing some chorus singing on my own, but I've never taken the lead on a song. Not until now. When I brought the song to Gavin, urging him to put his own spin on it, he refused. He said it was mine to sing and that it was time that I step up to the microphone. My voice is decent, but doesn't have that raw, sex-fueled tone that Gavin's does. Not that this particular song needs that kind of edge. This is destined to be a quiet song. And I likely won't even agree to put it on the album. It's just something I need to get out and, thankfully, the guys are all for it.

I keep playing and sing a bit more:

When it comes to that final goodbye
Will it come with a wink and a sigh?

It's melancholic, I know. But I have no other words to give this subject. Gavin knows the impetus of it. Felicity doesn't, though I suspect she will think it's about the fear of my own mortality in light of Christian's passing. That's not quite right, but I'll let her believe it is, because there probably is some of that coloring this song. It's just not the driving force.

I stop playing and singing when I see Felicity's eyes fill with tears.

"Honey, am I that bad?"

She laughs despite the emotion overtaking her. "No, love, your voice is wonderful," she says. "I can't believe I haven't heard you sing —I mean *really* sing—before this. And this song, oh it strikes me so deep here." She presses a hand to her chest over her heart.

"Glad you like it."

"I want more of it. More of you like this."

For a second, I think she's getting flirty, that I might be able to grab her and take her to the bathroom for a quickie. But the spark in her eye isn't about being turned on, it's about her thinking I'm sharing my emotions. She's long told me I don't have to keep my own counsel the way I tend to do. She wants me to turn to her rather than trying to be in control of everything all the time. I should, she's right, but it's not in my nature. I'm not one to complain or vent or share. I'd rather hold things close, at least until I feel like I've figured out the next step forward.

"I want more of *you* like this," I return, deciding to try to force this into something lighter as I pull her closer to me. Maybe I can get her into a more playful mood. I grab her backside with one hand and give her my sexiest smile. "There's a time-honored tradition of christening the studio, honey. Let's do our part, yeah?"

She laughs but disentangles herself from my touch. Again.

"I'll make it quick," I try, "like the old days." I'm referring to when we were first together back in school, a time she remembers as me not having lasted very long in bed. I've come a long way since then and we both know it.

"Con, they can all probably hear this, right?" She gestures to the microphone.

"Ah, if they can, they better mind their own bloody business." I try to pull her back to me, but she steps away.

That's my Felicity, always backing away from me.

15

Conor

Felicity doesn't stay much longer and when she leaves it's with a sense that we have purposely left things unresolved. Her glib attempt to give me an "out" in our relationship, or at least to feel like wanting that would be normal, is unsettling. It weighs on me so much that after a couple hours of work, I beg off, saying I need to run an errand and will be back in an hour.

I don't have Amelia Patterson's phone number. I could find it easily enough, but what I need requires an in-person visit anyway, so I go to her office with the hope that she'll be there. The waiting room is empty and I'm about to knock on the interior door when I notice the red glow of a light on what looks like a doorbell. I assume that means she's with a patient and isn't to be disturbed. Checking my watch, I see that it's nearing the top of the hour. Based on Felicity's appointment, that should mean that whoever is in there now should be wrapping things up.

I should have anticipated the reaction I get when the door opens, but my mind was elsewhere. A young woman, her eyes shining from lingering tears, looks up and does a double-take. She raises a shaking hand to her mouth as recognition sets in.

"C-C-Conor Quinn," she stutters.

This is the last thing I want. I don't want to take selfies with a fan, I don't want to put on my signature sexy smile, I don't want to charm the girl so that her impression of me is as she might have fantasized.

But that's exactly what I will do. Because if I don't, she might walk away disappointed and my image would be damaged. And God knows I care about my image. My concern with image—mine and the band's—has helped ensure we are where we are today. I've always made sure I'm in great shape and that I make every fan, journalist, and record executive—man or woman—feels like I'd be honored to take them to bed. It is amazing how much that has helped push along our career. And it suits me, too. I won't deny the ego rush I get in playing these games.

Ms. Patterson must have heard the commotion because she soon joins me and the awe-struck fan in the waiting room. I hadn't met her the last time I was here for Felicity, so I introduce myself.

"It's a pleasure to meet you, Conor," she says as I take her hand into mine.

As I release her, I let my fingertips trail over the inside of her wrist. I've found that extra touch tends to do something to a woman. When she hesitates, eyeing me for a second longer than necessary, I feel that thing I've known since I was a teenager. It's the heat of a woman's desire for me. With loose curls of long brown hair, intelligent blue eyes, and shapely legs, she's nice looking, if a little plump.

"Tammy," Ms. Patterson says, turning to her client, "I'll see you next week, yes?"

Though her eyes never leave mine, Tammy nods in response. She still hasn't made a move to leave. This isn't the first time I've rendered a woman incapable of functioning. It doesn't help matters that I smile at her and give her a wink.

"Next week, then," Ms. Patterson repeats.

Tammy blinks once, then several times rapidly. "Yes, next week," she says and hugs her tote bag to her side as she walks to the main office door. She turns and gives me another look before finally stepping out.

"So, what might I do to you?" Ms. Patterson asks. The rush of blood to her cheeks doesn't stop there. The blush runs down her neck and onto her chest.

Before she can stumble to correct herself, I speak. No need to let her stick her foot deeper into her lovely mouth. She and I know she's hot for me and that's enough for my amusement.

"I need to talk to you about my wife," I tell her.

"Is Felicity okay?"

"That's what I need you to answer, actually."

"Oh. Well, I see. But—"

"Before you say you can't answer because of a privacy privilege, she tells me she's no longer seeing you in a professional capacity. So, I would think that frees things up a bit, doesn't it?"

She assesses me for a moment, her posture rigid. Then she relaxes a degree and turns to her office door. "Come inside for minute, won't you?"

I follow her into the room. Except for the unfortunate color of the dark green walls, it's a welcoming space. The lighting is warm, and the furniture is comfortable. I don't take a seat, though. I didn't come here to be analyzed. I won't be sucked into that.

"I am seeing Felicity again. We have a coffee date at our regular appointment time," she says.

"Yes, I know that. And the way you both say it makes it sound like therapy is somehow continuing, but Felicity seems to think she's all better and has no need for any kind of structured help."

"You disagree with her decision to stop therapy?"

"I do."

"Have you spoken with her about that?"

"I have, as I said. She said she feels more herself now and that therapy isn't necessary. But I'd like your opinion on that."

"You sound concerned."

Her measured tones have struck my last nerve. "Of course, I do. This is my *wife* we're talking about. She's my partner, the mother to my children. The other day, she was incapable of caring for them and instead curled up at my feet like a shamed dog. I'm *incredibly* concerned. I came here because I can't trust her judgment about quitting therapy. I need to figure out how I can help her and whether she's any danger to herself or the babies."

She nods, and I can see her thinking of what she will say next. She strikes me as someone who tries very hard to be careful with their words, and rightly so. But there's some other layer of consciousness going on here that I can't quite pinpoint. It goes beyond the normal therapist caution because she should have pat answers at the ready. But she's struggling. When she speaks, it's clear she was telling herself not to say what she finally does. Because it's not what a therapist would say.

"When she came in this morning and said she was done with our sessions, I knew it was an overcorrection on her part. She feels good because she's on an upswing right now."

"An 'overcorrection'?"

"I'm guessing you know the number of issues she's dealing with—"

"Postpartum, right?"

She hesitates and her eyes flick over me, as if assessing what more she should say. "I can't diagnose her with postpartum. Partly because I don't know enough, but also because I'd rather her primary physician take on that role."

"Then, what good are you?" I snap. It's rude, but I came here for assurances, not excuses and shifting responsibilities of care to others.

Despite my tone, she doesn't flinch or even alter her pleasant expression. She must have had a lot of experience in maintaining that façade.

"I think I can be of help for her other concern. She's dealing with a lot. I think the children have brought to the surface a whole host of things and they're overwhelming her right now."

"Okay," I say slowly, trying to think of what else my wife hasn't been telling me.

"I do believe more therapy would be hugely beneficial to her. That's why I went to coffee with her. That's why we've got another coffee date. Because sometimes, it helps to get therapy in an unconventional way. Some people are more open in a different setting."

I take a moment to digest this. Though I'm grateful that she has taken it upon herself to step out of the normal confines of traditional talk therapy, it doesn't quite sit right.

"I'm a bit confused here," I admit. "Are you saying you're continuing to be her therapist, but in the guise of a friend? That you're deceiving her into getting help?"

She takes in a deep breath and slowly lets it out. "I suppose you could make that argument, but what I'd say is that I'm only interested in being her friend. If I can impart some of my training with her in the course of this friendship, then all the better."

"Fuck me," I whisper. I'm trying to wrap my head around this idea, but I'm thrown. Thrown by the fact that this woman is suggesting she treat Felicity in this way. It's either an incredibly generous act of kindness toward someone in need, or an irresponsible manipulation of someone too vulnerable to know better. And what does it make me if I go along with it?

"I understand that this sounds unusual," she says. "But I hope you will give me the benefit of the doubt because I really have nothing but good intentions. In fact, I don't have any big plan at all, other than wanting to be sure that Felicity is managing."

I examine her for some telltale sign of an ulterior motive but find none. What I do detect is a woman who wants to help. I think of the progress she's had with Danny Boy and wonder if her methods were similarly unconventional. Danny Boy's apology to me for having stolen my guitar at the end of the last tour comes to mind. There's no doubt in my mind he never would have made that effort if it hadn't been for someone like Ms. Patterson intervening to steer him in the right direction. That realization helps me accept this unorthodox arrangement. Though, I'm quick to make one thing clear.

"I'm not paying you."

Her brows crease. I've offended her.

"Why would you? Of course, you wouldn't."

"Will you let me know if you think I should be concerned?"

"I'm not in the habit of sharing my girlfriend's confidences with their husbands."

I roll my eyes at her sudden discretion. My evident frustration elicits a caveat from her.

"But, if she tells me something truly worrisome, I will make sure you know about it."

"Good."

We exchange mobile numbers and I start to take my leave, but she seems to want to say more. I worry it's to do with Felicity and urge her to speak.

"It's nothing," she says with a smile.

"You're sure?"

She hesitates a moment longer. "I just wonder if you might keep from telling Daniel about this, about my involvement with you and Felicity."

"Daniel?" I'm stumped at the name for a second. "Oh, Danny Boy? No worries on that, honey. I'm not after involving Danny fucking Boy in my personal issues, that's for sure."

"I see."

"I'm sure you know him better than most at this point. So, you can understand why I wouldn't trust him with something as delicate as this. I mean, no offense, he has come a long way and I give you all the credit, but in the end, he's still Danny Boy, isn't he?"

She tilts her head rather than nods and I can see I've offended her once more. She seems protective of him. She must have pride in their work together. I have no desire to muddy that up.

"He has become a part of our crowd, you know?" I say. "So, I'm allowed to take the piss."

This seems to have the effect I wanted. She relaxes into a smile and gives me a nod.

"Listen, don't take this the wrong way, but I really hope I don't hear from you."

Now she laughs. "I hope I don't need to get in touch, either."

16

Felicity

The bit of independence I found in my two sessions with Amelia have made me realize I need to allow myself more of that. Being housebound with the babies has been both wonderful and difficult. I am a mother, but I also need to take care of myself, and part of that means having some time away.

It's with this in mind that I tell Conor I need him to watch the babies while Sophie and I go out for a drink and dinner.

"Em, I was going to go back to the studio," he says.

He had come home unexpectedly again and I suspect he was trying to check up on me. Our visit earlier at the studio hadn't ended with any clear resolution, leaving us in an uneasy spot. It's clear he doesn't want to continue discussing how he thinks I'm pushing him away, but rather, would like to simply bypass it all together. He'd be happy to ignore the whole thing as long as I signal to him that all is well again.

I'd normally dig into the issue to find some resolution, but I'm not ready to right now. I'm more focused on repairing the damage I did to another relationship. I called Sophie when I got home from the studio and suggested that just us girls go out, and she quickly agreed.

Now I'm in the en suite of our bedroom, the door open and Conor watching me as I get ready. I've made a big effort to look put together—showering, carefully drying my shoulder-length auburn hair, and dressing in jeans fresh from the wash that cling to me. The peacock-blue silk blouse I've got on makes my eyes pop, and the black YSL high heels I wear give me height. I've done my makeup for the first time in I don't know how long, and I feel good.

Glancing over at Conor where he's seated on the side of the bed, I can tell he likes what he sees, too.

"All this for Sophie, then?" he asks as I join him.

"Just trying to look halfway human for once."

He stands and eyes me lustfully. "You look much more than that, honey."

"Oh really?" I ask. I'm fishing for a compliment and curious how he will respond.

"Yes. In fact," he says and wraps his arm around my waist, pulling me to him, "you look incredibly fuckable."

That was a *very* good response. I smile and feel a tingle. My long-dormant desire has suddenly showed itself. I wonder if it's because of his forceful tone. He's been so sweet and patient with me that I've almost forgotten the way he could take command.

I wrap my arm around his neck and look up at him. "And what would you like to do about that?"

He leans to me and gives me a lingering kiss that brings me to my tiptoes as I yearn for more. But then he pulls away and kisses my neck just below my ear before whispering an answer to my question.

"What I'd like to do is peel those jeans off and eat your pussy until your thighs shake against my face."

"Oh," I say, the word escaping as a soft sigh.

I'm ready to take advantage of this moment where we are both—finally—wanting each other at the same time. I'm also aware that connecting physically would go a long way toward improving our relationship. It also just might keep him from drooling too much over Lizzy who is downstairs with the babies.

I run my hand down his abdomen, over the waistband of his jeans, and to his crotch where I find him ready to finish what we started in the shower the other day. He's hard and thick and hot against my grasp.

"Fuck yes," he moans.

There's a quick double tap at our bedroom door but neither of us reacts to it. Until it opens.

Lizzy pokes her head in, sees the intimate way we're positioned and retreats behind the open door.

"So sorry," she says. She clears her throat. "Sophie is here for you, Felicity."

When I hear the click of the door closing, I release the grip I had on Conor and lean my forehead into his chest.

"There's time," he says and pulls me into a kiss.

"I should—"

"Fee, we can still—"

I shake my head with a weak smile. "When I get back? The anticipation will be worth it," I say.

"I've had months of anticipation. We can make this quick. *Please.*"

I'm mortified. I've made Conor Quinn beg for sex. I can see in his face that he's not happy about it either. Before I can think of how to make this situation better, he turns away. He's found his limit.

"Go ahead," he says. "Sophie's waiting."

"Conor—"

"Is Lizzy staying for a bit? I'll need to call Gav and the guys to say I can't make it."

"Em, yes, she said she can stay to help get you settled with the little ones but has plans later."

He nods. I watch as he rubs his bottom lip and gets lost in thought.

"Sweetheart, I . . ."

I'm at a loss for how to make this better and he doesn't step in to help me.

"I'm sure you'll be fine," I continue, changing the topic, "but call me if you need to and I'll cut things short with Sophie."

Conjuring up one of his confident smiles, he winks at me. "I'll be grand. You go ahead and have a good time."

17

Felicity

"So, Lizzy's back?" Sophie asks.

She's waited to say anything until we are seated at a table in the back corner of a lively shared-plates style restaurant, each of us with a gin-based specialty cocktail as a starter.

"Yes. We thought having her come back would give us a little more flexibility. You know, to do things like this," I say and raise my glass in the gesture of a toast.

Sophie smiles and raises her glass in return and we both take a sip. I sense her hesitating to say more and I scramble to think what I've told her before about Lizzy. What I may have told her about my mixed feelings over the young woman who has clearly caught Conor's eye. Have I told her before that it makes me uneasy to allow this beautiful young woman access to my sex-starved husband? And now I worry that I've just set up the worst-case scenario, having left those two together after I worked him up into unresolved desire. I've left him with the hot nanny. It's actually quite funny, the thought of that scenario. Such a cliché.

"He won't do anything."

Blinking, I focus on Sophie. She's looking at me with compassion, urging me to believe what she's said. And I realize I said out loud the last part of what I thought was only racing through my mind. What happened to the clarity I was feeling after seeing Amelia just this morning?

"And if you're really concerned, I can help you find another au pair," she continues. "Someone older, maybe?"

"Oh, em, no, I know he wouldn't," I say.

"Right. We both know Conor is one of the good ones."

"Right." I take a long sip of my juniper and mint-infused cocktail, savoring the bright flavor. This is the first alcohol I've had since before I became pregnant. I'll have to pump and dump later, but I've taken a cue from Amelia's unabashed indulgence at the donut shop and decided this is another bit of freedom I should give myself.

"This tastes amazing, doesn't it?"

I look up to find Sophie grinning at me. I smile back, and we share a moment of silent connection. Us sharing in this simple thing reminds me why we are such good friends. She's been there for me ever since I returned to Dublin, and especially during my pregnancy and these early days of motherhood, even as she's expanded her own family.

"Thanks for coming out tonight," I tell her.

"I'm glad you called. It was well-timed. The kids were especially exhausting today."

"Really?"

She laughs at my unmasked incredulity. "I don't know why you think it's all so easy for me, Felicity. It gets to me just as much as it does you. I'm only human."

I start to disagree with that but stop short and try for praise instead. "Well, you certainly make it look just the opposite."

Sipping her cocktail, she watches me for a moment. "Have you ever considered that I've spent a good number of years creating that impression?"

"What do you mean?"

"I mean, my life with Gavin has been so scrutinized by the media that I've had to learn to project a certain image. There have been many times when I was literally falling apart but I had to pretend I was just fine because there were likely cameras watching my every move in public."

I know that Sophie and Gavin have received a ridiculous amount of attention over the years, but this still sounds like a bit much. My expression must telegraph my skepticism because she proves her point in the next second.

"There are at least two people either photographing or recording us right now," she says. "Look there—the bartender at the far corner and the man sitting alone over on the opposite side. If they don't work for the tabloids, they'll either sell what they get tonight or sell the tip that we're here and we'll soon see a real paparazzi show up."

I see that both the female bartender and the solo diner have their mobile phones pointed in our direction. I wave dumbly before catching myself and slumping back into my chair. I've never been good at this. It's a cruel irony given that I run the media strategy for the band and yet I can never spot these things when they're focused on me. Of course, if I wasn't with Sophie McManus, world-famous supermodel and wife of the notorious Gavin McManus, I probably wouldn't have rated a second glance. I only ever get this kind of attention when I'm with Conor. But even then, it's always Conor who spots the spies and points them out just as Sophie has done.

"So, em," I mumble, struggling to get back to our conversation, "you're saying that you put on a front? That your perfect demeanor is all pretend?"

"I don't know if I'd put it like that, exactly. I'm just saying appearances don't always tell the whole story."

For some reason, this strikes me as ominous and I jump to conclusions. "Is everything okay with you and Gavin?"

She pushes aside her glass and leans forward over the table. I brace myself for some terrible news. For her to tell me that she and her husband are splitting up again, this time for good. And if Sophie and Gavin—the couple everyone, even me, describes as *destined* for each other—can't make it, then what hope do I have?

"Gavin and I are," she says in a hush, her green eyes gleaming in the low light, "better than ever."

I should be reassured, but I had prepared for the opposite and am left oddly disappointed. "Is there something more you're not telling me?"

"Well, Gavin and I have been talking and we made some decisions about the future."

"Go on?"

"After this tour, which they'll push to be no more than a year, I'm going to go back to school."

I can't comprehend what she's talking about. Firstly, I've never heard of Rogue doing a tour as short as a year. The worldwide demand they face calls for tour dates that will stretch to at least eighteen months. And secondly, Sophie is a married mother of two. Married to a rockstar, no less. Why would she go back to school?

Once more, all this must be clear on my face because she answers my questions before I can ask them.

"It's something he and the guys have been kicking around—the shorter tour. Everyone's on board. It seems like we all have so much to want to be home for. There's us, of course, with our kids. Then Marty and Lainey are really getting serious. And Shay's committed to Jessica out in San Francisco. So, it makes sense to do this tour, then take a bit of a longer break. An unofficial hiatus. Just to actually live life."

The fact that Conor hasn't talked to me about this is something I'll have to take up with him. And I have no desire to make it clear to Sophie that I've been completely in the dark. Instead, I focus on the other thing she had mentioned.

"And you'll go back to school?"

She nods with a beaming smile. I can see it gives her pleasure, the very idea of it.

"You went to Trinity for a time, right?" It was so long ago now that I'm not sure if I even remember what she studied, so I don't try to guess it.

"Yes, I studied art history. But I took a break after Gavin and I got married so I could go on tour with him. And then I got scouted for modeling, and my whole world changed. I said at the time that I could always go back to school, no matter how old I was. Now, I'm finally going to prove that's true."

"That's, em, fantastic," I say. "What does Gavin plan to do with himself during this time?"

She shrugs like it's the least of her concerns. "Be at home with the kids," she says with a laugh. "Maybe he'll write a book or a hundred songs or a play. Who knows? I'm just so excited that he suggested this to begin with. He says he wants me to have the time and space to focus on what I love. It's—" She stops herself as tears rush to her eyes. Smiling, she takes a deep breath and blinks away the emotion. "It's taken a long time to get here. But everything finally feels so right. Balanced, you know?"

I nod but stay mute about how once again she appears to have everything lined up perfectly. All is well in Sophie-land, despite what she tried to tell me earlier. Here she is with two gorgeous children and a husband so supportive he's willing to halt the momentum of his band and career so that she can return to the studies she casually abandoned a decade beforehand. By contract, I'm just hanging on from moment to moment, desperate to keep from driving my husband away but also unable to keep from pushing him from me for fear that I can't possibly be enough for him.

"That's such good news," I force myself to say.

"It'll be good for all of us, I think. You know, give you and Conor real time together as a couple and as a family? You've had such a disjointed sort of road, so far, haven't you? I mean, he went on tour almost as soon as you got together. And then he's been living in the studio for so long now. Imagine having a real period where you can just be together. It'll be a lovely thing."

That kind of simple, stable life was all I once wanted. And then I fell for Conor and had to reset my expectations. I had to settle for taking what I could get from him, including snatching a few days spent with him here and there, either when I met him on tour or when he made a mad dash home to see me. My previous penchant for early, cozy nights in was replaced with tagging along with him to parties that lasted until dawn. I soon found my routine changing from rising early in the morning for a brisk swim to desperate for a coffee with an espresso chaser just to get moving. It's a completely different lifestyle, one that I never expected to have. But it's the cost of being with the man I love, and I've accepted it as the new norm.

The prospect of being able to create a different kind of life together, one that might more closely match what I have long craved, is both thrilling and terrifying. Terrifying because I fear it isn't who he is. What if we live the life of regular folks and this is the thing that finally makes my rockstar husband realizes it's not enough? That *I'm* not enough?

"It will be lovely, sure you're right," I force myself to say.

ANOTHER COCKTAIL EACH, and we relax into our old, familiar way with each other, chatting easily and laughing over the silliest things. It feels good, like our old friendship. I realize that, while I may never meet the standards of perfection Sophie seems to embody, that won't stop me from loving her as my dear friend.

She and I had always been opposites, starting from when we met in school. She was a head-turner even then—the epitome of what we Irish imagined a California girl to be, with her blonde hair and tanned skin and bright white smile. But what made defining her by her looks alone impossible was how she challenged Gavin. He has gone from using his sexiest voice to chat her up, to questioning whether she had come to Ireland on some sort of high horse. After the briefest hesitation during which I saw a flash of vulnerability, she pushed right back, shutting him up. That moment of her struggling with deciding whether she would be toyed with, along with the forceful way she answered him was enough to instantly endear her to me. Most girls would have withered under his shift from flirting with her to antagonizing her. He and Conor ruled that school, after all. Whether they were in a band or not, they were the boys everyone looked to, the ones all the girls wanted. And Sophie, being the new girl, might have chosen the path of least resistance in order to assimilate into her unfamiliar school, but instead, she chose to stir things up. We were thick as thieves after that.

It's with these memories washing over me that I ask, "What was your first impression of me when we met that day in class?" My curiosity about this is probably because I've been so foggy lately. My sense of self has felt out of reach, intensifying the anxiety I can't seem to shake. So, I'm genuinely curious how she saw me all those years ago.

"Oh, god, Felicity," Sophie says with a smile. "I was so in awe of you."

I laugh. "Me? Really?"

"Yes, of course. Well, first because you came to my rescue when Gavin was being a jerk to me. And then because you just seemed to have everything figured out."

"Don't all teenagers put on that front, though?"

"They might," she concedes. "But yours wasn't a front. You knew what you needed at that age. You knew falling for Conor wouldn't work because you wanted more stability from your partner. You knew the best way to create your own life was to start new far away. You were just so wise beyond your years. It was admirable. And brave."

"Brave?"

"Because I couldn't do those things. I couldn't resist falling for Gavin even though I knew it wouldn't last and I'd get hurt. I couldn't take a leap and start fresh by staying here when the school year was up."

"Well, you were still young," I tell her.

"Not much younger than you were when you left for Toronto."

"I think I was just stubborn, really."

Sophie laughs. "I wanted to *be* you. I wanted to know my own mind the way you did and forge ahead with big plans the way you did. I even wanted to be out at all hours with the boys like you did. But other than one time staying out all night with Gavin, I just couldn't *not* play by the rules."

I think about the fact that she has this view of me and it makes me wonder if I'm still that headstrong girl, willing to do what I please. I'm not sure. I do know that I'd like to get closer to being her, if nothing else. I'm just not sure how I'll go about it.

18

Conor

Coming downstairs to find myself alone with Lizzy is not exactly the ideal scenario. Not after my wife has left me with a serious case of blue balls while she's off with Sophie for a girls' night. I had lingered in our bedroom making a few phone calls for long enough that it seems the children are already down for the night. It's half-eight, meaning if I'm lucky it will be four hours before Ella wakes wanting to nurse—or a bottle if Felicity is out that late. Romeo has his schedule down to closer to six hours, which is great progress, though Felicity can never seem to get enough rest in between.

I'm lost in wondering at Felicity's shift from messily sobbing at my feet one day to looking gorgeous and going out for drinks without me the next when Lizzy waves her hand to get my attention. She's looking sporty today with her hair in a high ponytail, wearing tight jeans and trainers along with a Shamrock Rovers tee shirt she's pulled taut in a knot at her slim waist.

"You off, then?" I ask.

"If you're all right?"

"Yeah, I'm good. Thanks, Lizzy. Big plans tonight? Rovers playing?"

She eyes me for a beat before nodding.

"You'll have missed the start. Go on, then."

"I just want to be sure you're set. You seem . . . distracted."

"Ah, I'm fine. Tell me, you have a favorite player?"

I'm talking about her football team, the Shamrock Rovers, but she seems to deliberately misinterpret me.

"You, of course," she says with a sly smile. "You've always been my favorite of the band."

I smile reflexively. Lord knows, it's good to be a guitar player and have the adoration of beautiful girls.

"I used to have your posters up on my bedroom wall," she continues, color coming to her cheeks.

"Don't break my heart and tell me you've taken them down."

The instinct to flirt is so ingrained that I rarely notice when I'm doing it. It's usually only when Felicity gives me her bemused smile that I realize I'd better watch myself. I've never been addicted to anything other than the rush brought on by the little spark that happens with flirting. It's hard to give up, not that Felicity has ever tried to curb it. The only thing she's ever been threatened by is my history with Sophie. Other women throwing themselves at me or me flirting with them has never raised her jealousy. I take it as a mark of the confidence she has in me, in us. But what would she think of this scenario if she were here? Likely, I'd get one of her trademark smirks and eyerolls.

"I've got my own flat now," Lizzy says. "I left those childish things behind."

"Childish? Surely you haven't left your love of Rogue behind. Don't we rate as your top band?"

"I have a theory about a girl's first band, actually."

I raise my eyebrows. "I'm intrigued."

"It's that even when you sort of grow out of the music, it'll always be a part of your heart." She places her hand on her chest, drawing my eyes. Her hand isn't quite where her heart is, but lower, on the upper swell of her breast.

I stare longer than I should, my imagination quickly constructing a fantasy in which she starts with a slow caress of her breasts and escalates to letting me watch as she masturbates. Of course, she won't want to do it alone. She'll *beg* for my touch. But I'll stay still, enjoying the show. Enjoying the excruciating tease of *not* being able to run my hands over her body. *Not* being able to explore her with my fingers and tongue.

"So, what do you think?"

I drag my eyes to hers and find she's breathing a little quicker than she should be, maybe because she can see my desire. I am so fucking sexually frustrated. I'd love nothing more than to pull Lizzy to me, to feel her eager body pressed against mine as I ravage her. It would just be lust and a release on my part. Not some kind of affair.

"I think," I say, making up my mind, "that you're probably right."

"Am I?" There's hope in her voice. She takes a step closer to me.

I can smell her perfume. Her need. I bet she likes to play submissive. She'd probably call me daddy at some point and ruin it all.

"About a girl's first band being a part of her forever," I continue. "I think that happens with the lads, too. Happened with me, that's for sure."

Her posture sags and I realize I've been a little cruel by toying with her. Then again, she may be young, but she knew what game she was playing with me. She'll have to take the rejection along with the bit of fun.

Taking a deep breath, she nods to herself and steps back. "Right, well, I'd better go. My boyfriend is at the stadium."

So, she does have a boyfriend. And yet, that hasn't stopped her clear signals of wanting me.

"Don't keep him waiting on account of me," I say.

"Oh, he's definitely not waiting on me."

"No?"

"He's a footballer. A forward, in fact."

There's a bit of defiance in the way she reveals this. Her chin is tilted up as if she wants to get the point across that she was never really interested in me, not when she's got her man running the ball over at Brandywell Stadium. I give her a small smile, the one I know has an effect on women, because she and I both know that though her boyfriend may be a minor celebrity, he and I are not remotely on the same level. I could have her with the snap of my fingers.

"I'm sure you'll be his good luck charm tonight," I say, making it clear our moment is over.

"Right. I, em, I'll see you tomorrow."

"Have a good night, Lizzy."

She nods, gathers her coat and bag and heads out.

I POUR myself a healthy tumbler of Knob Creek 25th Anniversary bourbon, put Bon Iver's self-titled album on the living room stereo system, and sit by myself on the sofa with the dual baby monitors on the coffee table. Taking a sip, I close my eyes and savor the rich flavors. It's cinnamon and charred oak and even hints of leather and sweet vanilla. It leaves me wanting more and I take taste after taste until I'm ready for a refill.

But I don't pour another bourbon even though I'd love to get drowned in it. Because I don't ever get drunk. Or, at least, I can count on one hand—*maybe* one and a half hands—the times I've been well and truly pissed. I don't like the lack of control of being drunk, so I just tend not to go there. I take pride in my willpower.

This willpower was put to good use earlier with Lizzy. But honestly, there's a less than zero chance that I'll ever do more than fantasize about her. I admit that I've not always understood my motives in matters of love and lust, but I do understand I'm drawn to her both because I'm fucking horny as hell and because I'm looking for an escape.

Not an escape from my marriage, exactly, but from all the other things going bad in and around my life. That list includes the shaky mental state of my wife. I wish I had a clear answer of what was happening with her. I wish she was willing to seek traditional treatment for her problems. The uncertainty of her stability weighs heavily on me. And that's on top of the news about my father.

My father. He's part of the reason I lingered so long upstairs after

Felicity left. First, I called Gavin to let him know I wouldn't be going back to the studio tonight. Then, I called to check in on my father.

My father was Rogue's biggest fan from the very beginning. I think he's enjoyed a bit of a vicarious thrill with it all, including his imaginings of my wild bachelor days. Whenever I try to downplay his notions, he dismisses it.

"Let me have my ideas, Son," he says. "It keeps things interesting for us." This type of comment is usually said in conjunction with a wink at my mother and makes me cringe. He loves to tease my mother and horrify me by saying things like this.

Then there are his oft-repeated boasts about his own bachelor days, which always start with him asking, "Did I ever tell you that I was my own version of a rockstar with the ladies at the school way back when?"

He had been the principal of a public school that I, thankfully, didn't attend. To hear him tell it, he had a field day with the mothers who would come in with any random excuse just so they could flirt with him.

We share the same features, including good height, dark hair, bright blue eyes, and high cheekbones. And the love of flirting, apparently.

Even with that, he's been happily married to my mother for ages. That happiness seems to, at least in part, come from the way they indulge each other. She indulges him in his flirting, and he indulges her by taking her dancing.

Those dancing days may be numbered now, though, since he's been diagnosed with Alzheimer's.

I'm happy to be distracted from these thoughts by Felicity returning home. Looking at my watch, I see it's already almost eleven. The music I'd put on had ceased long ago and the babies haven't stirred. I've occupied myself for hours in the silence of this house with just my thoughts.

"There you are," Felicity says with a lazy smile.

It's a smile that matches her unfocused eyes. She's drunk.

I laugh and stand to greet her. "Had a few, yeah?"

She throws one arm around my neck dramatically, and then the other as she teeters in her heels. "Let me tell you, a few goes a loooong way when you haven't had any in so many months."

"I bet." I lean down to kiss her because even in her high heels, she's petite. "You didn't drive, did you?

"Sophie gave me a ride."

I raise my eyebrows. "You got the ride from your girlfriend, did you?"

"You dirty-minded boy, you," she says with a scoff. But she's still smiling and holding onto me.

"A boy has fantasies, is all."

"Yes, I'm sure you do. Lizzy get you set up, then?"

That switch to asking about Lizzy seems deliberate and makes me rethink whether anything piques her jealousy.

"Yes, didn't take much. They've been sleeping well since you left. Easy, really."

"Easy," she repeats and pulls away from me. "Of course."

I can see that didn't come off the way I intended. She's somehow taking it as a judgment against her own difficulties managing the babies. "*Lucky*, I should say. I got lucky tonight."

She eyes me for a moment, clearly struggling to let this go.

"And I'm going to get even luckier, amn't I?" I ask with a wink before reaching for her.

But she steps backward, out of my grasp. "I need to pump. Since I had a few drinks."

"Okay, I can wait."

"It'll be about twenty minutes or so."

"I've waited a lot longer than that, honey. I'll be only delighted to wait twenty minutes. After all, you're worth every bit of it."

This gets me a smile and when I reach for her this time she lets me pull her to me for a deep kiss. It doesn't take long to reignite the passion we had before she left as I soon feel the pressure of her hand on my cock. The friction as she rubs me over my jeans is so intense I feel like a teenager again, barely able to contain myself.

"Fuck," I hiss in between kisses. I reach for her breasts and that's when she pulls away once more.

"Twenty minutes," she says, her sexy smile a promise of more to come. "Come up in twenty minutes."

"*Hurry*," I tell her.

I watch the time go slowly by for the next eighteen minutes before grabbing the baby monitors and following her up the stairs to our master suite. The door is partially open, and the lights have been dimmed. She's put Sade on the sound system. I like where this is headed and start to pull off my shirt.

I stop when what I find is not Felicity lying naked on the bed, ready and waiting for me to do all manner of naughty things to her, but rather curled up on one of the arm chairs in the sitting area of the room, wearing a ratty terry cloth robe and fast asleep.

"For fuck's sake," I mutter, unable to stop myself.

I get it. She was out drinking with her mate. She's got no tolerance for alcohol. She's been through a roller coaster of taxing emotions lately. But still. Can *I* get a break here?

Letting the door shut a little louder than I normally would, I then kick off my boots and let them drop with a thud on the hardwood floor. The noise doesn't even make Felicity flinch, let alone wake. Without much hope, I go to her and firmly nudge her shoulder. She. Does. Not. Move.

Once again, I'm left to take matters in my own hands. I decide a shower is in order if I'm to get any kind of release tonight.

19

Felicity

I'm early to the donut shop, eager to make sure Amelia and I have a table. Once again, the place is full of university students. They come in groups of twos or threes, laughing and joking with each other, seemingly with no obligation in the world other than the present one of getting a sugar fix. Their youth and freedom are intoxicating.

I used to be one of them. I used to be fearless. That was back in my school days, when I boldly made my friends-with-benefits arrangement with Conor, when I would run with the boys all over Dublin late into the night, when I made a plan to escape from my mother's dependence on me. And I did escape. I went all the way to Canada to be on my own, convinced the distance would give me everything I need.

I was right for a while. The freedom was magnificent. I had no one but myself to consider for the first time in more years than I could count. Every decision was based on what *I* wanted and what *I* needed. It was a heady time of friends and parties and explorations of Toronto life. Before long, I met Richard and he quickly became my world. Before I realized it, I had once more taken a back seat in my own life, much like I had done with my mother.

Have I repeated that pattern once more with Conor? I know he hasn't forced me away from myself. But have I willingly given up on who I am?

"You look deep in thought this morning," Amelia says as she joins me.

I hadn't seen her come in, but I'm delighted that she's here. I realize that I've been looking forward to this visit. It's been several days since the last time we met and I'm keen to share with her the recent happenings in my life.

"Will you want your lemon meringue, then?" I ask.

She waves for me to sit back down. "I'll get this one. Coffee? Anything else?"

I request just coffee and she moves away to get our order. Watching her at the counter, I see her present the same positive, pleasant manner I encountered with her at our first therapy session. She's obviously at ease chatting with anyone she comes across, including the young pierced and tattooed woman behind the register.

It occurs to me that it would be a good idea for Conor to meet her. That way, he could see that she's becoming a real friend, not my therapist. He could see that that's all I need and stop worrying about me.

There's no ring on her finger, but I wonder if she has a partner. Perhaps we could attempt a double-date sometime.

"No lemon meringue today," she says as she sits down with me. "So, I'm trying a s'mores."

I'm so caught up in my own thoughts that I ignore her cheerful explanation of the donut *du jour* and launch instead into my own agenda.

"Would you ever want to have dinner with me and my husband?" I ask. "You and your boyfriend, if you have one?"

"I, em," she says with a patient smile, "I don't have a boyfriend, but it's a lovely thought."

"Ah, well, you don't have to have someone to join us. I just think it might be nice. I'm sure Conor would love to meet you."

"You've said he's very busy in the studio, right?"

"He is, but he'd make time for a dinner. So, you're not seeing anyone? Maybe I know someone I can fix you up with."

She's laughs. "No, please don't."

"You never know. It could be just the match. And not everyone I know is associated with the music world, if that's what you're worried about."

"No, I'm not worried about that. It's just, I am sort of attached to someone at the moment. I've been trying to get over it, actually. So, until I do, there's no use in trying to push it."

"Oh, this is interesting," I say. "What's the story? I hope he didn't break your heart."

I had said this with what I thought was the conspiratorial tone of girlfriends, but she seems to withdraw into herself, dropping her eyes to her hands. I should take this cue and retreat. Instead, I say the first thing that comes to mind.

"Was that him who called when we were here last? You know, when you grabbed your phone so quickly?"

After a moment's hesitation, she nods.

"So, you're still in touch?"

"In a way." She tears at her donut and takes a small bite. "He leaves me messages. Voice messages. They're these long, rambling calls where he's just filling me in on his life and asking me about mine."

"And do you return the calls?"

"No. Never. But he's kept at it for months."

I can see in her expression that she isn't bothered by this. This isn't some case of an ex stalking her. She enjoys the connection, despite it being so uneven.

"But it must make it hard for you to let go," I say gently.

"Yes, that's true."

She shrugs and smiles, making it clear that she doesn't really want to let go.

"Tell me about him."

"I don't know. I shouldn't really get into all that."

"Shouldn't?"

She opens her mouth to speak and then stops, trying to formulate her response. "Well, like you said, it makes it hard to let go."

"Perhaps there's a reason for that. Maybe you aren't meant to let go?"

Again, she picks at her donut and this time we share a moment of silence. Finally, she takes a deep breath and smiles at me. "Tell me how you've been."

This time, I follow her lead and change the conversation. "I've been very well. I've been getting good rest—well, it's still interrupted at night, but I get naps because of Lizzy. And I realized after our last visit here that I deserved more time just for myself, so I actually went out with my friend Sophie for dinner and drinks."

"That's great. And how are things with Conor?"

Now, I can't help but hesitate. "He and I, we're okay."

She nods but is silent. I watch some kids come stumbling in through the front door. They're trying to trip each other.

"I mean," I continue, suddenly feeling the need to unburden myself, "there is this whole subtext with us, this stuff we don't really talk about. And we've had these disastrous attempts to have sex."

"Disastrous?" she asks with a wry smile.

I laugh. "It's ridiculous, really. I told you, didn't I, that I've had zero sex drive since I got pregnant? Well, it's been a lot to ask to have Conor waiting so unsatisfied. I mean, any man would get anxious, right? But, he's not just any man. You obviously know what he looks like—"

"Obviously?"

I'm stumped by the question. "Because he's Conor Quinn. He's one of the most famous guitarists in the world. Everyone knows—"

"Ah, yes, I see what you meant. Yes, I know what he looks like."

"So, I'm just saying he's not only a famous guitarist but he's drop-dead gorgeous. Women are constantly throwing themselves at him. And I'm not exaggerating about that. It's quite a thing to be around.

Anyway, he has all these options, all these temptations, at the same time that I've put our own sex life on hold."

"I'm sure he understands the nature of your . . . disinterest."

"He does. He's wonderfully patient. But, the worst thing is, I had this amazing rush of desire the other night. It felt like how it used to. But we got interrupted and had to push it back to later in the night. And then I ended up falling asleep before we could get back to it."

She raises her eyebrows. "He didn't wake you?"

"He tried but I was so out of it there was no use."

"And since then?"

I sigh. "Since then, he's spent every spare moment in the studio. Which is just as well, because I seem to have lost that desire once more."

"Have you considered that part of your lack of desire could be because you aren't feeling connected with him? If he's spending so much time focused elsewhere at precisely the time that you've been struggling to find your balance with the kids, your father, and everything else, that could be off-putting."

I take a moment to absorb this theory. I don't want to cast blame on Conor, but I can see how our different focuses might have sent us in opposite directions. I can also almost hear him scoff at the notion. He'd likely tell me I'm using this as yet another excuse to push him away. I tell Amelia as much.

"He thinks you don't want to be with him?" she asks.

"He thinks I have a bad habit of feeling like I'm not enough, and that turns into me finding ways to push him away. Like, the other day I visited him at the studio and for whatever reason—I'm still not quite sure why I said it—I told him I'd understand if he had regrets about how quickly his whole life has changed by suddenly becoming this family man."

"How did he react to that?"

"Angrily. And then he reverted to his old playboy ways and started flirting shamelessly with our nanny," I say with a laugh.

Amelia doesn't see the humor in it, though. "He did what?"

Though I appreciate her indignation on my behalf, I wave it away.

"It was just Conor being Conor. I really find it silly. It doesn't mean anything other than he still gets a thrill out of playing those games."

"Well, then, how did you resolve this?"

"We didn't. That's what I'm saying. We have these things we don't resolve. Things we aren't saying to each other."

She nods and falls silent, tearing up bites of her donut and licking her fingers unselfconsciously.

"Do you think," she says, "you two could try dating each other?"

I laugh. "What?"

"I think a lot of couples could benefit from going back to the beginning, recreating that dating ritual as a way to reconnect."

"Therein lies our problem, perhaps! We never dated. Not properly. We were friends for a long while when he was engaged to someone else. But we were close in a lot of ways. So, finally, when he was free, we just went right to it. I basically moved in with him right away because I had nowhere to stay."

Nodding thoughtfully, she wipes her hands on a napkin and then balls it up. "Then, you'll just have to start from scratch."

"And date my husband?" I asked, amused.

"Who else would you rather date?"

"No one."

"There it is."

I smile and once more feel lighter for having spent time with her. I wonder if she could possibly feel the same in return, but don't know how I might have been of any use. Just then, her mobile rings and she reaches for it quickly. I watch as she looks at the screen, silences it, and the puts it face down on the table.

"Was that him?" I ask.

"Em, no. No, not this time."

She's struggling to hide her disappointment.

"Were you together long? You and this phone fella?"

That nickname makes her laugh. "It was complicated. Not a traditional relationship, I guess you could say."

"Tell me something about him."

Her eyes drift away from mine as she looks out the window. Rain is coming down and the gray clouds feel especially low today.

"He's absolutely unique, that's for sure. And funny. Perceptive. Thoughtful, too."

"Sounds like a very interesting man."

"That he is. He's lived quite a life. But he's only just getting started really."

"Shame it didn't work out."

She nods. "Yes. In the end, there was just no way to make it work."

I'm about to respond when she thanks me for the chat and says she needs to get back to her office.

"Thursday, then?" I ask. "Same time, maybe different donut?"

She laughs. "Love to. See you then, Felicity."

20

Conor

"Tell me something—and don't get all defensive about it," I say.

I'm sitting with Gavin in the little lounge area of the studio. The others have gone but we stayed to work through Christian's song. It's still not done, but we're so close. That's what keeps us here at all hours, that instinct that we *almost* have it.

At the moment, however, we've taken a break for a Guinness.

"Why would I get defensive?" Gavin asks mildly. He leans back in the chair opposite me, putting his feet up on the coffee table.

"Just tell me it's not true that Sophie doesn't let more than two days go by without making sure you get off."

"What?" Gavin asks with a laugh. "What are you on about?"

I feel a sense of relief that he seems to be rebutting Felicity's claim. She and I never did find our way back to that intense attraction we toyed with the night she went out to dinner with Sophie. It's been three days and we've both been ignoring the issue. I'm not sure why I haven't pressed her more. Probably because I'm sick of being turned away. It's not just that she makes it clear she's not attracted to me, but in doing so, I feel how off balance we are. And I don't know what to do about it.

"Where did you come up with this?" Gavin asks, pulling my attention back to him.

He looks worried. It's a look I've seen too many times before, one where he's hit in the gut over the ways in which his wife and I have betrayed him. He thinks Sophie shared this intimacy with me.

"Felicity told me," I say quickly, hoping to ease his mind over the matter. "She told me because she's been spiraling with insecurity and comparing herself to Sophie. She was going down a whole list of ways in which she feels like she doesn't measure up to her."

Gavin is slow to relax with this explanation, so I throw it all out there, saying, "Including the fact that while she's all but lost her own sex drive, Sophie makes sure that no matter what, she takes care of you."

This has the effect I intended. His shoulders loosen, and he leans his head back against the chair. There's silence between us and I fill the time by finishing my beer.

"I suppose that's true," he finally says with a laugh. He looks at me. "Hadn't ever really thought of it, not about the timing and consistency thing. But yeah, I don't go wanting. In one way or another, she makes sure I'm completely satisfied."

The way he says this, there's the slightest hint of him lording it over me. I can't blame him for taking a bit of pleasure in the fact that he's got an incredible sex life. And I don't begrudge him at all. But then he takes it a step too far.

"So, heartbreaker Conor Quinn is hard up, is he?" he asks with a wicked smile.

"Very funny," I say without humor.

"And is this why you're always muttering *fuck me*? It's a plea, is it?"

"Enough, Gav."

"Jesus, do you think she's taking her cues from Celia? She's got the ring and the babies. What does she need your cock for anyway? Oh, you're done for, man!" He covers his eyes with one hand, tosses his head back, and laughs until he's breathless.

"Fuck off."

Wiping at his eyes, he looks at me with a pitying smile. "It's okay,

Con. I, too, was once the King of Wank. Only, it was 'cause my wife and I were separated. As in not even on the same continent and headed toward divorce."

"I'm sorry I said a word."

"Ah, come on," he says, finally letting it go, "I'm sure it'll all right itself soon enough."

"Yeah, it's fine."

Gavin's still amused by it all, smiling and staring at some middle-distance. I ignore him as I try to decide whether I should cut things off here and go home or if I should get another beer. It's almost ten o'clock. I realize I'd better get going and stand.

"I'm away," I say.

He looks at me and recognition that he's helped make my decision to leave colors his face. Standing, he slaps me on the back.

"Just fucking go all out and romance her, man," he says. "I'm sure with a bit of that, along with your pretty face, she'll be powerless to resist you."

My pretty face. Gavin's held onto calling me pretty since we were kids. Felicity has always said it was because he was jealous of my good looks. Jealous over how he thinks it's given me an advantage in life. The only problem with that theory is that he's a good-looking guy. On top of that, he's got a singing voice dripping with sex, not to mention an ability to charm a fish out of water, and a bleeding heart, fix-me magnetism. He's done just fine for himself. After all these years, there is absolutely no reason for him to be jealous of anything I have. For him to revisit this kind of thing somehow feels related to his feelings toward me over what happened with Sophie.

"Hey Gav?"

"Yeah?"

"You got the fucking girl."

He squints at me. "What's that mean?"

"It means you can relax. You and me, we got no issues. *Let it go.*"

The emotion drains from his face as he examines me. I've never—not *really*—asked him to let go of the damage I did to our friendship when I slept with his wife. He's made strides toward forgiveness in his own time. There have been setbacks along the way, but the forward momentum has always been there. At this point, however, with us each well past that episode, I need him to drop it. I've got bigger things to deal with, anyway. Like a wife who can't seem to decide whether she's fully committed to our marriage.

When Gavin nods, there's hesitation in it. "Yeah, sure," he says.

"Listen," I tell him, "you told me once that I was your brother. I don't know if you remember that because you were fucking wasted."

He eyes me for a moment. "I do. It was when that *Vanity Fair* article came out about my mother."

"Well, I haven't always lived up to that. I will always regret the ways I fucked up. But, no matter what, you've always been *my* only brother. That goes beyond any of this." I gesture to the studio we're in. "It goes to my dying day, man. You are my brother."

His eyes drop from mine but only for a second. When he speaks, I can tell it's coming from the heart. "I know that, Con. I do. You're right, we're good."

"Thanks." In the past, I would have been dripping with relief over this, but I'm just too tired to give more than I have.

"Go on home. I'll see you tomorrow?"

"Yeah. Tomorrow's the day we finish this fucking song."

"No doubt."

IT'S NOT ALL that late when I get home but all I want to do is get into bed and sleep.

My family has other ideas for me, however.

I hear the crying coming from the monitors sitting on the kitchen island. A glance at the little screen shows me a night vision picture of what's happening. Felicity's there in the kids' room, holding a child in each arm while they both wail. She's swaying back and forth and shushing them.

Taking a deep breath, I exhale and go to help.

When Felicity turns to me, I see the babies aren't the only ones crying. She's got tears running down her face.

All I can think is, *not again*.

"Ella's been crying for over an hour. I think it's gas, but I can't get her to burp," she says in a rush. "And Romeo's . . . just crying. I don't know why. I can't seem to make it better. I can't make it better."

"It's all right," I tell her, taking Ella from her arm. I kiss the baby's cheek. She's got the softest skin, but now it's slick with her tears. I put her against my shoulder and tap her firmly on the back. I don't suddenly have the magic touch. Ella keeps crying but with Felicity giving Romeo her full attention, he soon quiets. I start singing my little song to Ella about everything being okay even as she cries on.

Felicity puts Romeo down in his crib, gives Ella a kiss, squeezes me on the bicep, and shuffles out.

With my burping technique going nowhere, I shift Ella forward into the crook of my arm and examine her for signs of hunger. Not that I can tell that cry from any other. Still, I wonder if Felicity has somehow failed to realize that's what Ella needs. Second-guessing her this way doesn't feel very good, but I can't stop from doing so.

I offer the tip of my pinky finger to Ella's lips and she eagerly suckles it. A wave of anger passes through me. This must mean the baby is hungry, but Felicity has withheld milk from her for some unknown reason. The fear that she's incapable of properly providing for our kids comes at me full force once more.

And then I realize that my finger isn't the only reason Ella has calmed down. She's apparently not hungry at all and had been simply unable to calm down from her discomfort. Now she's sleeping and only sucking on my makeshift pacifier as a reflex. Felicity has been adamant that we don't give the babies pacifiers, having read all kinds of literature decrying the damage they do to not just the child's teeth but to the soft palate as well. I've always deferred to her in these matters. But I'm beginning to realize that things like pacifiers and formula are not the enemy. And that Felicity may be making some of this harder on herself than it needs to be.

Once I'm confident that Ella is in a deep enough sleep to put her down, I gently remove my finger and place her in her crib.

I find Felicity exactly where I had wanted to be when I got here: lying in bed.

She's not asleep, but rather staring at the wall, letting her own tears fall over her face and onto the bedding.

I strip down to my boxer briefs and climb into bed behind her, pulling her into my arms.

"How was your night?" she asks with a weary, tears-congested laugh.

"I'm sorry you were on your own with that. You could have called me."

"I had my hands full."

I laugh but she isn't after joking about this.

"You weren't there, Conor. You aren't there when it matters."

I close my eyes and press my forehead to the back of her neck. "You don't mean that," I whisper.

She takes in a deep, shaky breath. "I'm all on my own. I've got no one."

"You have me, honey. You *do*."

She's quiet.

I'm quiet.

My heart aches at the blame she's casting. I try to think of a reason to excuse it. I've accused her of pushing me away, but wouldn't I have to be there for her to do that? I have prioritized the studio. I come and go on my own terms. Am I to blame for the troubles she's had?

Then I feel her hand gripping my forearm. It's not much, but it's enough reassurance for the time being.

I'M MOSTLY ASLEEP and only really wake when I feel Felicity forcefully push me away from her. It takes me a moment, but I realize I had been rubbing myself against her backside. I've got an enormous erection straining against the front of my boxer briefs. She's asleep or pretending to be asleep. Either way, I've made yet another unwanted advance and am left aching.

I turn onto my back and glance over at the bedside clock. It's just past two. The house is quiet. Felicity is still and breathing steadily. Might as well finish what I started in my dreams.

Pulling down my underwear, I free my cock, fisting it firmly. I can't remember what kind of fantasy I had been having that made me this hard in my sleep, but I definitely won't take long to finish.

I've quickly resorted to imaginings of what I had wanted to do to Felicity the other night, conjuring up the throaty moans she's so good at giving in response to how I tease her. For a second, I think about trying to ease down her panties so I can make my fantasy a reality, but I remember that she's more likely to respond by kicking me in the face than writhing her thighs against me. Still, I indulge in the idea of it. In the idea that she'd respond to my tongue toying with her by grabbing my hair and pushing herself against my mouth.

I hear the bedsheets rustle but don't think much of it, too invested in the quickening pace of my strokes. But then I feel Felicity throw her arm around my waist. I stop and listen in the dark. Her breathing isn't coming at its usual sleeping pace.

"You awake?" I whisper.

She snuggles into me, burying her face into my neck and taking in a deep breath. Just when I think she's fallen asleep, I feel her lips on my skin. She's giving me slow kisses and soon her hand has replaced mine on my cock.

Jesus. *Finally.*

The only problem is I'm already so close to coming that it's hard to pull back. I reach for her but she mumbles, "It's okay."

"Honey," I say when she starts pumping me faster, "you're going to make me come—"

She bites the skin under my ear. "That's the idea."

"I want more," I insist. I mean I don't want just a hand job from her. I need more of *her*. I want my cock deep inside her, to feel our hips against each other, to lean down and take her nipple into my mouth as I grind on top of her. But she misinterprets what I've said because she squeezes my balls with her other hand and then it's all too late as I can't stop from coming with a low moan.

Releasing her hold on me, she pats my chest and moves back onto her side, facing away from me. As if she's done her duty. As if she had only wanted to appease me. As if she's checked that box and now her part is done.

What. The. Fuck.

Did any of that even turn her on?

I grab several tissues from the bedside table and quickly clean myself up. Then I move closer to her once more and put my hand on her hip. She's wearing basic cotton bikini panties but all I want to know is if she's wet. Sliding my hand over the curve of her ass, I slip my fingers between her legs. She doesn't recoil or push me away. Instead, she parts her thighs to give me better access. So I can discover that she is definitely wet.

I have more motivation than usual to go slowly because I not only want to make sure I arouse her as much as possible, I also need a little time to recover myself if I'm going to make love to her the way I want. I kiss the side of her neck and her shoulder as I gently play my fingers over her damp panties. I want her to need my touch. To need *me*.

Pulling her onto her back, I finally do what I've wanted for a while now by easing off her panties and spreading her legs wide. I lean over her, my cock pressing down on her belly, and kiss her chastely until she's the one who thrusts her tongue into my mouth. There it is. There's the passion I've been missing.

I break free so I can move down the length of her body, kissing her reverentially as I go. She doesn't believe it, but I still think she's sexy as hell. When I'm where I want to be, my face between her legs, I go slowly, savoring the taste of her desire. And I get the reaction I wanted as she fists my hair and a moan escapes from her mouth.

I realize I haven't had this pleasure since very early in her pregnancy. The thought gets me hard all over again as I suck on her clit. Her thighs quiver when I push a finger, then another deep inside her while tonguing her tender spot.

"Con," she whispers breathlessly.

And then it's over. She's trembling and pulling on my hair, and then she slowly goes slack.

I trail kisses over the inside of her thighs, on her hip, along her belly and up to her full breasts. They're not just large, but firm from needing to nurse. It means I'll have to have a light touch. I kiss around the outline of one breast and circle my tongue over her nipple, biting the tip gently.

"Sweetheart, maybe not—"

"I know, honey. It's okay. We're just getting—" I stop when the baby monitor lights up and the sound of crying comes out of the tinny speaker. "Started," I say with a sigh.

She smiles at me in the pale light of the room and touches my cheek.

"I want more," I say, letting my head fall to her shoulder. "I need more of you. I need you."

"I know, Conor." She says this while stroking my hair. While now both babies are crying.

I nod against her and then pull away, giving her the space to get up.

I had wanted her to need me, but I realize that I'm the one left wanting.

21

Conor

When I wake it's with the sense that I've been sleeping well past my usual time. The bedroom is bright, even with the drapes closed. Felicity is not in bed with me. I was out cold when she came back from nursing the babies. And it seems she's let me sleep until after ten o'clock. Stretching, I turn over on my side and reach for the remote control on the bedside table, manipulating the buttons to open the drapes. It's a clear, sunny day and I wonder if I have time for a quick run before I need to get to the studio.

Felicity's accusation from last night comes to the forefront of my mind: *You aren't there when it matters.*

That motivates me to jump out of bed and head straight downstairs to see if she needs my help with the babies.

I find Romeo in his exersaucer in the living room and he squeals when he sees me.

"Hey, big man," I say and pull him out of the contraption.

He's a sturdy fellow and feels so good in my arms. He's started to do this cute thing where he nuzzles his head into my shoulder. It's a mixture of shyness and lovey-ness. It kills me every time, including now.

"Where's your sister, then? And your Ma?"

He, of course, has no answers. But I do get a big smile as he gazes at me with a kind of wonder. I had imagined I'd love my kids, but I had no idea it would feel like this. This is a love that is all-encompassing and unlike anything I've ever felt before. I'd do anything to ensure my kids have everything they need in this life.

I wiggle my eyebrows and contort my lips, earning a hiccup of a laugh out of my boy.

There's a noise coming from the deck, so I take Romeo with me to see if that's where Felicity and Ella are. Turns out it's Lizzy with Ella. She's got her in both arms, bouncing her lightly and humming.

"Everything okay?" I ask.

She turns to me and starts to speak but stops abruptly. It's only when she slowly takes in every inch of me that I realize the only thing I'm wearing is form fitting boxer briefs. I imagine what she sees when she examines me is my mostly naked body, including the defined muscles of my abs and the sculpted 'V' leading into my low-slung underwear. In my haste upon waking to get downstairs I hadn't dressed. And I hadn't thought that Lizzy might be here, though I should have known better. She's been getting here every day but the weekends by nine.

"Hi baby girl," I coo to Ella. I catch Lizzy reacting for a second as if I had addressed her. Her face lights up in a smile and she leans toward me. But as I go to her and lean in to kiss my daughter, she seems to realize her error and stands stiffly, waiting for me to be done with this routine.

"Good morning to you, too," I tell Lizzy with a small smile.

"Good morning." She gives me another quick once-over. "Em, it's such a beautiful day, I just wanted to give Ella a look."

It's not sunny but the clouds are high, and the air feels good. The view of the sea in the near distance is mesmerizing.

"Yeah, of course. Is Felicity here?"

"No, she stepped out about ten minutes ago. Said she had a coffee date with a girlfriend."

"Ah, okay." Must be her recurring "appointment" with her therapist friend. "Well, I should probably get dressed."

I've turned to go back inside when I hear her say softly,

"Oh, please don't."

I smile but keep walking.

I SHOWER AND dress in anticipation of going to the studio. Gavin's already texted, saying he thinks he's got a solution on Christian's song. I decide, at the risk of interrupting Felicity's coffee date, that I'd better phone her to be sure she's okay with me spending the day away. After last night, I have no idea how she'll react. But I don't see how she would be in favor of me sitting here in the house without her just for the sake of it.

She picks up after the second ring.

"Honey, sorry to bother you," I start.

"No bother." Her voice sounds light, untroubled. It's a stark contrast to how she sounded during our conversation last night.

"So, I really need to get to the studio today. I wanted to make sure you're okay with that."

"Why wouldn't I be?"

This baffles me and I'm silent for a moment. I have the sinking feeling her nonchalance is just a pretense and that I'd better tread carefully.

"Because of what you said last night," I tell her gently.

"It's fine, CQ," she says. "You're going to do whatever you please anyway, won't you?"

I shake my head in frustration. She has a tell that exposes when she's trying to distance herself from me. It's using the nickname "CQ." I had thought we were well past that. Now it's made a timely reappearance.

"Tell me what I should do," I say as calmly as I can. "I need to get some work done. Lizzy is here with the babies. You're doing your thing."

I wait, but she's silent. I have no choice but to push through.

"I'll ring you later, then. Maybe we can do a late dinner together?"

"Sure," she says, "if you can find the time for that."

The rebuke stings. It pushes me where I don't want to go, and I lash out.

"What do you want from me, Felicity? I'm trying to wrap up this album so I can be around more. Can't you see that?"

The line is quiet again except for some ambient noise from wherever she is. Then, she replies, "What I see is that you will, as I already said, will do whatever you please. Let's not pretend you're *accommodating* me with this call."

She disconnects before I can say anything more and I'm fuming. I throw my mobile hard against the wall. It falls to the floor, its screen a spiderweb of cracks and bits of the frame scattered.

"Fuck me."

22

Felicity

My hand is shaking when I set my mobile down. The sugary air of the donut shop is suddenly overwhelming, the university student's chatter too loud. I look up to find Amelia watching me. Our coffee date had started off benignly enough, but after that call with Conor, I can't look at her. I'm at a loss. I cannot understand why I say these things, why I'm pushing my husband to be someone he's not and penalizing him at every turn.

Oddly enough, I had woken in a good mood. I'd cast off the despair I'd felt when I was home alone the night before with two inconsolable babies. I'd pushed aside the accusation I leveled on Conor, taking heart in his quick rejection that I meant it. Because I didn't mean it. Not really. It was just my fatigue and frustration coming out in a way he didn't deserve. And then after we had that intense exchange of orgasms, well, I thought we were good.

I think it was the careful tone he used when pretending to ask for my permission to go off to the studio for God only knows how long that set me off. He's still tiptoeing around me, acting as if he thinks I'll fall apart at any moment. And sure, I've given him reason to worry about that with the one very bad night I had when he came home to find me practically catatonic. But that was *one* bad night. I've got a handle on things now. I don't even need therapy. Though, I will admit that Amelia's friendship has been especially helpful. Her calm, patient way, along with her ready ear has been just what I needed.

"Everything all right?"

I look up to find Amelia eyeing me.

"Oh, sure. It was just Conor saying he's off to the studio. Yet again."

She smiles sympathetically. "His time away seems hard on you."

"He says he's trying to wrap it up so that he can be around more, actually."

"Well, that will be nice."

"Only, he and I both well know that once they do finish the album, he and the lads will be busy with media appearances, and rehearsals, and touring. So, it's really a false promise."

"I get the sense you're dissatisfied with the way your husband's job keeps him from being as present as you'd like."

I laugh. "That's a diplomatic way to say it, I suppose." I pause, trying to sort out my thoughts. "The thing is, I *knew* this is what I'd be getting. I *knew* this was his life. And I still jumped in and pretended I'd somehow be okay with it."

"What bothers you most?"

"At the moment, it's that we had a bit of a row last night about this very thing and exactly nothing has changed."

"A row?"

"I was home with the babies after Lizzy left. Conor was at the studio, of course. An hour after I got them down, Ella woke. And then Romeo woke. And I couldn't settle either of them. This went on and on to the point where I was in tears myself. Conor will never understand how truly painful it is for me when I have these episodes where I am incapable of soothing my children. I wouldn't wish the self-loathing it triggers on my worst enemy."

"All that because you couldn't settle them for a bit?"

"It wasn't for just a bit. It was for over an hour. I fed them, burped them, changed them—walked them all over the house, put them in their swings, took them outside to get fresh air, gave them a bath with lavender scented soap but nothing worked."

"Sounds exhausting."

"It was. Which is why Conor came home to find me crying right along with them. His concern was for the babies. It's always for the babies first." I take in a shaky breath. "As it should be, of course. But I can't help feeling jealous because I just want someone to rush in and take care of *me*. I realize, though, that this is terribly selfish. And so, that gets me even more upset. It was all this that had me accusing Conor last night of not being around when it matters. I think I broke his heart a little bit with that."

"What did he say?"

"He told me I didn't mean it."

"Did you?"

"No, not really. I mean, the reactionary part of me did. But if I think about it, I know it's not really true."

"Did you tell him that?"

"No, not exactly."

She nods her head and waits for me to go on.

"We fell asleep. For a while, anyway."

"The babies woke?"

"Em, no. He woke me up when he was, well, you know." I raise my eyebrows and hope she takes my meaning. After a couple seconds, she gasps and then tries to nod seriously to cover for her reaction. "So, I helped him out. And he helped me out. And it all felt very good. I sort of thought he would be satisfied then. That we could just move on from the row."

"But then he called."

"Then he called. And it was this overly precious way of checking in with me, trying to get my permission for him to go to the studio. And I just reacted badly."

"What would you have wanted him to do instead? Put off the studio to stay home to care for you and the babies?"

"I—" I stop and take a deep breath. "I wish I knew what it is that would ease this anxiety I feel. But I don't. I don't want to fault my husband. He's good to me. And he's good to the babies. I fear I'm pushing him away, like he said I was." I have to stop again as tears rush to my eyes.

"Why do you think you're pushing him away?"

She deftly hands me a napkin and I dab my eyes. Shaking my head, I shrug. We are quiet for several minutes as I try to compose both myself and an answer. Finally, I say, "I'm sure it's to do with this sense that . . . no matter what he says, in the end, he'll find that I'm not enough for him."

She nods and lets that admission hang in the air between us for a moment. And then she connects the dots for me, saying, "Which is the way things ended with your first husband?"

This strikes home and I take in a sharp breath. My mind starts racing with thoughts of how the stakes are so much higher this time. Because now we have children involved. It would be one thing if Conor rejected me and our marriage, but I couldn't stand for him to in some slight way also reject the babies. To walk away. The way my father did.

Amelia's phone vibrates. It's on the table and she grabs it quickly just as she has done before. I catch a brief smile crossing her lips before she clears it away.

"I'm so sorry about that," she says.

"No, I'm glad for the interruption," I say. And I am. I need something else to think about. "Is it him?"

"Him?"

"Your phone fella?"

She laughs. "It is."

"Answer it!"

"No, I can't."

"Oh, it kills me that you won't speak with him."

She shakes her head slightly, but with a pleased smile.

"It's romantic, isn't it?" I suggest. "That he keeps up with these calls, despite not getting a response from you."

Though she tries to hold back, she can't resist agreeing. "It is. He's . . . persistent, that's for sure."

"And he's here in Dublin?"

"Yes."

"Mightn't you run into him sometime? Ah, I love the very idea of it. That you two would meet on the street somewhere, lock eyes, and just know without saying a word that you are meant for each other."

Laughing, she says, "You do have a very romantic vision of this. It's much more complicated than you can know."

"Tell me. Oh, please, Amelia. Tell me all about it, just as I've told you all my troubles."

She opens her mouth to speak but stops short when her phone chimes to signal she has a voicemail.

"Oh, or better yet, let me listen to what he's said!" I suggest.

"I'd never—"

"I know, I know. But you can go ahead and listen. I don't mind."

There's only a moment's hesitation before she pulls up the message and puts the phone to her ear. I watch her as she gazes out the window, intrigued by the emotions that cross over her face. She's by turns delighted, intrigued, and amused—even laughing out loud at one point. When the message is over, she holds her phone in two hands and looks at it wistfully.

"God, it's so obvious you're still in love with him," I say with a grin.

"I don't think I'd go that far. I told you, we never had a traditional relationship, so—"

"Is he married?"

"What?"

"I mean, I just assume that's what's kept you apart. I've got no judgment against it. I understand how tricky these things can be—"

"No, he's not married," she says firmly.

"Oh, okay. I just thought, with all the secrecy it was the likeliest explanation. And really, I wouldn't hold anything against you—"

"He was my client, Felicity. That's why I can't have a relationship with him. We were never together because it's not appropriate."

That has me sitting back in my chair in surprise. I never expected this explanation.

"I lost my professional objectivity when it came to him, if you want to know the truth. I mean, I do believe I was able to help him. But we got too close. So, I've been trying to impose boundaries, to get back to the training I had. Though, I can't say that I've been all that successful with it."

"What does that mean?"

She shakes her head. "Nothing. Just that it's going to take some time and better discipline."

Silence overtakes us as she picks at her donut—back to lemon meringue this time—and I turn my now cold coffee in circles.

"Thanks for telling me, Amelia," I finally say. "I hope you know that as your friend, you can share anything with me."

The smile she gives me is conflicted—both grateful and full of regret. I wish there was more I could do to ease her mind. And then something occurs to me.

"Wait, he's not currently your client?" I ask.

"Em, no. Not for some time."

"Then, isn't it okay now?"

She shakes her head. "It wouldn't be right."

"Sometimes what's right isn't what you need. Sometimes, you just need to listen to your heart."

She sighs. "That's easy to say."

"It's what I did. I slept with Conor when he was still engaged to another woman. I wanted him but didn't think he'd choose me. My heart pushed me to try anyway. And it worked out." I take a deep breath. "Now, look. Here I am, ever so happily married to him." I've put on a big smile and my tone is overly cheerful. It makes her laugh, which was my intention.

"Thanks for the chat, Felicity," she says, gathering her things to go.

"Wait. Come for dinner on Saturday? I still want you to meet Conor and the babies."

"Eh, Saturday?"

"Are you busy?"

I can see her thinking, trying to come up with an excuse.

"No, I'm free," she says at last. "It'll be just us?"

"Yes. I promise I won't try to set you up with anyone. Not yet, anyway."

She laughs again, and I tell her I'll text her with the time and address.

23

Felicity

Once home, I check in with Lizzy, nurse the babies, and head upstairs for a nap. But what I see stops me in my tracks. It's Conor's mobile phone, cracked and busted to pieces on the floor. I can see the mark on the wall where he'd thrown it.

He's left it for me to find. No doubt, wanting me to see how upset he was by our phone call earlier.

Sitting on the side of the bed, I gaze at the mess and regret all I've done to push him away. My talk with Amelia has been clarifying. I don't want to make him feel like he's in the wrong. I've still got things to sort out for myself, but I don't want to further damage our marriage while I do so.

"Right," I say out loud. I stand and quickly make a plan.

After taking a shower, I carefully put myself together, including doing my makeup and pouring myself into the sexiest lingerie I have. I put on a black dress that dips low enough in front that the upper part of the pink lace bra I'm wearing peaks through. Putting on high heels, I turn to face the full-length mirror and have to admit that I look a whole lot better than I thought I have. My legs are slim, and my waist looks narrow, if only in comparison with my large breasts.

I just hope it's enough for him to forgive the surprise appearance I'm about to make at the studio.

WHEN I GET THERE, the whole band is in the Wood Room. I say hi to James, the band's manager, the sound engineers and Danny Boy, who is sitting right alongside them.

Danny Boy lets out a whistle. "Don't you look a sight," he says.

"Thanks. What are they working on?" I ask with a nod toward the boys. I, of course, don't recognize the song. Conor hasn't shared anything with me so far. And I realize I haven't asked to hear any of the new music—another failing of mine.

"'The Point of No Return,'" he tells me.

Christian's song. The song that I am aware enough to know has been troubling Conor for quite some time. He's said they can't quite seem to get over the hump with it, struggling with the right feel.

"They came to some sort of epiphany today," Danny Boy says. "It's bloody magnificent."

Danny Boy works one of the sliders on the soundboard to raise the volume even higher. Roscoe, his dog, stirs in his sleep but doesn't wake.

I keep my eyes on Conor, watching the way he's playing the guitar. The instrument is slung low against his hips and he fingers it with such command, his talent undeniable. He's got his eyes on Gavin who has an acoustic guitar, and it's clear they are communicating somehow without speaking, urging each other on with the tempo they're manipulating.

Then Gavin leans into the microphone and sings, and the hairs on the back of my neck stand up.

Why did you have to care so much?
You answered my call but I did nothing at all
You've left an imprint and this touch
Won't fade away, you're more than your pall

When Conor joins him as backup for the chorus, I feel a burn in my chest. Both men are using the song to expose their broken hearts.

When you ca-a-ame to the point of no return
The point of no return
Did you know you weren't alone?
You're never alone, never a-lone
Because I'll be searching for you on the dawn patrol,
The dawn patrol
And we'll ride the crest
The never-ending crest, my friend

It all clicks. They sound raw and powerful and amazing. It's exactly the right combination of music and lyrics to express the pain and love they feel for the song's subject—Christian Hale, the friend they lost too soon, too suddenly.

When the song concludes, it's eerily still and silent. No one moves. Each man is frozen at his instrument, and everyone at the soundboard is just as motionless. Then, I see Gavin go to Conor and wrap an arm around his neck. He whispers something to him that we can't hear out here and Conor nods, his eyes closed. It's an intimate interaction, somehow, between the two men.

James clicks a remote control-like button so he can be heard in the Wood Room and claps loudly. "That's it, boys. That's *it*."

That's when Conor looks up and sees me. He's justifiably surprised and his brows come together in confusion.

As soon as I see that Shay has gotten up from his drum kit and is stretching and that Martin has taken his bass off from around his neck, I make my way into the room. I go straight to Conor and throw my arms around his neck, not caring about the lads in the room or even that his guitar is between us. I step up on my toes and kiss him full on the mouth.

Though I've surprised him, he puts one arm around me and kisses me back before asking, "What's this?"

"I need you, Conor," I whisper urgently. "I need you so much."

"Time for a break, yeah?" I hear Gavin ask. He and the others quickly file out.

"Hang on," Conor tells me, pulling away so he can take his guitar and put it in a nearby stand.

"Can we go somewhere?" I ask.

"Somewhere?"

I pull on his waistband. "Somewhere private, love."

That's all it takes to get him to spring into action. He grabs my hand and pulls me out of the recording space, down a hallway, and into the empty toilet. It's spare and purely functional, but has a lock on the door, which is all we need.

"You're all right?" he asks.

But I don't want to talk. I just want to show him how much I want him. How much I need him. Instead of pushing him away like I've done for so long, I pull him to me hard. He takes this as the sign I had intended and stops talking. Instead, he matches my desire by kissing me and pulling the shoulder straps of my dress down, exposing my breasts.

All those months of feeling numb, of not having any sexual desire disappear in this moment and are replaced by such an intense need to have him that I can barely contain myself. My body is warm and aching for his touch. His hands are on my breasts and down along my sides and gripping my ass and between my legs. But it's not enough. I'm practically panting from the need I feel.

I pull off my G-string and hop up on the sink counter. I fumble to try to help him open his jeans, but he's got it under control and is soon fisting his hard, dripping cock. If I didn't want him inside me so much, I'd drop to my knees to lick, tease, and suck him dry.

Next time.

This time, he pushes himself deep inside of me and I gasp and moan at the same time. He fills me so completely that I dig my nails into his back with the sheer pleasure of it. As anxious as I am, he's the opposite, content to go slow with measured thrusts that go deep before pulling almost all the way out.

Holding his face in my hands, I kiss him, my tongue exploring his in time to his thrusts, over and over again. I'm lost in the overwhelming sensation of his body joined with mine when he surprises me by grabbing me and pulling me up, turning us so he's got my back against the wall. He can fuck me harder this way and I hold onto him tightly as I feel my orgasm building.

"Yes," I moan.

I can tell he knows I'm close because he keeps at the rhythm that's working so well for me, grinding and pushing up against me at just the right angle until I cry out, incapable of being quiet. In the next moment, he's found his own orgasm and has buried his face into my neck, breathing hard.

I don't know how long we stay that way, but it feels like a while. Stroking his hair, I can feel his breath slowly return to normal. When we finally separate, he smiles at me.

"Hi, honey."

I smile back. "Hi."

"It's good to see you."

"Hope you don't mind the interruption," I say with a poor attempt at an apologetic smile.

"*Never*," he says emphatically, and kisses me.

It's not a kiss of burning passion anymore, but one of sweetness and tenderness. Both kinds of kisses make me realize they're everything I've been missing. *He's* everything I've been missing.

We each take a minute to clean up, but I don't want to leave the bathroom yet.

"I heard the song," I tell him.

"Yeah?"

"It's incredible."

"Thanks."

"No, I mean it. It does him justice, Conor."

He takes a deep breath and exhales slowly before nodding. "That's all we wanted."

"What did Gavin say to you afterward?"

"Hmm?"

"He hugged you and said something?"

"Oh, I, dunno."

My brows come together as I try to sort out why he won't tell me what Gavin said. I try to convince myself he's allowed to keep some things to himself, but it still gnaws at me.

"What made you come, Fee?"

I smile and glance down at his crotch suggestively. "You know perfectly well what made me come."

He laughs. "Yes, I'm glad for that. *Really* fucking glad, in fact. But you know what I mean."

"I, em, I went home after seeing Amelia. And I found your phone all smashed up."

"Oh, right. I've got Teddy getting me a new one."

Teddy is his assistant, but I don't care about the replacement efforts.

"Seeing that made me realize the effect I've been having on us" I say. "I don't want to smash up our relationship—"

"You're not—"

"Con, I've been mixed up and having a hard time. But you're not to blame. I'm sorry for taking things out on you. I love you so much."

"I know you do. And I love you, honey. I'm not going anywhere, no matter how you push me, okay?"

He's bent at the knees slightly so as to look me in the eyes and I smile. I wrap my arms around his neck and press myself to him. He holds me close and his strong arms feel so good, so reassuring.

"How embarrassed will I be when we go out there?" I ask into his shoulder.

"Hmm?"

"You think they heard all that?"

"Nah," he says dismissively. "Anyway, you're my wife. There's nothing to be embarrassed about."

It's a nice sentiment, but when we go out to the little seating area in front of the sound boards, all the guys are there, and they burst into a round of applause and wolf whistles. I bury my head into Conor's bicep, my cheeks on fire from blushing.

"Yeah, yeah," Conor says. "Fuck you very much."

I look up at him and see him smiling broadly. I take comfort in the fact that I've, at last, made him happy.

24

Conor

It takes some time to get my focus back after Felicity leaves. The guys give me hassle over it, but I don't care. For the first time in what feels like forever, I've got my wife seeming like my wife again. I wonder if I've got Amelia and her sneaky therapy sessions to thank for it.

It's with this in mind that I manage to find time to query Danny Boy later in the day. He's usually the one that runs out to get us lunch, but I volunteer to go with him with the excuse that I want to see if the restaurant can make the special smoothie I want.

He and I walk along with Roscoe at our heels. I let Danny Boy go on, in his typical excited way, about Christian's song. He's hyped by it, declaring that it will be an instant hit. I don't think he's necessarily got his pulse on such matters, but don't dismiss his enthusiasm out of hand either. There does feel like something special in this song. I just know I'm too close to it to be objective.

"We'll have to see, man," I tell him.

"Yeah, you'll see. I'm telling you, it's going to be a fucking block-buster," he says quickly. As usual, he's always got more energy than he knows what to do with. This time, he's funneling it into his enthusiasm for this song. "I mean, it's balls-to-the-walls rock 'n' roll but with all that *soul*. And it's not just Gavin's voice. I mean, fuck, where'd *you* come up with that voice, anyway? Been hiding it away all these years?"

"Okay, got it. You like the song," I say with a laugh.

"No, really—"

"Anyway, I wanted to ask you something." We've got just two more blocks until we'll be surrounded by people in the restaurant, so I want to get to this. "Em, Shay mentioned you're seeing a therapist, is that right?"

"Ms. Patterson? Yeah, I was. But not anymore. Why?"

"Oh. Why'd you stop?"

"You want a referral? Got some head shrinking that needs to be done?" he says with a laugh.

"Fuck's sake, Danny Boy. I just meant it as a compliment. That I could see you've found some kind of peace lately. Thought it was good that you had someone who seemed to help."

He considers this for a minute and I feel like I'm going to lose him into his own thoughts, but then he speaks again, saying, "She's something special, that's for sure. And yeah, she definitely helped me figure some shit out."

"But?"

"But what?"

I sigh with impatience. Danny Boy can be so painfully obtuse. "What made you stop seeing her?" I ask slowly, elaborately enunciating every syllable just to fuck with him.

"I was done with therapy," he replies in the same manner I had used. He throws in bullshit sign language moves with his hands. Just to fuck with me.

"Ay, you may be better, but you're a long way from fixed, I can tell that much."

"Fuck off, Mr. Perfect," he grumbles.

We get to the restaurant and as Danny Boy deals with the food, I sign some autographs and take selfies with the crowd of fans who seem to have sprung up out of nowhere. It's one of the reasons why

Danny Boy is usually the one to do these errands. I can't remember the last time I went out and wasn't recognized, even if it's only from a gawking distance.

On the way back, I realize I don't need to dissect what kind of therapist Amelia is. She's proven herself with Danny Boy. And she's already proven herself with Felicity.

"I actually phoned her earlier today," Danny Boy says.

"Phoned who?"

Now it's he who treats me as if I'm being obtuse. "Ms. Patterson, my former therapist," he says with exasperation. As if we had never stopped talking about her. As if we hadn't had the interruption of getting the food and the rush of the fans to deal with.

"Oh. So, you're still in touch? Friends, then?"

"Something like that. I keep her updated on how I'm doing, that sort of thing. Call her fairly often."

It's then that I remember Amelia requesting that I don't tell Danny Boy about her seeing Felicity. In fact, she seemed quite concerned that he not know anything about her. It makes me wonder about his evasive answer.

"Danny Boy, does *she* actually think you're friends?"

"What? Of course," he says quickly.

I stop walking and after a few steps he does, too. "For fuck's sake. Tell me you're not stalking her."

"Stalking her?"

"Jesus, man, does she answer the phone when you call her?"

"Well, no."

"You fucking idiot. You're going to get yourself in trouble with that."

"No, she's good with it, I swear. I mean, the thing is, we have a connection. It's just with me having been a client, she can't really give in to it, is all."

"What is wrong with you?"

"Nothing. You said yourself I'm good now."

"Wake up, wanker." I flick his forehead and he steps back. "If she wanted to hear from you, she'd answer the fucking phone. You're harassing her and she's too kind to tell you. Don't you know a single thing about women?"

He blinks, considering this. But then he shakes his head. "No. You don't understand. You don't know how it is."

I roll my eyes. "First you fuck up with Julia. Then you go and set your sights way too high with Amelia."

His eyes widen. "Amelia? How'd you know her name is Amelia?"

Fuck. That was a misstep. "You said it. I dunno."

"I don't call her that. She's my 'dear Ms. Patterson'."

"You sound like a loony person. She's not your 'dear' anything. She's the one you're stalking."

"I'm not. And you can fuck off, already. It's none of your business. I don't need to stand here and convince you of anything."

He's abandoned the issue of how I knew his therapist's first name, and I realize it's the right time to end this conversation.

"You're right," I say. "I don't know. And I don't need to know."

"That's more like it."

We start walking again, but then he stops abruptly and looks at me. I worry he's about to question me again, but in typical Danny Boy fashion, he's moved on.

"Who's the idiot now?" he asks.

"What are you on about?"

"You didn't even remember to get that smoothie you wanted."

I laugh and then try to feign frustration. "I completely forgot, damn it."

"You want me to run back?"

I slap him on the back. "No, I'm good. But thanks for the offer, man."

As has become the case in recent months, it's hard not to enjoy Danny Boy. He and his dog Roscoe are a perfect mirror of each other. They've both been abused and lost. But now they've found their home—together and with us, and there's no turning back.

25

Conor

I've got Ella in the crook of my arm while I watch Felicity in the large walk-in closet of our bedroom. Lizzy's got Romeo downstairs and will be leaving for the night soon. Amelia is coming over and Felicity has woken later than she planned from a nap, so now she's hurriedly hunting for something to wear. If I had my choice in the matter, I'd have her keep on what she's wearing now. The oversized Rogue concert tee shirt falls to just above mid-thigh and her bare legs are shapely and sexy.

In the last few days, we've had a lot of fun making up for lost time with our sex life, keeping up the intensity we found when she dropped by the studio. We've made a bit of a game out of it, carving out time early in the morning or late at night—or even in the middle of the day—when the kids are asleep. She woke me once in the middle of the night with her mouth on my cock. After such a long dry spell, it was one of the best blowjobs of my life.

Despite this part of our marriage roaring back to life, it's clear there are still issues we need to work on. I know she's not suddenly got a handle on everything that had thrown her off. And I've got my own worries. But neither of us has been stepping up to communicate those things. Baby steps, I tell myself. It's somehow easier to have patience with this when I'm not suffering from blue balls.

Or maybe, focusing on our sex life is not just easier than working on our issues, but a sort of escape from them. I've been down that road before with my former fiancée, Colette. In the end, there was nothing between us but our physical connection. If I didn't know better, I might worry about history repeating itself now with Felicity.

I just don't believe that's the case, though. Colette and I never had a deep connection. Felicity and I have a connection that goes back to when we were teenagers. Nothing will change that. At least, not if I have anything to do with it.

"And, I've got everything to do with it, don't I, Ella girl?" I ask my daughter. She opens her mouth into a reflexive smile and I give it right back to her.

"Dress or trousers?" Felicity asks, still in the closet.

It's a showpiece of a room, having been designed by Colette , who had wanted not just enough room for all of her designer clothing, but specialized lighting and custom cabinets as well. Felicity, even after these past few years living here, still hasn't filled her side of the room. She's never been especially into fashion. My side, on the other hand, is full with bespoke suits, all manner of dress shirts, rows of jeans and trousers, and tee shirts and jumpers neatly folded in drawers. I also have an extensive display of high-end watches that sit under a spotlight that originally seemed a ridiculous indulgence but now I secretly love it.

"Whatever you're comfortable in," I tell her. "It's just a simple meal, right?"

"Yes, right."

I look down at Ella. She's been quietly hanging out with us. As usual, she's happiest when being held. I pull her up to my face and look into her beautiful blue eyes. She studies me curiously. When I smile, she coos. And my heart melts. This girl will forever be able to twist me around her little finger, that I know for sure.

"Okay," Felicity says as she comes out dressed in black linen trousers and a loose maroon top. "Is that what you're wearing?"

I look down at my clothes. I've come from the studio for this dinner and haven't bothered to change out of the black work trousers and black and gray camouflage long sleeve thermal I was wearing.

"Is this a job interview? Or is this a dinner in my own home?" I ask.

She laughs. "You're right. I don't know why I'm nervous about this."

"Maybe because she knows so much about you," I suggest with a tease in my voice. "And you've probably told her all kinds of intimate things about me. Now she'll have to see me and put it all together."

"Ha ha," she says.

"Why don't you tell me a choice thing or two about her, so we're all on even ground here?"

"What do you mean?"

"I dunno. Maybe tell me some secret your friend has shared with you that might be on par with what you've likely told her about me?"

She sits with me on the side of the bed. "Eh, well, she did tell me something surprising."

"I'm intrigued."

"She's got this ex-client who she seems to have fallen for, but she won't really admit it."

Jesus, no. This can't be what I think it is.

"What do you mean?"

"Well, I guess there was a fella she was working with and she says she ended up crossing professional boundaries with him somehow. Though they were never actually together. And she won't date him, even now that he's no longer her client. But he calls her quite often and leaves her these long messages that she seems to adore, even though she never answers or calls him back."

For. Fuck's. Sake.

"What is it?" she asks.

I know I didn't say anything out loud, but my expression must have exposed my thoughts. "I, em, nothing. Just thinking about studio stuff, sorry. We're getting close to the end."

"Uh huh." She's not convinced but lets it go, taking Ella from me and suggesting to her that they go find her brother.

I don't move to follow her. I need a second to think about what I've just learned. So, this means that Danny Boy was telling the truth. He and Amelia—his *dear* Ms. Patterson—really do have some kind of connection that goes beyond therapy. That is definitely a clear violation of her duties. And it suggests the ease with which she offered unconventional therapy with Felicity was rooted in a history of playing fast and loose with professional boundaries. And I didn't just go along with it, I conspired with her to make it happen.

Fuck. Me.

WHEN I GO DOWNSTAIRS, it's not Felicity and Lizzy I find with the babies, but Felicity and Amelia. I remind myself to act as if we've never met and do a good job when Felicity introduces us.

"Thanks for having me," she says. "You have a beautiful home—and a beautiful family."

Felicity's done her best to soften up the modern decor, including bringing in plush area rugs where the babies are now lying side by side on the musical-themed playmat in the middle of the living room.

"We're glad to have you," I say. "Can I take your coat?"

"Oh! I should have asked," Felicity says with a laugh.

Amelia shrugs out of the heavy wool coat. "No, it's fine. You've got your hands full with the babies and dinner."

I take her coat and walk it back to the closet by the front door. It gives me a minute to try to think how to approach this situation. It feels like an opportunity to test Amelia. To prod her on what exactly she's doing with her visits with Felicity. Is she really helping? Or is it some kind of simple incompetence from someone who doesn't know the proper way to do her job?

Of course, I have to tread lightly, no matter what I do. I can't have Felicity understanding the bargain I struck with Amelia at the start of this.

The women are seated on the sofa, staring appreciatively at the kids who are both in their pre-bedtime wind-down.

"You're saying these are the very same babies who gave you such trouble the other night?" Amelia asks with a put-on look of skepticism.

"That's their best trick—making you think they're always this angelic," Felicity says with a smile.

"Can I get you ladies a glass of wine?" I ask.

"We have a great Bordeaux," Felicity says.

"Sure, I'll take a glass."

As I turn to the kitchen, I hear Amelia telling Felicity, "He's very kind."

I'm only trying to be a good host. But it might not last, depending on how things unfold.

I come back with a glass for Amelia and myself, reserving one for Felicity once she's nursed again. Conversation is mostly about the babies. Amelia shares a bit about her nephew, and it's clear she's good with children.

"I'm sorry, but I need to leave you for just a few minutes," Felicity says after a time. "I'm going to get them off to bed."

"No problem. Take your time," Amelia tells her.

I help Felicity take the kids to their room but then leave her to nurse them once more before getting them down for the night.

Amelia is looking out at the view when I return. The sky has grown darker, and the houses below ours and along the coast are lit up. The moon is also full and starting to reflect brightly on the water.

"Gorgeous view," she says when I join her at the wall of windows.

"We like it."

I wait to see if she's going to say anything about this odd situation we're in. She's quiet, though, and I suspect it's a tactic she uses quite well in her therapy sessions. It makes one want to fill the void, to say something just to keep from feeling uncomfortable.

Despite my desire to do otherwise, I fall into the trap and speak first. "I'm glad I haven't heard from you." That had been our agreement, that she'd call me if she thought Felicity's troubles were getting worse.

She laughs and glances at me. "I am, too."

I turn to her. "Listen, I have to tell you I've got some concerns about what you're doing."

"And what am I doing?"

"That's the question, isn't it? *Do* you even know what you're doing?"

She stares at me without saying anything, her eyes scanning over my face to try to make sense of what I've just said. I'm painfully aware that the time we have to talk freely like this is draining away. It won't take Felicity much longer before she joins us.

"It's just as I said before. I'm being a friend."

"That's it, huh? Is that the same with you and our mutual friend, Danny Boy?"

Her eyes drop from mine at the mention of his name.

"He's under the impression that you're friends," I continue. "Only, that seems to be defined as him calling you and you not answering. Doesn't sound like the healthiest—"

"Does Felicity know?"

"What? That it's Danny Boy you get these calls from?"

"Yes."

"No, I haven't told her. I can't even comprehend it myself. I can't imagine what she'd say."

"And does Daniel know about me working with Felicity?"

"No, I didn't tell him."

She's visibly relieved by this news. But the reaction only makes me more curious about just what is going on with her and Danny Boy. I open my mouth to ask but stop when I hear Felicity descending the stairs.

"We've only lived here for a couple years," I say, as if we'd been talking about the house.

Amelia is slow to understand but finally realizes she's to play along. "Well, it's magnificent. I'm sure it will be great to raise your family."

"They're both asleep," Felicity tells us with a grin. "Time for a glass of wine and dinner."

"I'll get your wine," I say and step away.

It's not likely I'll get another chance to speak privately with Amelia now. That means I'll have to couch my queries to her very carefully during dinner.

26

Felicity

There was something odd happening between Conor and Amelia when I came downstairs. They both took pains to pretend it wasn't there, but I have to assume Conor was trying to get her to tell him her thoughts on how I've been. I feel secure in the knowledge that Amelia will safeguard the things I've told her in confidence. After all, that's what girlfriends do.

Now we've gone through almost two bottles of the Bordeaux and have filled up on the beef bourguignon with fresh pasta I had brought in. Another way in which I fall short in comparison with my friend Sophie, is that I am not a cook. Conor has never minded, especially as I *am* good at finding the best restaurants and caterers to have food delivered or made on the spot.

I'm feeling the happy and warm effects of the alcohol and have finally relaxed with Amelia being here and getting to know Conor. They've been bonding over their shared love of Ella Fitzgerald and other jazz and blues artists. He's even gone so far as to put on his original press vinyl copy of the 1956 album *Ella and Louis*. It seems they are getting along like a house on fire. Which is why it is so odd that he suddenly starts a line of conversation that changes the tenor of the dinner.

"Do you have a boyfriend, Amelia? Someone to share your love of jazz with, maybe?" he asks.

"No, not at the moment," she says, smiling down into her glass of wine.

"No? No one special? Maybe an admirer trying for your attention?"

Amelia squints at him and slowly bites her lower lip, considering what to say. When her eyes flick my way, I realize she's wondering if I've told Conor about her ex-client who has kept up phone calls to her for months. I never should have betrayed her confidence. Guiltily, I scramble to head this off.

"Sweetheart, I've already suggested fixing Amelia up, but she's not interested. If that's what you're getting to." I squeeze his hand under the table.

Conor nods and is quiet, but I can tell it's because he's gearing up to say more.

"You know who's also single?" he asks. "Our own Danny Boy."

I laugh out loud, both at the idea of fixing Amelia up with Danny Boy of all people, and with the relief I feel that he's dropped the subject that bothered me. "Yes," I say, "and he's single for a reason."

He gives me an amused smile. "Meaning?"

"You know very well what I mean." I look at Amelia. "Danny Boy is Shay's brother. And you know Shay is Rogue's drummer, right?"

"Of course," Amelia says.

"He's become a part of our lives in the last couple years. But he's a rough sort, if you take my meaning."

"You're being unusually harsh," Conor says. "You've always been the one to beg for him to have another chance, haven't you, honey? Like when he, I dunno, *stole* my guitar? Then there was the time he showed up at our house in the *middle of the night* as if that was the proper way to make amends. Oh, and remember when he was so reckless during our live show that he came crashing down and *broke* his brother's wrist? You wanted him to be given a pass for all of those things."

"Well, yes, I'm always in favor of granting him another chance, but that doesn't mean I'd consider him suitable relationship material." I look at Amelia, whose face is a frozen mask. "Conor just loves to give Danny Boy a hard time, always making him the butt of the joke."

"Now, that's not true. I never thought I'd say this, but I actually *like* him. He seems to have changed his ways in the past few months. That's why I thought, well, he's single . . ."

"That'd never work," I say. I'm about to say more, to dissect why Danny Boy is unfit for my refined friend Amelia, when she interrupts.

"Because I'm not interested in dating." She levels her eyes on Conor. "But thanks for thinking of me."

They maintain eye contact for a long beat before he pivots the conversation once more.

"Tell me, how long have you been a therapist?" he asks.

"Let's see," she says, "it's been almost ten years now."

"Wow. That's impressive."

Conor's tone is strange. It's almost mocking. But Amelia smiles and shakes her head in wonder, saying, "Yes, I can hardly believe it myself."

"What got you interested in the profession?"

"I suppose it was just . . . a natural curiosity I had about people and a desire to help those in need," she says.

"Have you ever heard the theory that those who go into the field of psychology often do so in order to heal themselves?" he asks.

"Conor!" I slap at his arm and look apologetically at Amelia.

"It's just a theory," he says with a laugh.

"It's rude, is what it is," I say. I examine him for signs of drunkenness but other than the inappropriate remark, he seems totally in control. He's always in control. It's a permanent condition with him, and likely why he's so put off by anyone—including me—who doesn't share that trait.

Amelia seems unruffled, though. "It's okay, Felicity," she says. "I've heard worse."

"Really? Like what?" he asks and leans back in his chair.

"You don't have to answer that," I say. "Conor, how would you like it if she questioned your motives for getting into a band, suggesting something dark about it?"

"What? Like that I have demons that only the music can exorcise?" He's amused because he hasn't described himself. He's described Gavin and we both know it. "Nah, that's not me. I wouldn't worry about such an accusation. Why would anyone, if it's false?"

"It's still not nice."

He turns to me, smiling benignly. "What shall we talk about then? I can't help it if Amelia's work interests me."

"What would you like to know, Conor?" Amelia asks.

She looks composed, with a pleasant look on her face. It's the demeanor I found so comforting when we had our one and only session. It's the look that invites you to bare your soul, while somehow assuring you it will all be okay.

"I dunno," he says. "How about, do you ever treat family members? Or would that cross the boundary of professionalism?"

"That's a very odd question," I say. "Of course, she wouldn't."

"No, I've never treated family members."

"What about friends—"

The baby monitor lights up and Ella's crying fills the room, interrupting the odd exchange. Conor stands and says he'll check on her and I'm glad he's stepping away.

I lean across the table and say in a hushed tone, "I'm so sorry, Amelia. I don't know why he was going on like that."

She waves away the apology. "It's fine."

"The only thing I can think is that he's worried about how our friendship came to be. You know, that we started in a therapy session and then became friends. Like it crosses some boundary he doesn't agree with? But there's nothing wrong with it. Right?"

I don't like the way she hesitates to answer. Her eyes leave mine and focus on the inky darkness of the night. It feels like she does indeed believe she's done something wrong, that Conor is right in disparaging her professionalism. The thought that she'd turn away from me, from our friendship, because of this issue Conor has somehow seen fit to bring up, has tears stinging my eyes.

"Amelia?" I say softly. "There's nothing wrong with us being friends, is there?"

Taking a deep breath, she exhales and looks at me. "Well, the truth is—"

"It was nothing," Conor says, his voice louder than it needs to be as he returns, causing both Amelia and me to jump. "She never really woke. It was just fussing." He sits and looks from me to Amelia and back again. "Ella. She's fine."

"Oh, okay."

"I need to apologize, Amelia," he says.

I watch them lock eyes for a long moment, wondering what I'm missing. Again, there's some subtext that I've been left out of.

"I was just playing devil's advocate, really. I'm sorry if that came off as rude."

An excruciating ten seconds passes as they stare at each other. I'm so relieved that Conor has realized he's been unfair and apologized. I silently urge Amelia to accept his offering and let out a breath when she finally nods.

Amelia leaves not long after that. I'm ready to lay into Conor for the way he behaved but before I can, he gets a phone call and I finally learn that I'm not the only one who has been keeping secrets.

27

Conor

By the look in Felicity's eyes after Amelia leaves, I can see I've got hell to pay. I briefly consider trying to redirect that energy into something sexual but then my phone rings and I automatically check it. The caller ID shows it's my parents' house. It's almost eleven o'clock, so the call sets off alarm bells.

My chest has tightened in anticipation as I answer.

"Conor," my mother says, "I need your help. I don't know what to do."

"What is it?"

"Your father. He went to take out the rubbish and he hasn't come back."

Incongruously, I want to laugh. It seems silly that she's "lost" my father in this fashion. But it's not funny. It's a part of the Alzheimer's.

"I'll be right there. In the meantime, round up your neighbors to help look."

I assure my mother that the late hour won't bother her neighbors and beg off.

"What's going on?" Felicity asks.

"I need to get over to my parents' house."

"But why? I don't understand."

"Fee, I can't explain it all right now. Let me just go and I'll be back as soon as I can."

I turn to go but she grabs my hand, imploring with her eyes me to share more.

"It's my Da. He's gone missing."

"Missing?"

"He's recently been diagnosed with Alzheimer's. For years he's played off his memory issues as a silly game he meant as a laugh, but my Ma had him see a doctor and it's not a joke. Now, he's gone and wandered away from the house."

Felicity covers her gaping mouth with her hand and her eyes well with tears.

"He can't have gone far. It'll be okay."

"Let me know if I can do anything."

I kiss her quickly and hurry out the door, relieved she hasn't asked me why I didn't tell her any of this sooner. In my haste and distress, I might well have blurted out that she's been too unstable lately to rely on.

WHEN I GET to the house, I see a smattering of pensioners in their robes walking the neighborhood with flashlights. Checking in with my Ma, I find her sitting in the front room, one hand tightly clasping the other.

"Stay here and call me if he finds his way back," I tell her.

"You will find him, won't you?" she asks.

I'd been so eager to go join the motley crew out on the streets that I hadn't taken time to properly absorb the state I'd found her in. She's terrified. His symptoms up to this point have been relatively minor. Yes, he has trouble remembering some things, he's had short moments of disorientation, and will repeat himself without realizing it. But he's never done something like this.

Crouching down, I take my mother's hand and rub it gently. "Yes, I will find him, Ma. All will be well, you'll see."

She nods but her eyes are glassy with tears.

"After this, I'll look into some kind of tracking device for him. Won't that be a laugh?"

Though she shakes her head, the corners of her mouth turn up. I kiss her soft cheek and head back out.

After speaking briefly with a few of the neighbors and learning they haven't seen or heard anything, I get back in my car and circle the block, then the outer perimeter, both without any luck.

Fuck. Where could he have gone? I try to put myself in his place. Think about the fact that the night air is cool. Even if he was disoriented, he'd feel the chill and want to get out of it, wouldn't he? With that in mind, I drive back toward the house, toward his local pub. It's an easy walking distance and a place he's spent countless hours over the years.

The pub, Mulligan's, is a sea of dark wood paneling, posters of old beer and spirits adverts on the wall, and an accumulation of disparate memorabilia ranging from Mohammed Ali's 1970s visit to Dublin, old movie posters, and personal snapshots of the Irish coastline. This is where I had my first beer. I'd come with my father on one of his usual "stop-ins" after work when I was fourteen. He had been in a good mood, as one of the newer bartenders, a cute young woman, had indulged him by flirting. Then, he asked her to pour two Guinness and suggested it was time for us to share a drink. I'd had the odd sip—or gulp—before, but this was different. It made me feel like I was a man. But it also meant something to have that first, full drink with my father. It showed me he had trust in me and that I could trust him in return because now, we were on a different, more mature, level with each other.

That feeling of equality dissipates as I see him sitting at the far corner of the bar, clad in his pajamas and robe. He looks happy as can be, to tell the truth, hunched over a pint and smiling at something that Joe, the pub owner, is telling him. I make my way toward them and catch Joe's eye.

"There's your boy now," he says with a nod to me.

Joe's always had a smile as big as the belly he hefts around over a low-slung white apron. The pub is a family business, having been his father's and grandfather's before him. He's always treated my father and his other customers as an extension of family. It's one of those places you feel comfortable whiling away the hours in, and I can see why my father ended up here.

"Hey, Joe," I say as I take a seat. "Having a pint, are you, Da?"

When he looks at me, his eyes go wild for just a split second. It feels like he's trying to place me. Or place why I would suddenly be here. But recognition soon floods his face.

"Joe, get my son a drink, won't you?" he says.

I nod when Joe looks to me for confirmation.

"Gerard was just by for a stop-in," Joe says, and gives me a meaningful look. He's suggesting I don't force my father to understand what he's done, how he's shown up here in his nightclothes without even realizing it.

I nod. "Of course, he has. Just like always."

"I was going to ring your Ma. Should I go ahead and do that now?"

"Appreciate that." I get the sense he's been stationed at the bar with my father all this time, wanting to make sure he was okay. "Thanks a million, Joe."

The bartender nods, places my still settling Guinness before me, and moves away. I watch him go, taking a deep breath as I try to release the anxiety I've felt since I answered my mother's call.

"So, you're in town, then?" Da asks.

"Eh, yeah." He's forgotten that I have been home from tour for quite a while. He's forgotten that I'd visited him and my mother not long ago. "We won't do any touring for a few months yet. Still trying to wrap up the latest album."

He nods and takes a drink off his pint. "Did you bring the babies with you?" he asks, suddenly looking past me as if I'd hidden them in one of the nooks of the pub.

"Not today. I'll bring them next time I visit you at the house. You'll be shocked by how quickly they're growing."

"They are sweet little angels, aren't they?"

"They sure adore you." I feel a flood of emotion threatening to overwhelm me as I think of the fact that my father may never really get to know my children. His fleeting memories will no doubt impact his ability to have a meaningful relationship with them.

I clear my throat and then down half my pint. "Listen, Da, our next tour will be shorter than the usual. I want to be home more these days, you know?"

"For the wee ones, no doubt."

"Well, it's all about family, isn't it?" I squeeze his shoulder and he smiles at me.

"Had enough of all that running around and chasing skirt, have you?"

I laugh. "Had plenty."

"Your Felicity is a keeper, isn't she, though? Your Ma and I always liked her."

That he's remembered her name makes me beam, but I stop short of complimenting him on the simple act. Instead, I agree with him, saying, "She's my one."

Da laughs. "Like the song goes," he says and whistles a bit of Rogue's biggest hit, "You're My One."

"Let's get on home now, yeah?"

After another drink of his Guinness, he nods. "Your mother will have tea ready, I'd think. You should stay. You must be hungry."

We get up and I help my father adjust his robe to brace against the chill outside. Of course, I'm not hungry for the dinner he's offering. But there's no need to get into explaining that to him, nor do I need to tell him that it's after midnight and that he'll be going straight to bed.

"This way, Da. I drove, so we'll be home before you know it."

"Oh, I always like driving in your sports car," he says with glee.

I laugh. "It's your lucky day, then."

28

Conor

I've slept hard and without dreaming. I've also slept, once again, far later than I should have. The bedside clock tells me it's almost eleven. The routine I had long established of rising no later than eight in the morning to work out—regardless of how late I was out the night before—has fallen by the wayside.

When I came home last night, Felicity was waiting up for me. I knew we needed to talk, but I didn't have the energy. I slumped down on the sofa next to her and was grateful that instead of pushing things, she simply pulled me into her arms and held me tight. We'd fallen asleep that way until Ella woke us. Felicity had pushed me toward our bedroom while she'd gone to the babies' room.

I know I should get up. Not only should I be checking in with Felicity and the kids, but the studio awaits. Yet, I don't move a muscle. Instead, I stare up at the ceiling and picture my mother's face last night when I brought my father home. The anguish she'd been feeling was slow to depart, but finally her relief won out and then turned into gratitude. She'd hugged Da and he'd joked about her getting frisky with him.

I've never seen my mother look so vulnerable. She's always been a figure of strength. She was the one to set boundaries and discipline me, but it was always with the aim of getting the best out of me, of making sure I lived up to the potential she saw in me. So, to see her so fearful was a blow. But more than that, it brought home the fact that she's getting on in years. They both are. And they are at the point where I will have to step up and be the one to take care of them. That shift—as inevitable as it may be—is tough.

Add my concerns for Felicity into the mix, and I've got my hands full. I can only hope that talking with her about my father will help and that it doesn't instead add to her own worries.

There's no other choice in the matter now. I've kept all this from her long enough.

I'm careful to put on some clothes before going downstairs. Lizzy doesn't come on Sundays, but I wouldn't be surprised if Felicity had called her in to help since she'll likely want to have the freedom to speak with me.

Lizzy doesn't appear to be here, however. I find Felicity in the kitchen with Ella strapped to her chest in a sling and Romeo in a high chair at the center island. Kodaline is playing on the remote speaker sitting on the counter and she is humming along as she loads carrots into the blender.

"Morning," I say, and she turns to me.

"Good morning." She leans over and kisses me quickly before starting up the whir of the blender.

I give Ella a gentle kiss, not wanting to wake her and surprised that the noise hasn't disturbed her. When I go to Romeo next, I'm rewarded with the sweetest smile ever created.

"What are you up to here?" I ask once Felicity has finished with the blender.

"I am making carrot puree for Romeo. It just needs to cool down a bit now." She glides over and offers Romeo Cheerios to gum.

"Homemade baby food, huh?"

"Yep. I figured I'd start off easy and see what else I can add in. Tea or coffee for you?"

I hesitate, thrown by her supermom routine. "Tea. But I can get it."

"It's no bother," she says quickly and gets to work preparing it.

I join Romeo at the island and we have a conversation in gibberish for a few minutes.

"Here you are," Felicity says, setting a tea cup in front of me. She's already prepared it with the perfect amount of milk by the looks of it. "I'm making a bit of a fruit salad. Just give me another second."

I watch as she slices a banana to add to a bowl already full of blueberries, strawberries, and peaches. She brings it and a bowl of the carrot puree to the island and sits next to Romeo. Raising a spoonful of the carrots to her mouth, she tests it for heat by touching it to her lips. Satisfied that it's cool enough, she offers a bite to Romeo.

"Do you want some toast or something else?" she asks after Romeo's had several bites.

"No, I'm grand. Thanks."

I'm still struck dumb, watching Felicity expertly manage everything. Then Ella begins to stir. Felicity shushes and bounces her and the baby settles.

I sit back in my stool and try to think of how I should phrase my question delicately. Because, basically, what I want to ask is, *what the fuck is going on here?*

This is not my wife. *My* wife is not on top of things like making her own baby food while satisfying both children and catering to her husband. She's slapdash and barely got her head above water but still making it all work, despite how she tears herself down over it.

"So, I was thinking," she says before I can speak up, "it might be time to let Lizzy go again."

"What? Why?"

She eyes me with a playful smile. "Well, I do know you *appreciate* her, but I think I've got a handle on things."

"Fee, there's no need to push aside good help. And I know you're joking about thinking I have any interest in her like that."

Shrugging, she gives Romeo another bite, and then uses the spoon to wipe clean the bits at the corner of his mouth. "It's okay. I'm on solid ground now. You don't have to worry about me."

Ah, so that's it. She's *overcorrecting*, to use Amelia's diagnosis. She thinks that if she proves herself to be fully capable and without any need for help, it'll make my life easier. Because with my father declining, she doesn't want to add to *my* burden.

"Honey, this isn't helping."

She looks at me, confused.

"*This*. Whatever this is that you're doing. I don't need you to put on some act for me. You are fine just the way you are."

"I don't think you really believe that," she says quietly.

I raise my eyebrows in surprise. "Excuse me?"

Instead of answering me, she takes Romeo out of his high chair and places him into his walker where he immediately starts pushing buttons, causing high-pitched nursery rhymes to play. Then I watch as she carefully releases the straps on the sling and pulls Ella into her arms. She heads upstairs where I assume she will put Ella in her crib.

I wait impatiently for her to return to the kitchen. When she finally comes back, I expect to pick up right where we left off, to get an answer from her about why she doubted me when I said she was fine the way she is. But instead, she's mute, busying herself with gathering the spoon and bowl from Romeo's snack. I lose patience.

"Well?" I demand.

"How can I think you believe that when I wasn't someone you could talk to about what your father is going through? I wasn't *fine* enough to confide in."

Fuck. Here we go.

"You're one to talk."

"What does that mean?" She doesn't just drop the bowl and spoon into the sink, she does so with enough force to make an angry clatter. It's a clear indication of her frustration. But I'm a long way from finished with this issue.

"It means, *I'm* apparently not fit for you to speak with about your issues, am I? No, you've turned to a stranger for that."

"Amelia is not a stranger," she says, as if the thought is ridiculous.

I throw up my hands. "Okay, sure. That makes a lot of sense. The point is, though, that you haven't been able to talk to me. So, let's not pretend this isn't going both ways."

"The difference is that I haven't even been sure *what* I'm feeling. That's why it's hard to talk about. You always want cut and dried answers. And I can't give that to you. I just need to sort it out myself."

"I—"

"I know that lack of control drives you crazy. That was clear enough with the way you were trying to assert yourself with Amelia. That kind of pressure doesn't help me, so it's just better to leave you out of it."

The words have flown out of her mouth faster than she can control and she looks like she wants to retract them. But it's too late.

I nod. "Good to know."

"Wait—"

"No, really. It's good to know my place. Thanks for helping me to understand that. I'll stay out of your way, shall I?" I say and stand.

"Conor, I don't mean it in the way it sounded."

I laugh and it's a bitter sound, even to my own ears. "My father is okay, by the way." I've said it as a parting shot, ready to walk away, but she speaks and stops me.

"I know. I spoke to your mother this morning."

I turn back to her.

"She told me about his diagnosis," she continues. "She also told me she's worried about you."

"Me?" I ask with surprise. "Why is she worried about me?"

"Because you always bottle things up. You're always so busy being the strong one that you never let yourself feel—"

"That's bullshit."

"Conor, she's right. You always take things on by yourself. You never lean on me. You never share your thoughts and feelings with me."

"You don't know what I feel? You don't know that I'm *terrified* right now? You don't know that it fucking scares me that my father is going to deteriorate? That it scares me that I'll have to watch my mother experience that? Well, it does. And if you want me to share it all, you should know I also worry that, for all I know, I'll end up the same way as him down the line. Oh, and here's another fun thing— it's that I feel profound *sadness* over the fact that our children will never know him the way I have."

There are tears in her eyes as she watches me.

"Yeah, I was really supposed to share all that, huh?" I ask. "I was supposed to put that on you when you were having your own difficulties? Sorry, but I just didn't think that was the best way to help you."

"I can handle it—"

"Really? You can handle it? When? Like when you were cowering at my goddamn feet that night?"

That was a step too far and now I want to retract my words. But it's too late.

"Will you forever judge me by my worst moment?" she asks. "Is that it? Because, I'm sorry I'm not perfect."

"Fee—"

"I . . . *fell down*, for lack of a better description," she continues. "I had a *really* bad patch, I'll admit. But I'm only human. Can't you allow me that?"

"That's all I want from you. I don't want this nonsense idea of perfection you have. How can I convince you of this? You seem to relentlessly assign me these notions and it's just not true. I fucking *love* you. I think you're an amazing mother. I love our life. I love the family we've made. What will it take for you to believe that and stop pushing me away?"

The tears fall from her eyes and down her cheeks now. "You really won't walk away?" she asks in a whisper.

My heart cracks a bit at that. I can feel a tear in my chest as I see quite clearly the fears that have been stirred up in her. It's her father having walked out on her. It's her first husband having walked out on her. It's me not being as available as she needs.

"Oh, honey," I say softly. We had been standing with some distance between us, but now I close the gap, pulling her by the waist to me and sliding my fingers into her hair at the nape of her neck. I kiss her, pressing my lips to hers for a long moment, wanting her to feel in my touch what I'm going to say with words. Breaking away only slightly, I fix her in my gaze. "I *really* won't walk away. This is it. *You're* it for me. You're stuck with me." I take a deep breath, close my eyes for a second, and then look at her again. "Will you believe me?"

As an answer, she takes one of my hands and draws it to her lips, kissing my palm. It's tender and sweet, but I need more.

"Tell me, Fee. Tell me what I can do to convince you that no matter what happens, I'm staying." I think better of adding, *I won't be like those other men who disappointed you.*

"Just keep staying," she says. "And give me time to sort it all out."

"I can do both of those things. You know why?"

"Why?"

"Because I'd do anything for you."

She smiles and touches my cheek before raising herself on tiptoe, so she can kiss me. When she pulls away, she leans her forehead into my shoulder.

"I love you so much. I honestly do," she says.

I wrap an arm around her shoulders and press her to me. "We're going to be okay, honey. I promise you."

With a shaky inhalation of breath, she nods. And then she says something that further sets my mind at ease, because it indicates she's returning to herself.

"You were right before. It's ridiculous to make my own baby food when we can buy the same thing."

I laugh. "Definitely. I mean, let's be rational people, here."

I take comfort in the way she smiles up at me. Nothing has really been fixed. But we're on a better path.

29

_____

Felicity

Conor doesn't go to the studio today. Instead, we spend a quiet day at home with the babies, talking mostly about his father. He tells me stories I hadn't heard before, tells me about other concerns he has for the future, tells me this is part of why he's in favor of an abbreviated tour for the new album.

He also takes out an acoustic guitar, playing and singing for me the song he wrote about memory, the song about his father. It's both a beautiful tribute and melancholy exploration of loss. I understand why he felt compelled to write it and urge him to include it on the album, but he's not yet convinced it should be.

It's late in the afternoon when I get a call on my mobile. Before I can shield the screen, Conor sees who's calling.

"Your father?" he asks, surprised.

I haven't told him about my father's renewed interest in being a part of my life. Of wanting to be a part of Ella's life—but *not* Romeo's. He does know that we've had the odd communication over the years and that I usually hesitate to engage with him, so he doesn't find it unusual when I tell him I'm in no state to talk to him today and decline the call.

I don't know why I haven't told him about that upsetting call from my father. I know Conor would feel the same as I do: outraged. It occurs to me that I should see what Amelia makes of this. She's obviously got a keen insight into all that I've been going through.

When a tone sounds, I assume it's a voicemail notification, but a text shows instead. It's Amelia, as though her ears were burning. I smile before I'm able to absorb the words, and when I do, I feel all the emotion leave my face. She's canceling our coffee date for the next day.

"What is it?" Conor asks.

He must have seen my disappointment. I shake my head, trying to cast off the outsized reaction I feel. It feels like some kind of rejection, especially given the odd evening she spent here just the night before when Conor interrogated her.

"It's nothing," I say. "Just—Amelia has to cancel our plans for tomorrow. Something came up, I guess."

He watches me for a moment and it feels too much like he's assessing my response to this. I look away from him.

"It's fine. I'm sure I'll catch up with her another time."

"Sure, you will."

"I think I'll lie down, if you don't mind."

"No, of course not. I'll take the kids with me while I get a run in on the treadmill," he says.

I almost laugh. Not because I don't think this could work, but because of how easy it is for him to assume that it will. I seem to default into focusing on the hardships with the kids, thinking first and foremost of why something won't work or how difficult it will be. It means that even little things like taking the kids with me to the store seem like an insurmountable task. Whereas I start in negativity, he begins with the idea that everything is possible. This thought process has only ever dragged me down and I know I need to figure out a way to change it.

After he comes with me to the bedroom and changes into workout gear, he tucks me into bed and kisses me tenderly.

"Sleep well," he tells me. "I'll figure out bringing dinner in later. Maybe we can watch a movie, too?"

"Sweetheart," I protest, "I should be taking care of you right now." It's been an emotionally draining day, not to mention the night before when he had to hunt for his wayward father. He has to be exhausted, but yet again, he's either better at managing it or better at concealing it.

"We take care of each other," he says simply. "And this run will do me good. Now, get some rest."

Once alone, I curl up on my side and close my eyes. I try to relax, but thoughts of Amelia preoccupy me. I fear she's choosing to abandon our friendship, that my unanswered question to her last night about whether it was okay that we even be friends given how we met is to blame. Trying to talk myself out of getting too worked up, I reason that there's no need to be this emotionally invested in her. I enjoy her company, of course, but this isn't the end of the world. I should probably take this as a sign to tend to my friendship with Sophie. After all, she and I have so much in common, what with each of us having two kids and rockstar husbands.

I laugh out loud at myself, just as a tear escapes my eye and is absorbed by the pillowcase.

Waking an hour later, I feel better. Sleeping has cleared my mind of the intense emotions I was feeling about Amelia. That sense of abandonment is gone.

I grab my phone and see another text from Amelia. She says her conflict has been resolved and she hopes we can still meet tomorrow.

An involuntary smile spreads across my face.

30

Felicity

"Fancy a walk? We can take our order to go," I say when Amelia joins me at the donut shop the next day.

She looks back out the window. "It is a lovely day. Let's do it."

Once we have coffee and sweet treats in hand, we walk along Westland Row. I don't have any particular destination in mind. It just seemed a shame to miss out on the clear skies and sunshine.

"I'm so glad you were able to make it, after all," I say. "To be honest, I thought Conor might have scared you away from being friends with me." I laugh, but it comes out hollow. I'd rather allude to her possible skittishness as being Conor's fault than suggest that our possibly inappropriate friendship is to blame.

"Ah, no," she says dismissively. "He just seemed like he was looking for a debate."

"It's just—he's not usually like that. He's not a contrarian. It was out of character, so I'm glad he apologized the way he did."

"Really, don't think another minute about it."

I nod and smile, happy to have put this blip behind us. "So, how was the rest of your weekend? Get any more calls from your Phone Fella?"

"About that," she says. "I've been thinking that I probably should stop telling you about him."

"Why is that?"

We've come to the end of the street and we both naturally turn right.

"For confidentiality. It's not right that I share those details."

"Oh, come on. You can trust me. I'd never betray your confidence." The minute I say that, I realize that I have already done so by telling Conor. And it's clear by the side-eye glance she gives me that she suspects as much, though she's doesn't actually say so.

"At any rate, I still think it would be wise to hold off."

"If you think so," I say. "But I promise I won't say anything more than I already have to Conor about it."

She looks at me quickly, her long brown hair flying a bit at the sharp motion.

I try to give her a sheepish smile. "I'll be honest. I did mention you have this former client who seems to be holding a torch for you."

Her expression is hard to read, but her mind is clearly at work.

"I'm so sorry. He was teasing me about how I've confided so much in you, that you probably know these intimate things about him and so, I told him about that just to make him feel more comfortable. But it was only in those broad strokes. I mean, even if I did know more about the situation, I'd never say anything to him."

We keep walking but it's in silence now. I drink my coffee and wish I'd gotten an iced version. The sun feels warm on my face and makes my long sleeve blouse feel too heavy.

"How was the rest of your weekend?" Amelia asks at length and I nearly sigh at the way she's moving on.

"Well, it was . . . eventful," I say with a laugh.

As I launch into a rundown of all that happened after she left our home on Saturday night, we turn left onto Kildare and I realize we've been gravitating toward St. Stephen's Green, the city center public park. I keep talking as we stroll through the grounds, past the people lounging wherever they can soak up the sun. There are men with their shirts off, exposing blindingly white chests, and women with their trousers or skirts pulled up, their skin just as pale. This kind of clarity and warmth is so rare that Dubliners take advantage any time they can.

Amelia is sympathetic when I tell her about Conor's father, even suggesting she can refer us to an occupational therapist who would offer recommendations for how to prepare for the issues to come. Then, I tell her about the fight Conor and I had where we both accused the other of not communicating. She's encouraged by the way we got to some resolution, that I admitted to my fear that he would walk away and his promise that he wouldn't.

"And then," I say, "I got a phone call from my father."

She raises an eyebrow. "Was this the first time since he called that day and said he only considers Ella his family?"

"Yes."

"How did that conversation go?"

"I didn't answer."

"Did you ever tell Conor about that?"

"No. I know how he'd react."

"Angrily?"

"Yes."

She's quiet for a moment. "And you don't want to risk that."

"What do you mean?"

"Well, if you tell him your father is eager to be a part of your daughter's life but not your son's, he'll reject him out of hand. He won't stand for the discrimination."

"Right," I agree. "And neither will I."

"And so, why haven't you told him?"

"Because. Because . . ." I drift off, trying to sort it out and failing.

"He's your only living parent," Amelia offers. "Your only immediate family."

"Yes. So?"

"If you tell Conor about this, you will either have to completely cut off your father for good, or you'll have to go against your husband's wishes—maybe *your* own wishes—in order to create some kind of relationship with your father."

"But, why would I do that? Why would I give my father that chance? After everything he's done? Or *not* done by not being part of my life?"

"Why do you think?"

"I don't know. I honestly don't know what you're getting at."

She's quiet for a long moment and I fear she plans to keep me waiting forever. But finally, she says, "My guess would be that, imperfect as it may be, family is a very strong draw. Especially when you've just created your own."

"You're saying I'm willing to accept a relationship with my racist father simply because we're related, and I want some kind of family?"

"Felicity, only you really know the answer to that. I'm just suggesting that could be a possibility."

I look down, disturbed by this thought. The thing is, she's not wrong. Should I deny Ella her grandfather out of principle? Or should I give this a chance with the hope that he'll come around to understanding that Romeo is as much his grandchild as Ella is?

"There's no timetable for making your decision," Amelia says gently.

"And, what if," I start and then stop. I take a deep breath and try again. "What if I did choose to have a relationship with my father. What would I do about Conor?"

"We can work on that together, if you like."

"And what if I decide I don't want anything to do with my father?"

"Then we can work through that, too. There's no wrong decision."

This sounds so reassuring. So . . . *therapeutic.* I hear Conor's unanswered question from our dinner with Amelia in my head: *Do you ever treat friends?*

"So, I have a confession to make," Amelia says.

I look at her quickly, wondering if I've done that thing where I've spoken my thoughts out loud.

"It's about my ex-client."

Relieved that she's changing the subject of her own accord and not because of my absent musings, I say, "Oh. But you said you didn't want to talk about him."

"I . . . well, what you said is correct. You are my friend."

I nod eagerly, happy that we are returning to a give-and-take friendship and leaving behind the feeling that her advice during this walk was her being my therapist. "Yes, of course."

"Let's sit there," she says, pointing to a bench. It's the first one we've seen that hasn't been occupied. The park is crowded with locals and tourists alike.

Once seated, I wait impatiently for Amelia to tell me more, but she's obviously trying to find her wording.

"The thing is, he's a mutual friend," she starts.

I have absolutely no idea who she could be referring to. I can't think of anyone I know who would have been seeing her, let alone have fallen for her.

"He is the 'rough sort' as you mentioned," she continues. "But there's a lot more depth to him than that."

"Danny Boy?" I nearly shout, causing her to look around as if the people in the park will instantly recognize how absurd this is.

But then she gives the slightest nod of her head. And I'm floored.

31

Felicity

"Well, I actually call him Daniel," Amelia says, and looks away. "I think it suits him better."

I shake my head in wonder as I ponder the idea of Amelia with Danny Boy. I can't think of two more different people. Whereas Amelia is educated, thoughtful, and purposeful, Danny Boy is streetwise at best, inconsiderate, and rash. As far as I can tell, she's spent her life working to create a meaningful career. He's spent his life living from fix to fix. What could she possibly see in him?

"What? I mean, how? How did you—" I stammer.

"I know, it's a bit surprising," she says. "But, it's not as odd of a match as you might think. Not when you consider the man I got to know."

I nod dumbly.

"Anyway, I knew after our first session that I'd have to stray from the normal confines of talk therapy with him. He wasn't a typical client. He needed more provoking to understand his motives. So, I suppose it was with that decision of mine to treat him differently that led me to thinking of him differently, too."

Again, I nod. I'm not quite sure I follow what she means about treating him in a different manner, but whatever she did seems to have worked wonders. He's continued to maintain his sobriety, he shows up at the studio every day, and he hasn't pulled any kind of wild stunt in a long time. That last bit reminds me all too keenly of Conor's taunt at dinner the other night, when he said Danny Boy was single like Amelia.

"Conor knew Danny Boy was our connection?"

I can see her thinking, though I'm not sure why the answer requires this much contemplation. Finally, she says, "He seems to have figured it out."

I think of how I betrayed her confidence by telling Conor she had an ex-client who still called her. That was the reason for his odd reaction. He realized it was Danny Boy somehow, or wondered if it could be. Which was why he then went overboard with trying to get her reaction to the idea of setting them up.

"That means, he was being quite cute at dinner, wasn't he? With him suggesting Danny Boy could be someone you date?"

She shrugs. I seem to be more bothered by it than she does. In fact, she seems serene about the whole thing, perhaps enjoying the freedom of having told me this much. I realize my incredulity hasn't been the kindest reaction and that I should be a better friend than that. I should be taking the time to absorb what she's revealed and see what I might be able to do to help.

"What is it that draws you to him?" I ask.

"His humor. His humanity. His, underneath it all, decency. His striving to do better. To be better."

I smile. Those are wonderful attributes. She really has seen a side of him that I probably haven't taken the time to try to see. I feel a pang of sadness that she's denied herself a relationship with him.

"And what keeps you from being with him?"

Amelia takes a deep breath and smiles wearily on the exhale. "Well, there's the obvious, of course."

"You mean that you treated him and so it would be inappropriate, if not a career-threatening move? Oh, and also that he's a recovering addict? And that he goes on tour with a rock band and so will be gone for months at a time?"

"That about sums it up," she says with a shake of her head.

"And what's the not-so-obvious?"

She's quiet for a moment, thinking through what she will say next. "I worry that I will disturb his recovery. He's still creating routine. He's still understanding what's in his control. And to be honest, the last time he had a romantic relationship, it nearly derailed all the progress he had made."

My eyes widen at this last bit of information. I had no idea Danny Boy had any kind of romantic life.

"I couldn't bear to be the cause of him losing focus," Amelia continues.

"But, should you really take that on? Isn't all that his responsibility? His burden to bear?"

"It is. You're right." She pauses. "But, I still couldn't stand it if I, in any way, contributed to him struggling."

A chill runs through me as I realize how she's sacrificed her own chance at happiness to ensure his well being. It's a grand gesture that he will never really understand. And so romantic, really. It makes me sad for her. And for him. It also makes me want to rush to Conor, to have him hold me, so I can savor all I have.

32

Conor

I've told her about Daniel.

I shake my head at Amelia's text. What does this even mean? I really don't even care that she and Danny Boy have this weird thing going on. I mean, it does still make me wonder about her issues with professional boundaries and judgment. But my recognition of how much Felicity needs her has outweighed any of those concerns.

I'd gone after her during dinner at our house, wanting to get at just how she justifies this slippery line she seems to walk. She'd held her own, so I pushed it and asked whether she treated friends. Thank God Ella interrupted that because it gave me a chance upon my return to see Felicity's face when she thought Amelia was going to declare their friendship inappropriate and therefore off-limits. Felicity looked ready to slip right back into that defeated, helpless version of herself I found on that awful night when she was neglecting the babies.

I did a good job of changing the subject, even apologizing. But what I thought was settled, was disturbed once more when Amelia canceled their coffee date. Felicity had done a poor job of trying to hide how much this bothered her. After tucking her into bed, I'd taken the kids with me to the home gym, set Ella up on her playmat and Romeo in his door frame bouncer, and called Amelia.

I launched right into it when she answered, saying, "You need to text Felicity back and say you can make it to see her tomorrow, after all."

"This is inappropriate," she replied. "You are not in any position to tell me what to do."

I took a deep breath, knowing I needed to adjust my approach. "Listen, I apologized the other night and I meant it. I'm sorry I was pushing things. I just—I had found out from Danny Boy about him calling you and it made me rethink everything we were doing. But all that is meaningless in comparison to how much Felicity gets from your talks. She *needs* you."

"This has gotten to be a bit much," she said.

"No, it hasn't. You're doing good. You're helping her."

"But, Conor, we should tell her about this arrangement. It's only right."

"*No.*"

"If—"

"I thought you wanted her friendship? Don't you share things about yourself with her? It's not all one-sided, right?"

She sighed. "No, it's not all one-sided. And I do value her as a friend."

"See! It's like you said at the start. If you can impart some of your training as part of a friendship, then all the better. It's grand, Amelia. Just keep on with it."

There was some hesitation, but in the end, she finally agreed. She'd texted Felicity soon after and their coffee date was back on.

Now, they must have parted ways because I've gotten this odd text from Amelia. I'm at the studio, waiting for the lads to show up. I'd come early, anxious to make up for the lost time over the weekend. But now I'm sitting on a stool with my guitar in my lap and my phone in my hand, useless.

Then she sends a follow up text.

I told her he's how we're all connected.

I'm not sure where she's going with this, so I keep my reply short.
I see.

She continues on, texting: *I still don't want Daniel to know about all this, though.*

Won't say a word.

Thank you. Felicity and I had a good talk today. I'm glad we put the meeting back on.

I don't want to know more than the generalities about Felicity's meetings with Amelia. As long as I continue to see improvement, I'm happy. I send a text that I hope will put an end to our chat: *Grand. Cheers.*

And then Amelia further explains herself.

What I mean is, you were right. She has become a true friend. This is no longer an arrangement. I feel I'm only giving her the advice a girlfriend would.

There's something that feels off about this. My instincts tell me she's trying to convince herself she's not out of line, though I think we both know that isn't quite true. Still, I'll let her have her rationalizations. We all have them to some degree, don't we? Hers will ensure that Felicity has someone to lean on.

Glad to hear it. I mean it, but I'm also glad to be done with this chat. It feels too much like a violation of Felicity's privacy.

I see Roscoe before I see Danny Boy. The dog finds his way into the room where I am, sniffing and licking me like the old pals we are at this point. His wildly wagging tail is enough to get me to spend a minute scratching him behind the ears. Getting up, I place my guitar in its holder and Roscoe and I make our way out to the front of the studio. Danny Boy is there with Shay. They're bickering about something, but I don't register what, as I'm looking at Danny Boy differently now that I know he wasn't bullshitting me with his claim of having a connection with Amelia.

It occurs to me that Amelia is disregarding with Felicity the very thing that Danny Boy claims is his only impediment to a relationship with her: their previous history as client-therapist. So, why the two sets of rules? What makes her hold back in Danny Boy's case? I mean, besides the obvious of not wanting to get involved with an addict fuckup. Maybe it's just her way of letting him down easy. A lighter touch than rejecting him outright. It would be the prudent thing to do, especially after having made the mistake of getting too close to him when he was a patient.

"Aye, Con," Shay says with a nod.

"What's up, man? You guys good?"

"*I'm* good. Never can tell with this bastard," Shay says, punching his brother hard in the arm.

"Hey, fuck off with that," Danny Boy says with a groan. He rubs his arm vigorously.

Roscoe whimpers and we all look at him. He's leaning all of his weight against Danny Boy's leg. The dog is meaning it as a protective gesture, but all I see is that night when Felicity practically did the same thing to me. She wanted *my* protection and I wonder if I've really done anything to help. Has setting her up with Amelia been the right thing? Or am I just too deep in this thing, too hopeful, that I won't let up and recognize it for what it is: irresponsible.

"See that?" Danny Boy says with a sneer. "My Roscoe will bite your hand off if you go after me."

Shay tests the theory by offering his hand to the dog. Roscoe promptly licks him.

"Come on, boy!" Danny Boy says with a laugh. "It's just because he senses we're related. He's showing you pity."

"Of course, that's what it is," Shay says with a roll of his eyes.

Roscoe whimpers again, shifting on his haunches and making it clear his agitation is much more about needing to take a piss than protecting Danny Boy.

"All right, let's go, fella," Danny Boy says. He gives him a pat and then heads back outside.

I'm glad for the time with Shay. I hadn't ever planned on doing this, but now that I've got an opportunity, I feel I must go ahead and do it.

"So, listen, I don't know what Gav told you about Felicity needing someone to talk to?"

Shay had been doing some of his normal warm up stretches, pulling one arm behind his back with the other and stops now to give me his full attention.

"He didn't say much actually," he replies. "Just wanted to know Danny Boy's story with the therapist, if she seemed to know her stuff. Told him I wouldn't doubt it, not after seeing how Danny Boy's improved."

I nod. I should stop here. I should just be glad that she's making strides with Felicity. But I don't stop. "You ever meet her?"

"Eh, yeah, as it happens."

And then he tells me the story of how he and his brother got pulled into babysitting for Daisy when Gavin and Sophie were away, and their nanny got sick.

"Danny Boy ended up calling Ms. Patterson when he thought Daisy was sick, too," Shay says.

"Was Daisy sick?"

"Nah. I guess you could say he was being overly cautious by having her over. But it's more likely he used it as an excuse to see her."

"Because he's got something for her?"

Shay sighs. "It sure seemed so."

"And her? She return the sentiment?"

"Well," he says and tilts his head one way, then the other. "I dunno. Not that I could tell in what she said in that short time I saw her. But, you gotta figure her coming out in the middle of the night when he called is a pretty good sign that there was more going on for her side, too."

"You think it was these . . . *feelings* that ended the therapy?"

"He says it was because he reached his year of sobriety and felt he was good. But, I wouldn't be surprised if that other stuff played into it."

"He's managed pretty well since stopping the therapy, right?"

Shay nods. "Yeah, he's been doing great. Especially, though, I think, because of being with us. Having the studio stuff to focus on is a big deal."

"What'll happen when we're done with this? Tour won't happen for several months."

"Funny you say that because I was just talking with Jessica last night about having him come out to San Francisco to stay with us."

"To babysit him?"

"Well, more just to have him around. As much as I give him hassle, I like him being around."

I know Shay's had it rough with his brother over the years. He's spent more time cleaning up Danny Boy's messes than he ever did just being pals with him. I never thought I'd say it, but I'm happy Danny Boy is around, too. If only because he's given Shay some much needed peace.

"Is there some trouble with Felicity seeing Ms. Patterson?" Shay asks, taking me from my thoughts.

"Ah, no. I was just curious about what went on with Danny Boy and her. She and Fee are getting on well."

Shay eyes me for a minute. He's always been one to see beyond the surface level of things. It's a blessing and a pain in the arse, to be honest. But whatever he sees now must tell him to let it go because he starts stretching again.

Danny Boy and Roscoe return then and are soon followed by Martin and Gavin. We're days away from finishing the album. Time to put aside my lingering questions about Amelia. Time to focus.

33

_____

Felicity

Conor returns home at a little past eight o'clock, a welcome surprise since I assumed he'd be late. I'd been prepared, in fact, to wait up.

I greet him at the door with a lingering kiss that has him reaching for me when I abruptly pull away.

"Good to see you, honey," he breathes.

"I have a plan for us tonight," I tell him.

He grabs my backside and pulls me to him forcefully. "Can't wait."

"Not that. It involves a little outing." I nod to the side table where I've placed his motorbike helmet along with mine.

"What do you mean?"

"Lizzy's here. She's going to stay as long as needed. Tonight, you and I are free to do as we please."

He raises his eyebrows and smiles down at me. "You know what pleases me, don't you?"

I grab the lapel of his weathered leather jacket, pressing my body closer to his. As usual, he smells good. He has the ability to apply just the right amount of cologne so that it literally entices you into getting as close to him as you can in order to inhale his masculine aroma.

"I hope that's true," I tell him. I give him another kiss, and once again leave him wanting more. "Let's go out for a motorbike ride right now, though."

"Fuck," he murmurs, leaning into me. "Okay, okay. Yes. An evening ride sounds grand."

He checks in with the babies, changes into boots fit for riding, and grabs his motorbike jacket, before returning to where I'm waiting by the front door. I have a backpack filled with things to enjoy at our destination.

"Where shall we go?" he asks when we're standing before his bike.

"North."

"How far?"

"Let's go see Finn MacCool," I say, and he stares at me for a moment, thrown by this suggestion. Going that far will be a least an hour and a half, which is nothing to him. He loves long rides. But he knows I'm not the biggest motorbike fan, so for me to suggest this as what we do for our one night of freedom is unexpected, to say the least. "It will be fun," I tell him. After another moment, he smiles and tells me to hop on.

The earlier good weather has lasted, and the air still feels warm. I've got my arms wrapped tightly around Conor's waist as he confidently steers us onto the open road.

Though I don't love motorbikes, whenever I ride with Conor, I feel completely at ease. There's something about the way he handles the bike that dispenses with any worries I might have. I just know that with him, I'll be safe.

And so, we drive on, and the journey is smooth all the way until we get to Giant's Causeway, the World Heritage site consisting of forty thousand honeycomb patterned basalt columns. The hexagonal formations rising out of the sea and up against the cliffside were caused by volcanic eruptions, but legend has it that a giant named Finn MacCool lived there once upon a time. Not being a strong swimmer, he created the "steps" to aid in his journey across the water to challenge a giant in Scotland.

Being on motorbike helps us avoid the after-hours road barrier and we're soon parked and walking hand in hand on the stones as the summer sun finally sets. I've brought flashlights but the moon on the rise is full and there will be plenty of natural light for some time to come. We settle on what is known as The Giant's Boot—a lava formation which looks exactly like what its name suggests.

"Well, this is a treat," Conor says when I pull a bottle of wine and two plastic cups from my backpack. "What did I do to deserve being romanced like this, honey?"

"It's working, is it?" I ask with a laugh.

"The evening bike ride. This phenomenal location. The wine. All with my beautiful wife. Yeah, I'd say it's working."

I smile and reward him with a kiss. When I pull away, he gently touches my face and I freeze, locking eyes with him.

"Thank you, Fee," he says softly. "You're pretty good at making memories."

The last bit is something I've said to him before and we both know it. It takes me back to our early days when we were struggling to maintain the line between friendship and something more. But it also resonates with what he's been dealing with lately: his father's failing memory. The implication makes me tear up.

"Sweetheart," I say, "I will be the keeper of your memories. And you will be the keeper of mine. I promise you that."

I see a flash of emotion pass over his face before he can clear it. Before he can regain his legendary control. He looks out at the water. It's shimmering in the moonlight, a breathtaking sight. But I know that's not why he breathes in sharply at this moment. Without looking at me, he reaches for my hand and I give it to him.

We sit without speaking for some time, content to listen to the water splashing against the shore. Finally, he releases my hand and takes the bottle of wine, uncorking it and pouring us each a cup.

"What shall we toast to?" I ask.

He thinks for a moment. "To finding our way through, together."

I kiss him before tapping my cup against his and taking a drink of the pinot noir. I feel it slide down my throat in a warm trickle. I've brought bread, soft cheese, and a mix of nuts and dried fruit. I make a picnic of it as a late dinner. I still haven't regained my appetite, but the wine's immediate effect makes me realize I'd better eat something or risk getting quickly drunk.

"Jesus, I don't think I've been here since I was six or seven," he says.

"Did you come on a school trip like I did?" Though we were together in our upper grades at a co-ed school for girls and boys, our early years were segregated by gender.

"Ah, no. My parents took me. They were good about getting me out, exposing me to nature or museums."

I smile and take a sip of wine. "My Ma's idea of an outing was taking me to the shops to help her find a new frock for her latest man."

"You've been missing her lately, yeah?"

I watch as a wave crashes against the steps, sending a spray of water into the air dramatically. A gentle breeze brings with it the briny scent of the sea.

"I suppose so," I say. My mother has been on my mind ever since Ella was born. But not really at the forefront of my thoughts, more at the edges. Or at least, I haven't been able to really acknowledge her absence, not until now. Consciously doing so before, when I was barely hanging on, would have been too much to handle.

"I wish she were here, Fee," he says. "For you. For our babies."

"So do I."

"In a way, I'm sure she is, though. I hope you can feel her presence."

I think about that for a moment. Conor is more religious than I am and I envy him that. He takes comfort in the teachings of the church. But the certainty in his voice that my mother is with us still is strong enough to carry over to me. Closing my eyes, I picture her sitting in her front room on one of her awful plastic-covered sofas, a ciggie in one hand, and a smile on her face as she delights in watching our babies.

"I can," I say with a smile. "I do."

When he wraps his arm around my shoulders, I lean into him, enjoying the warmth and security of his embrace. We stay like that, quiet, for a while. I meditate on how well he's read me, how, even though he's spent all hours at the studio in these last months, he's still aware enough to see how the loss of my mother has affected me. He's incredibly special, and I know my mother would be delighted that we are together.

"See that moon right up there?" I ask.

"The big round one?"

I laugh. "That'd be the one."

"I do see it."

"Well, I can safely say that my Ma would be over it to have you as a son-in-law."

"Over the moon," he muses with a smile. He gives me a squeeze and kisses me on the temple. "More wine, honey?"

"Why not? I'm not driving."

"Not yet. Though, I would love for you to learn to drive a motorbike."

"Never gonna happen."

He raises his eyebrows skeptically. "I have great powers of persuasion, don't you know?"

"That's true," I concede. "But, we're parents now. We should be avoiding risky behavior, don't you think?"

"To a degree. Oh, talking of being cautious—I have a contractor coming to the house next week to look into putting in a covered pool. We'll make it childproof and all that."

"What?" I ask with an incredulous laugh. This is the first I've heard of such a plan.

"Well, I know how you've missed swimming. It's such a hassle to get over to the sports club. We have the land, so I thought, why not bring the pool to you?"

"Conor, are you serious?"

"I am, of course."

I take his face into my hands, cupping his cheeks so I can kiss him long and slow. That he would even think of something like this, let alone go through all the trouble that this kind of installation and construction will cause, is one of the most romantic things he's ever done for me.

"Thank you," I tell him, pulling away only slightly.

"I only want your happiness, Fee," he says, and I kiss him again.

We spend a good hour drinking and snacking as we chat idly and point out the sights around us. It's so nice to just be together, to be enjoying something that is just about us.

By this time, it's gotten cooler but still isn't cold—not with the scarfs I've brought and the wine warming us through.

The distinctive barking of seals rings out not far off from where we're sitting. With only the waves competing for sound, their cries are loud in the night.

Looking around, Conor smiles and then laughs. "This is incredible, honey. No one has ever done something like this for me."

"You deserve it."

"Do I? You really think so?"

I wince, thinking of the night I told him he was never there for me, that I had no one. I realize I never apologized for that.

"I do think so, Conor. I'm sorry about the things I've said. The way I've snapped and made accusations that had nothing to do with the truth. I . . . I've struggled. I've been struggling since I was pregnant, as you know," I say, and he nods. "But I never admitted how much harder everything felt for me once Ella was born. In fact, I didn't even *allow* myself to acknowledge the abject fear and self-recriminations I felt. I just forced myself to keep moving forward."

"Until you couldn't that one night," he says.

The image of that night is burned into my brain. It brings such shame and self-loathing. All I can do is nod.

"Why fear and self-recrimination?" he asks. "Where does that come from?"

"Well," I say with a lightness I do not feel, "Amelia pointed out that I have this ridiculous fear that I won't be enough. Not enough for you, not enough for the babies."

"Why would you think that?"

I shake my head and he says my name as a question, a gentle prod. "Because I wasn't enough for my father. I wasn't enough for Richard," I whisper.

"Oh, Fee."

He takes my hand and brings it to his warm lips, pressing a long kiss to my cool skin.

"Don't you know you're my whole world?" he asks. "You're more than I ever thought I could be lucky enough to have? And those babies, god you should see the way they react to you. Romeo's a mama's boy, no doubt about it. His eyes never leave you. And Ella, have you ever noticed the way she curls her finger around yours when you nurse? It's like she just wants to be as close as she can to you."

The words are sweet and comforting, but still manage to fall short. Because my insecurities are deeply ingrained, and I've only just recently begun to confront them. I tell him this because I want to be honest. I don't want to sit alone with those feelings any longer. I also tell him I will keep working on accepting not only the good things I have but that I have good things to give.

"I'm proud of you," he tells me. "You've come a long way. Thank you for sharing such difficult things with me."

It's this bit of praise that convinces me I need to tell him about my father. I finally delve into it and watch his expression change along the way. First, it's surprise when I say that I'd spoken to him the same day I had my bad episode. Then, it's anger when he blames my father for my troubles. That anger is only stoked when I tell him about my father explicitly stating he has no interest in a relationship with Romeo. Finally, it's confusion and dismay over the fact that I'm still undecided about what to do. I give him my arguments for and against the idea. Of course, he's against any contact at all going forward. He isn't moved when I remind him that my father is my only remaining parent.

"Fuck him," he snaps.

"I know. I know how you feel, because that's how I feel, too."

"So, what's to decide, then?"

"I just . . . I just want to consider things a little longer."

"You do this, and you're dividing your children into 'worthy' and 'less than.' And it's *not* okay."

"I knew you'd be upset," I say. "In fact, Amelia said the whole reason I've kept this from you is because of this. Because you knowing means I either have to reject my only family or reject you in some way by going ahead and having a relationship with him."

"I seem to be to blame for a lot of this—according to Amelia, that is."

"No, that's not true. It's just part of the big picture, part of the things I have to consider—"

"This so-called father walked out on you and your Ma. He rarely made time for you. He started a whole other family. But now that he's calling 'round, you're anxious to have him in your life?"

"You're right. You're right about it all," I say. "But Amelia says that family is a draw that's hard to deny."

"Jesus," he says with disgust. "He's not your family. Hasn't he made this clear over the years?"

"It's just that Amelia says that with me starting my own family, it's no wonder that I'm especially longing for that connection, and—"

"Fuck's sake," he groans, "I wish I'd never arranged for her to keep treating you."

My cheeks grow hot and the wine in my stomach burns. "What did you say?"

He stands and moves a few feet away.

"Conor, what did you mean?"

"Nothing. I just meant I wish I'd never set you up with her to begin with. Because I don't like her advice with this family thing, to be honest."

He's looking away from me. Because he's never been able to lie to me. He always said he was honest with me, whether that made him look like an arsehole or not.

"Look at me," I tell him.

There's a long moment before he finally turns to face me. He's trying to keep his face a neutral mask, but I can see the guilt in his eyes.

"You arranged for her to *keep* treating me. You're saying this friendship I thought I had is a lie? I've just been a client to her the whole time?"

He shakes his head slightly. But it's not a denial. It's resignation. He's been caught and doesn't know what to say.

I'm shocked. And saddened. And manipulated, by both the man I love, and the woman I had come to count on as a friend. I stare, glassy-eyed, at the small pools of moonlit water sitting in the concave tops of the stone steps all around us. I wish I hadn't helped finish that bottle of wine because I don't have the clarity I need for this moment. All I feel is devastation.

34

Conor

I want to rewind time. I want to be back in the moment not long ago when I was holding Felicity in my arms as we marveled at our luck of a cloudless, full moon night. When we took comfort in the heat of each other's bodies and simple company.

"Listen," I say, "I need to explain."

She stands, and I brace for some vitriol, some well-earned burst of anger. But instead, her shoulders slump in defeat.

"I want to go home," she says softly.

"That can wait. We need to talk. I need to tell you—"

"You've said plenty. You've admitted you've orchestrated something with her in order to deceive me. That's all I need to know."

"Fee, please. It wasn't even my idea at the start."

She doesn't hear me. She's turned away and is packing her bag. "I want to go home," she says again.

"I did go to her the day of your second appointment. I went to her because you said you didn't need her services. You said you were all better. And I . . . I couldn't *not* know what she thought of that. I had to know if I should worry about you."

Turning back to me, she says, "Why does it always have to be about you controlling things?"

Jesus, I wasn't trying to control—"

"That's exactly what you were doing. You should have let me sort it out. I'm an adult, not some child you need to mind."

"Honey, you have to understand how scared I was for you. I wanted to be sure you were going to be all right. That you'd be able to handle things after what happened that night. I couldn't risk you falling down again."

"You could have taken me at my word."

We lock eyes for a long moment. I struggle to hold back, but can't stop from saying, "Not when the babies could be at risk."

"I didn't hurt them!" she wails, suddenly wracked with sobs that are painful to watch.

"You didn't. And I know you wouldn't," I say as soothingly as I can. "But they weren't being cared for that night, Fee."

She covers her face with her hands and shakes her head. "It was just a moment. A bad moment." Her words are muffled by her hands. "But you're using it to define me."

"No. I told you that I think you're an amazing mother and I honestly believe that. I just wanted to take every precaution. For you. For the babies."

Dropping her hands from her face, she looks at me, pained. "Why didn't you talk to me, then?"

"You were so adamant that you were fine. You didn't want to examine it all. Not with me. You know that's the truth. You couldn't speak with me about what led up to that. I'm only just now finding out about your father."

"I won't be blamed for your manipulations. Your lies. What you did was inexcusable."

"I'm sorry, Fee. I didn't set out to deceive you. I went to Amelia with the simple request that she confirm what you told me—that you didn't *need* therapy. That you were well on your way to handling things. Then she said she wanted to use your coffee dates as a way to be sure you were okay. She suggested this arrangement because she said she liked you. She said as your friend she could also impart some therapy if she thought it would be helpful."

"Really?" she scoffs. "*She's* the one who just came up with this plan?

"Is it really so hard to believe? I mean, just look at her and Danny Boy. Look at how she's stepped out of line with him. She obviously has a very fluid sense of what's professionally appropriate."

She opens her mouth to speak but stops short. I can see her absorbing my argument. But then she shakes her head. "You're both to blame, then," she says. "I am not some plaything for you to toy with, Conor. You've *broken* my trust."

I reach out to her and try to pull her into my arms. I want to soothe her, to convince her with my embrace that all I ever wanted was to offer her the support I thought she needed. But she jerks away from me.

"I want to go home," she says one more time.

This time, I listen and give her what she wants. We go silently to the motorbike. Instead of wrapping her arms around my waist, she holds onto the chrome grip bars at her sides. It's the longest ride I've ever taken.

ONCE HOME, she drops her helmet listlessly to the ground and goes straight inside. I trail after her, waking Lizzy on the couch to tell her we're home, and seeing her to her car. She's sleepy but ready to be in her own bed and leaves quickly.

Going upstairs, I expect to find Felicity in our bedroom but she's not there. She's not in the en suite, either.

I go to Romeo and Ella's room and find her curled up on the love seat, her eyes closed. The babies are sleeping.

I don't know where we go from here. I don't know if Felicity will ever forgive me or if I've done the one thing she can use to justifiably push me away. All I know is that I'm not going to make it easy for her. I sit down on the floor, leaning up against the sofa where she's huddled.

35

Felicity

When I wake, my neck is stiff from the awkward angle I was curled into and Conor has his arm wrapped around my waist, his face pressed against the sofa. It's oddly quiet. The babies are still sleeping soundly.

Carefully, I ease Conor's arm away from me and crawl off of the sofa. I need to pump and throw out the alcohol-tainted milk. And I need to think.

The rhythmic noise of the machine doing its work to extract my milk lulls me into a near hypnotic state. It makes me incapable of truly thinking through what happened tonight. I'm left with the resounding feeling of betrayal, but I can't pick apart the pieces of it.

Once done, I climb into the shower and hope the hot water will help. It's three in the morning. I should be trying to sleep, but I don't want to disappear into that kind of relief. I want to examine what has happened and figure out what I'll do.

The water has done its trick and I feel revived as I pull my wet hair into a low knot at the nape of my neck and wrap myself into a thick terry cloth robe.

Conor is sitting on the side of the bed when I emerge from the bathroom, steam following me out.

"No," I tell him. "You need to give me some space."

"Can I just say something?"

"I don't—"

"I love you, Felicity. I love you with everything I've got. You may not believe that right now. But I hope you'll remember it soon." He takes a deep breath before continuing. "I fucked up by trying to be the one to fix you. It wasn't my place. I should have just been here. I should have been *here*." He pounds his chest with his fist for emphasis and I can almost feel his desperation in my own chest. "You're right, I like to be in control. And I've had none of that lately. Not with what happened to Christian, not with how you are faring, not with my father's condition, not with anything. I guess that affected my judgment. I second-guessed the whole thing a million times, but I didn't stop it. I saw how you reacted every time you visited with her. She seemed to be the key to your happiness, honey. I couldn't help, but *she* could. And that outweighed everything else. Because I just wanted you to be happy. I so wanted you to feel confident in your own skin again. I hope I haven't destroyed your progress. I hope I haven't destroyed us."

I see the tears in his eyes before he hangs his head. I've never seen him cry. Not when we got married, not when Christian committed suicide, not at the news of Romeo being placed with us, or at Ella's birth. Seeing him this way now, I realize how beaten down he's been. I hate to see him this way.

Going to him, I touch his face. Instead of looking up at me, he wraps his arms around my waist and buries himself into my robe, holding me tightly.

Though I stroke his hair, I say, "You can't expect it to be this easy. You can't expect that everything is okay now."

"I don't," he mumbles into me. "Just tell me we're not over."

The plea in his voice is heartbreaking. I drop to my knees, so he's forced to look at me. I smile weakly. "Dear boy," I whisper, "don't you know that I can be furious at you and still love you?"

Of course, he doesn't know that, I admonish myself. He's never had a long-term relationship before this.

"I'm sorry, Fee. I didn't want to hurt you," he says.

I nod. I know his motives were never malicious. I can't deny that, in his own clumsy way, he was trying to help. But I won't disregard the bigger picture of what his actions did. Of how shaken I feel.

"Give me time," I say and his face falls. He's ready to take this as me rejecting him. "Just, know that I love you. But that I need some space."

He sits up, pulling as far away from me as he can without getting up and leaving. I suppose it's his own self-protection move. He's bared his heart, pleaded his case. And now that I'm not ready to forgive and forget, he'll close up and decide it's better to rely on his usual cool and control. But that's all right with me. I've given him enough hand-holding through his mistake. Time for him to accept responsibility and live with the fact that he hurt me.

"Okay," he says and clears his throat. "I'll get up when the babies wake. You get some rest."

"You're sure?"

"Yes."

His voice is detached. He doesn't meet my eyes.

"Thanks for that."

Standing, he looks around the bedroom as if seeing it for the first time. Or maybe the last time. "I'm going to go downstairs," he says absently and walks out without another word.

A few minutes later, I hear him playing an acoustic guitar. That's where he will find some kind of peace.

I'm not sure where I'll find mine.

36

Despite all my worries, I sleep deeply and undisturbed for almost ten hours. Conor was good on his word to take care of the babies, but the freedom means I'm now overdue for a nursing.

When I go downstairs, though, I don't find my family anywhere. I check the whole house before texting Conor to ask where they are.

His reply surprises me. *At the park. Be back soon.*

He's taken our little ones to the park. I've never taken them to the park. Another failing, I think, shaking my head as I go to do the pumping routine once more.

With time on my own, I decide to go ahead and reach out to Amelia. I might as well rip the Band-Aid off the rest of this injury. She sounds light and airy when she answers and is quick to agree to meet me at our usual donut shop even though this isn't our regular day.

Though I've hurried, I find she's there when I arrive, saving a table. She's got a coffee for each of us and a donut in front of her. I don't usually like those overly sugary things, but the sight of it makes my stomach rumble and I ask to share it with her when I'm settled opposite her.

"Of course," she says. "It's a simple one today. Just chocolate with sea salt."

I take a bite and the thing practically dissolves in my mouth. The feeling is pleasant at first, then I'm overwhelmed by the sugar and regret my decision. I take a sip of coffee.

I'm stalling. I just don't know how to begin.

"Everything all right?" she asks.

I should have known she'd spot that I was off right away. She's had all kinds of insight into me, hasn't she?

"Well, not exactly," I reply. She offers me with a warm, compassionate gaze. It's the one that makes you feel like you can tell her anything. "Conor let slip the arrangement you two worked out. You know, the thing where you pretend to be my friend but are really giving me therapy?"

She had a piece of the donut ready to pop it into her mouth but has stopped in mid-air.

"As you might expect," I continue, "I'm furious. I'm hurt. I feel betrayed. By both of you. And I don't quite know what to do with all of those feelings."

"I feel like there's been some confusion," she says, her hand with the bit of donut slowly dropping to the table.

"Really? Conor seemed pretty clear on the fact that *you* proposed this arrangement."

"I just meant, I do consider you a friend—"

"Then do me the courtesy of not lying to me. Not at this moment."

She considers me, then her eyes drift to the window. I let her get lost in her thoughts, not entirely sure I want to go through with this confrontation. It would be so much easier to just walk out at this point. To simply let her know that she's ended our friendship with this deceit could be enough, couldn't it? I could walk away from this odd episode in my life and be done with it.

But I don't move, too invested in finding out what she thought she was doing.

Finally, she looks at me and asks, "Do you remember the state you were in when you came to my office that first day? You were overwhelmed by a half a dozen major issues, including possible post-partum depression."

"I remember it very well. It was the morning after one of the lowest points of my life. But it was just a *moment*. I was having a rough time because everything had built up on me. But you know I moved past it."

"I didn't know that for certain then, though. And a few days later, you declared you were perfectly well and no longer needed therapy. I *wanted* to believe that. But my experience told me I couldn't do so without knowing more. And then you offered an opportunity for me to do that by inviting me for coffee. I really did enjoy our time here that day." She gestures to the donut shop we're in. "And I really did believe it when I told Conor I thought this could work as a genuine friendship where I was also mindful to offer guidance where I could."

"That wasn't your decision to make, though. Don't you see?"

"Some people need less conventional therapy. That's *all* that was behind it. Trying to style some help into a different format. Into something you were comfortable with."

"Again, that should have been *my* choice. Not yours."

"Have I been any help to you in these last weeks?"

"That's not the point."

"I think it is."

"You really do have problems with professional boundaries, don't you?" I ask with a scoff. "Let me guess, this didn't start with me, did it? And it didn't even start with Danny Boy? You've probably been doing these sorts of things for quite a while."

"I'm only interested in being of help. To me, it's less about the formalities put in place than the results."

"You should have your license revoked."

"Do you really believe that? Am I a menace?"

I open my mouth to tell her she is exactly that, but I don't get the words out. Because, if I'm honest, I have to admit that she helped me immeasurably. But I'm still angry with how it all came about.

"Granted, I know this isn't ideal," she says. "Ideally, you would have agreed to this more unconventional approach. But I did treat you like a friend. I told you about my sister and my nephew. I told you about my parents' expectation of perfection in me and how difficult that was to deal with. I told you about Daniel. That was all real. I swear to you, my intentions were good."

"Everyone's intentions were so pure," I say snidely. "But it's not enough."

"I'm sorry, Felicity. I did suggest telling you at one point."

"But?"

"Conor was against it. He thought you needed me too much to disturb what we had already begun."

"And you were convinced by that?"

"That, and the fact that when I reflected on our conversations, I realized they were almost as much about me as they were about you."

"As a ruse, you mean? You told me things to lure me into thinking we were on equal footing. But it was only the pretense of sharing, right?"

"If you're suggesting I used my sister's past and all the other personal things I told you as some kind of shameless way to get you to confide in me in return, then *you* really didn't bother to know *me* at all."

"How am I to know what to think at this point? How am I to ever trust what you say?"

"I've only ever spoken to you about Daniel. Your counsel helped me."

"Helped you to do what? To keep from taking a chance in being with him? To keep the decision out of his hands for whether to make his own choices like you did with me?"

"What does that mean?"

"You said you won't have a relationship with him because you don't want to be the cause of him losing control of his sobriety. At first, I thought that was so romantic. That you were giving up a chance at possible happiness in order to ensure his well being. But I've come to realize it's just another way you are making all the decisions. Whether he screws up his sobriety would never be about you.

That's not in *your* control. No wonder you and Conor got on as thick as thieves. You're very alike in your insatiable need to control things."

This appears to resonate with her. Her eyes drop and shift back and forth as she absorbs the implications of what I've told her. I take no pleasure in this, especially when I see the devastation on her face as it all—finally—clicks with her. She only now, with *my* insight, understands the error of her actions. In the end, all the rule-bending, all the overstepping, all the misguided attempts to help, however well-intentioned, have meant she's not only harmed me, but sabotaged her own happiness.

I watch as she covers her mouth in dismay and tears rush to her eyes.

"Oh god, Felicity," she says in a whisper. "I am so very sorry. I am sorry for breaking your trust and manipulating you. I thought it was all for good. I thought I was helping a friend. But I can see I was abusing my position. It was wrong. I was wrong."

The acknowledgment and apology feels good. But it doesn't wash away all the debris of her betrayal. It doesn't make me feel any less hurt by the ways she and Conor conspired to "help" me. I keep returning to when she was at our home for dinner and how the subtext I felt was real. It makes me cringe to think of how they played things off, how clever they must have felt. And how dumb I was.

Standing, I shoulder my purse and look down at her.

"I hope you take the time to look at yourself," I tell her. I start to leave but need to say one more thing. "To answer your question earlier, yes, you did help me. But the ends do not justify the means."

She blinks slowly and nods.

Pushing the shop door open and heading out onto the street, I feel exhausted but lighter at the same time.

I feel like I've reclaimed a bit of myself.

I feel like me again.

And I won't let anything stop me from moving forward.

It's raining but I inhale deeply, feeling refreshed by it. It feels fitting—a way of starting fresh. My legs are strong and steady as I walk. I've got a good rhythm, one where I feel like I could walk all day. But I come to a halt when I glance at the storefronts on my right and see a travel agent with a gorgeous display in the window. They suggest sun-soaked European destinations like Italy, Spain, and France. But the photos of Portugal are what draws my eye. I've never been there. The mix of colorful buildings of towns and cities alike are charming. And the emerald ocean water along a Riviera-style coastline are breathtaking. It looks like a place where one could collect her thoughts.

37

Conor

"I'm fucking impressed with us," Gavin says.

We're standing side by side, each of us wearing our youngest child in wraps against our chests, while pushing our eldest child in swings.

I laugh, thinking of the sight we make. Two rockstars who can generate ear-splitting screams from rabid audiences have turned into park-going *dads*.

I'd gone downstairs the night before and did what I always do when things are troubling me—turned to music. Sometimes I play the piano, but most often it's the guitar. And that's what I did for hours. I pulled out one of my favorite acoustic guitars and played for almost two hours before Ella woke. I tended to her and then returned to the guitar. Playing has the extraordinary ability to either take me away from my thoughts or to focus them.

I stayed up the rest of the night, trying to figure out how I was going to save my marriage. No answers came to me, though, so I was glad when the kids were up. Lizzy had been given the day off since she stayed late the night before, so it was just me and the kids. I changed them, fed them, and played with them for a while, but the time dragged on as I waited for Felicity to get up. Too antsy to wait any longer, I called Gavin to say I couldn't make it to the studio until later in the day. When he asked what I was doing instead, I told him I needed to get out of the house and was going to take the kids to the park. He offered to meet me.

And so, here we are.

"Listen," Gavin says, "What's been going on?"

I glance at him and then give Romeo a gentle push. He's in one of those bucket seat swings, his chubby hands holding tight to the plastic-coated chains. It's not a casual question. Gavin has held his tongue for the most part, but he's astute enough to know I've been struggling with things.

"A whole lot of shite, is what," I reply, surprising myself. I don't tend to pour out my heart the way Gavin does. I don't look to vent or get advice. I keep things close to me, wanting that control. Which is exactly what Felicity says is at the root of our problems. I wanted to control her. Control her emotional state. When it was both never in my power and never my right to do so.

"Let's have it, then," Gavin says.

I shrug. But after a few silent seconds, I unleash, telling him all about my father first. He says all the right things and it feels good to share that burden. And then I tell him about Felicity and how I've mangled things.

At the end, Gavin laughs.

"What's funny?" I snap.

"It's just, Con, you have this thing where you lose sight of the big picture. It makes you a great fucking guitar player because you can focus in on it so well. But it makes you pretty shite at relationships."

"That's helpful, thanks."

"I get why you did it. I do. And I'm not above saying I wouldn't have done the same thing. You wanted to help her. You saw an opportunity, and you took it. But now you gotta face the fallout."

"What if the fallout is she's going to divorce me?"

"Nah," he says dismissively.

"No? What makes you so sure?"

"For fuck's sake, this is nothing compared to what I've survived."

"Yeah, well, you're a whole other story. There's nothing Sophie wouldn't forgive."

He thinks about that for a moment as the swings go back and forth. Daisy is reaching out and trying to catch Romeo's hand, but they miss over and over again.

"The only reason that might be true," he says, "is because we know how lucky we are to have ever found each other. To have ever had the love we have. You don't just give up on it and walk away."

I should have known better than to bring up Sophie. *Yes,* I want to say, *your love is epic, blah blah blah.*

"Felicity knows that feeling well, wouldn't you think?" he continues.

"How do you mean?"

"With her first husband having walked away. She knows better than most what a waste it is to give up like that."

"Lucky for me he did what he did."

"And lucky for you that she'll recognize the motive beneath what you did, Con. You'll see," he says sagely.

"I fucking hope you're right."

Before he can reply, Romeo gurgles and we both watch as a mix of milk and the morning's cereal comes shooting out of his mouth. It's projectile vomit that is, honestly, impressive.

"Well done, Romeo!" Gavin says with a grin.

I stop his swing and kneel in front of him, using the bib around his neck to wipe his mouth. "You all right? Swing got your belly upset?"

He rewards me with a smile and I have the sense that he's proud of himself.

And then he goes for round two, hitting me in the face with more vomit. I shield Ella, but the abrupt move wakes her, and she complains with cries loud enough to wake the dead. It's a miracle I can hear Gavin's laughter above her wailing.

"Fuck me," I mutter as Gavin lends me a tot-sized blanket to wipe myself.

38

Conor

I'm relieved Felicity is up and ready to receive us when we get home. She wrinkles her nose when she gets a whiff of us, though.

"You smell, em—"

"Romeo threw up all over me, so yes, I don't smell great," I say with a smile.

"Oh, goodness." She takes him from me. "How are you feeling, Romeo? All better now that you got that out?"

"I may have been pushing him a bit too high in the swing."

She laughs, and I want to pull her into my arms in gratitude at the sound. It feels like everything is back to normal. Like *we're* back to normal.

"You'd better clean up," she says

"I will."

Ella is asleep in her car seat. I take her into her room, so she can keep on with her nap. Then I head for a hot shower. Under the heat of the water, my spirits are fucking high as I scrub my face and vigorously brush my teeth on the off chance that Romeo tagged my mouth. I keep replaying Felicity's laugh in my head and realize I'm smiling my way through the shower. She was so herself, so . . . *not* angry at me. It was just a little cooling off that we needed, I realize. Now, we can move forward.

When I come out the bathroom, I find Felicity waiting for me on the side of the bed. I go to her, still dripping and lean down to kiss her, ready to turn this into a proper makeup session.

But she pulls away from me and looks off to the side. My heart sinks. And I'm confused. I thought we were on our way to moving on, but this is a step backwards.

"What is it?" I ask.

"You should get dressed."

She's still not looking at me and my heart aches at the implications.

"Tell me what's going on." I sit next to her on the bed.

"You should get dressed. I'll wait."

"Are you fucking kicking me out? Is that why I need to get dressed?"

"No," she says, and I breathe easier.

I step into our closet and dress quickly in clean jeans and a tee shirt. When I return, she's standing at the foot of the bed.

"Here's the thing. I told you last night that I need space and that's still true."

"Okay," I say warily.

"I'm going to take the babies and go away for a few days."

My heart stops beating. My chest feels like its caving in. I don't breathe or blink.

My wife is leaving me and taking the kids with her.

"I found a little rental in Porto."

"Porto?" I ask, unable to come up with anything more meaningful to say.

"In Portugal. It's a quick flight, but it'll make me feel like I have the space I need."

"You need to be away from me?"

"I need to be able to think, that's all. James says you're just about done with the album. You'll be able to focus on it with us away."

"I don't fucking care about the album. I need you and our children here with me. Otherwise, all of this is meaningless."

She reaches out and grabs my forearm, giving me a quick squeeze. "The babies and I will be there for two days. And then I want you to meet us."

"What for? So, you can make it official?"

"Make what official?"

"That you want to end this. End us."

"That's not what I'm saying. I just need a couple days, sweetheart. I just need two days where I can get my head together."

"So, go. Go and leave the kids here."

She shakes her head. "No, I need to have them with me. And I'm still nursing them. It's just two days. Then I want you to be with us."

"You're not making sense. You don't need to go to another fucking country to sort this out. I'll leave the house. Just stay here."

"Please," she whispers. "*Please*, just let me do this. I need this."

I watch her, trying to understand what is happening. All I see is a woman desperate to get away from me. A woman who is pleading with me to give her freedom. *From me.* I can't force her to stay. I can't make her want to be here.

"When do you leave?" I ask, defeated.

"As soon as I finish getting the kids things together. James arranged a private plane, so that will make the travel much easier."

"What do you need me to do?" My voice is dull. I just want to get this over with.

"You don't need you to do anything. I have a car service coming."

"You have it all sorted."

"I . . . I met with Amelia earlier. I had to speak with her about everything. And it felt good to do that. I walked away from her feeling more clarity than I have in a long time. That included this idea of a few days away."

I nod. I feel numb. I don't have any sense of what I should be doing. Finally, I take a deep breath and say, "I'll just go see the babies while you, eh, pack."

"Conor," she calls, and I turn back to her. "I'm not doing this to hurt you."

"I'm not hurt," I say.

I'm wrecked.

39

Felicity

The flight takes less than three hours, and the three of us are briskly chauffeured to our apartment in Foz do Douro, an historic area on the west coast of Porto. I had been in such a hurry to find a place for us to stay, wanting to move forward with this plan before I changed my mind, that I engaged a small rental without much research. That now means I'm surprised to find that rather than it being a private house, it is one of six rooms within a house converted to a bed and breakfast. Too anxious to get the kids settled, I decide to make the unexpected situation work.

Duarte, the middle-aged proprietor with a thick mane of dark hair and smiling eyes, greets us with a warm welcome, delighted to have us. I'm grateful for his offer to help with our bags and the double-stroller, as well as his assurances that he's already placed two cots in our room.

"It's so nice to have young ones staying," he says in good English. "You have the ground-floor double-bed room. It has a lovely little terrace—fenced, so it's safe for the children. You'll see that it offers some privacy, but you can also view out to the back garden where we serve all our communal meals as long as the weather is good."

"That sounds perfect," I tell him as I follow him down a short hallway. "Are you fully booked?"

"We are. Your room became available at the last minute. We get mostly college students, artists, and young couples here. Rarely do we have children, but as I say, I am happy to have yours."

I thank him once more when he unlocks the door to the room and shows us in. Though small, the room is clean and comfortable. The bed and cots take up most of the space, but beyond that, I can see through to the terrace Duarte mentioned. The back garden is flooded with sunlight and has a cluster of small tables with terra cotta colored umbrellas for dining. There are hanging lights strung overhead in a zig-zag pattern. It's charming.

"You can pull the shade down here," he says, and reaches overhead to indicate a roll-down privacy screen. "I'm afraid, though, that guests do tend to gather for meals and drinks. Nothing too loud, but it won't be completely quiet."

"That's fine." I haven't come here to engage with strangers, but I still like the idea of others being around.

"Is there anything I might get you?" he asks.

"I don't think so, Duarte. Thanks so much for your kindness."

"Oh! I know. I will bring a tub."

I look at him in confusion.

"For the babies," he explains. "There's only a shower. I will bring a tub so that you may bathe them."

"That's so thoughtful."

"My wife and I are lucky to have three grandchildren. We do not get to spend enough time with them, though." He says this wistfully as he looks at Ella and Romeo who are both sleeping in their car seats. "So, I gave you a map of the area when you came in, some suggestions of Michelin-star restaurants—but you can find many delicious traditional food options at Mercado da Foz, too. Whatever is your preference. Of course, a drink at sunset at one of the ocean-facing bars is hard to top."

"I appreciate all the suggestions. I think, for now, I'm just going to settle in."

He smiles and takes his leave.

Falling onto the bed, I curl up with a pillow. Duarte has left the terrace door open and I can feel the warmth and humidity of the afternoon, yet I'm shivering. Saying goodbye to Conor earlier runs on a loop in my head. The determined stoicism he showed was heartbreaking because I could tell quite clearly that he was torn to bits on the inside.

I meant what I said, I'm not doing this to hurt him. I just need space. Is two days too much to ask after all that has happened?

I suppose that two days *plus* taking the children out of country is a much more dramatic combination.

Rolling over, I reach into my purse and find my mobile phone. Though we agreed not to talk until he arrives here in two days, I have no concerns with texting him.

We've made it to our room. I think we'll take a rest, then go for a walk along the water.

He texts back right away, obviously waiting for this moment. **Thanks for letting me know.**

It's odd to communicate like this. It's so cold. I miss him. I want him here with us. I want to explore the area together and make new memories. I want to forget the way he lied to me and manipulated me with Amelia. But I can't.

THE BABIES WAKE me twenty minutes later. The short nap was enough. I've been getting almost too much sleep lately. Time to get back into a healthy routine.

Thankfully, Ella and Romeo haven't woken in tears. They're close enough on the floor in their car seats to reach out to each other. I lean over the side of the bed and watch them as they coo and squeal, using a language only they understand. They are the greatest blessings of my life. Being their mother has presented challenges I never thought I'd experience. It's made me doubt myself and fall down in unexpected ways. But that was never because of them. It was always because I was overwhelmed by a torrent of emotions that were exacerbated by postnatal hormones. I know a large part of it all was brought on by the fact that I don't have my mother any longer. Even though I was an only child, my mother was a natural at taking care of babies. She was the one the neighborhood mums consulted whenever they had a question about how to get their child to nap or sleep through the night or eat something other than chips. I smile, thinking of her easy way with any baby she'd come across. She had such an impressive ability to soothe them.

Once, when I asked her how she could manage to comfort a crying child so quickly, she said, "Because it's not mine."

"What does that mean?" I'd asked.

"When it's your own child, you can't help but live and die by every little thing. Your heart sings or crashes based on whether they are happy and content. You'll see that when you have your own," she'd said. "That nervous energy is bound to be picked up by the baby, making the soothing harder to come by. But when it's not your child, you are much freer. You don't transmit your worries the same way. So, I just do what I know *eventually* worked with you when you were only little."

I realize with this memory that my mother was the one thing I never really got into speaking about with Amelia. I imagine she would have pushed me to see that her absence had been having a profound effect on me, despite my denials. I even brushed it off when Conor suggested I was missing her especially now that we had the babies.

It's funny what the mind will do to itself. I wasn't ready to think about her, to think about the fact that she would never know my children, that I'd never have the chance to apologize for leaving and staying away, to say sorry for blaming her for so much. I went across the globe to get away from her, to find a life of my own, all because I wasn't strong enough to do that in her presence. That was another thing Conor had suggested—when we were only teenagers—that I could make my own life in Dublin, that I didn't need to leave. But I was too headstrong. Too invested in finding the easy out. A change of location meant I could move forward without looking back.

I laugh out loud and both babies look at me.

"Is that what I've just done now, sweethearts?" I ask softly. "Have I repeated the pattern of running away, but convinced myself this is the only way? Just because staying seems harder?"

Ella does her thing where she works herself up into a cry. It's her signal that she's hungry. I get out of bed and quickly pull diapers and wipes from the diaper bag. I'll change them both and then nurse. After that, we'll all go out for some fresh air. It's just what we need.

40

Felicity

From the apartment, I'm midway to the two destinations I had hoped to view. I don't mind the extra walking this will take. The afternoon is beautiful with clear skies and warm air. I push the double-stroller south along the esplanade toward Jardim do Passeio Alegre. Along the way, I keep to my side to give the joggers, cyclists, and skaters room to enjoy the wide path overlooking the Atlantic Ocean. Both Ella and Romeo are facing out in the stroller and seem to enjoy all the activity around us as much as I do.

When we get to the garden I was looking for, I'm overwhelmed by the romantic feel of it. It's a mix of raked dirt paths, enough trees to offer relief from the heat, sculptures, fountains, gazebos, plenty of benches for relaxing, and even a bandstand that is currently being setup to host a philharmonic concert.

It's the kind of place Conor would love because even though it's well planned, it also has untended trails that would be good for exploring.

I have a small, thin blanket and I spread it out on the grass in front of the bandstand. Taking Romeo out of the stroller first, I then put Ella next to him, both on their bellies. Romeo's already a pro at raising his head during tummy time but Ella is still strengthening the muscles she needs to be confident at this. As we listen to the musicians warm up their various instruments, creating an uncoordinated but enjoyable mix of sounds, I wonder what Conor is doing. He's likely in the studio. I want to call him, to tell him to hop on a plane as soon as he can so we can enjoy this together. But I wonder if his hurt has turned to anger. I realize this dramatic gesture of taking the kids and leaving may have been the wrong thing. I was always accusing him of wanting to walk away, but in the end, I'm the one who walked away.

A breeze sweeps by and I close my eyes and tilt my head back to enjoy it, taking in a deep breath.

The realization of what he and Amelia had done to basically trick me into treatment was devastating. Not only did I feel betrayed, but it made me feel like this inferior being that had to be managed and manipulated. And it all came about at precisely the moment when I felt like I was getting a sense of myself back. It threw everything into question and I couldn't chance falling down again. I needed to be free to think and be myself. I couldn't do that with Conor by my side, clearly wanting desperately to fix things all over again.

I watch as Romeo rolls himself over onto his back. He smiles at me and I squeeze his hand.

"Well done, baby boy," I tell him. He's been able to roll over for some time now. Ella has been working up the rocking motion to follow in her brother's footsteps but isn't quite there yet.

I've been trying to separate Conor's intentions from how his actions made me feel. I have no doubt he thought he was helping, that this was a relatively innocent way to get me the guidance and support I needed. But there were so many lies around it and that's a big part of what hurts. He lied by omission mostly when he *didn't* tell me he had gone to see Amelia, when he *didn't* tell me they had come up with this plan, when he *didn't* tell me he knew all about her and Danny Boy, when he *didn't* tell me he urged her to keep seeing me after that awkward dinner that almost drove her away.

The orchestra begins in earnest now, complete with a conductor in tuxedo tails up front. I look around and realize I'm surrounded by others also enjoying the free concert. Ella perks up as the music plays, raising her head high to try to see who is making the music. I pick her up and hold her to me so she can see better. Romeo moves back to his belly and then goes up onto all fours, rocking his body. He's been making this attempt at crawling for a while now, but the music seems to bring him new intensity.

"Look," I whisper to Ella. "Is he? Is he going to do it today?"

Romeo keeps up with the motion for another few seconds, and then he's off, crawling like he's been doing it for months.

"Oh my goodness!" I say with a laugh, thrilled.

And then I realize I'd better set off after him before he gets too far.

We don't stay long after that to listen to the orchestra. Though there's still daylight left—the sun won't set until almost nine o'clock —I want to take in more of the area. I push the stroller back toward where we started and once we are past the midway point, the water-front avenue becomes Avenida do Brasil and the wide-open space is populated with large houses, beaches with cabanas, and cafés. It feels like a resort, especially when I choose a restaurant and am seated at an outdoor table overlooking the water. Romeo gets a high chair and I hold Ella. I eat ravenously. The simple soup consisting of potato, shredded kale, and pieces of spicy Portuguese sausage is the comfort food I've needed to stoke my appetite.

I give Romeo bits of soft potato and bread while Ella nurses. As I sit there admiring the view, I realize the anxiety I've long felt in being able to care for these two has gone away. I had worked myself up from the start, so consumed by the worry that I wasn't capable of handling their needs that I made it a reality. It's like my mother said, my fears were transmitted to them and so we were all worked up into a state where it made every little thing more difficult than it needed to be.

My poor mother. She never got over the fact that my father

walked away from her. She spent her life assuming she had to conform to be whatever it was the man she was with wanted her to be. That desperation to please always ended up being too much and each new man would leave, too. She never felt comfortable in her own skin because of it. I wasn't kind in my assessment of her, judging her harshly, and figuring I had it all sorted. But I lost myself just as she had, first in my marriage to Richard where I became what he wanted, and then after the babies came along when I couldn't see who I was any longer. I lost the person I had reclaimed when I returned to Dublin. That was the person who boldly talked her way into a media position for one of the biggest bands in the world, and through hard work and determination managed to be successful at it. That person was the one who saw through Conor's games and refused to let him keep on with them at her expense. That person was the one who took a giant leap in being with the vagabond rock-star because she wanted to follow her heart above all else. That person went fearlessly into motherhood, first with adoption, and then with the most unexpected but joyfully received surprise pregnancy. That person isn't perfect, but she keeps fighting to get better and to move forward. I *like* that person.

It's time to reclaim her.

THE SUNSET I watch from the Pergola da Foz, an expansive structure reminiscent of a Grecian style with its columns and gentle arches, is spectacular. It's not just the beauty of the yellow orb lighting up the sparse clouds over the deep blue sea, but the sense of peace I feel. The kids are sleeping in their stroller beside me as I sit on a bench and watch the yellow sky morph into orange, then a rusty red, before fading to pink and violet. Before leaving this wonderful spot, I send Conor a text. It's a video of Romeo crawling. I write a note with it.

Can't wait for you to see this in person.

I don't get the immediate reply I expect and wonder if it's because he's angry that he wasn't with us for this milestone of Romeo's. Realizing I don't have the power to change things at the moment, I get up and start to retrace my steps.

BACK AT THE APARTMENT HOUSE, I'm struggling to get the stroller over the main door's raised threshold without waking the babies when Duarte intercepts me. He leans down and gently lifts the front wheels.

"Ah, they are *precioso*," he says in a whisper, smiling down at the babies. "Did you have a good outing?"

"We did," I say. And then, because I'm feeling happy and grateful for his company, I go on to tell him of our little adventure.

"That sounds wonderful," he says. "I'm so pleased you enjoyed yourself. I must apologize in advance, but some of the guests are gathered out back. We have a fire pit, some wine. We'd love to have you."

"Oh, I don't—"

"Just for a few minutes? I bet the children will sleep right through it. Please, I think you'll like these people."

This man has been so kind to me that I can't refuse his simple request. I agree, and he smiles and leads me to the back garden. He introduces me first to his wife, Isabel, who promptly coos over the babies and makes space for me and the stroller in the circle of chairs around the fire pit. Duarte then goes around and introduces me to the others, including Boris, a German university student and Johan, a young traveler from Switzerland. There's a woman artist from Spain named Carmen, as well as two young couples: Hannah and Bryce from America and Armand and Geoffrey from France.

I wave my hello and smile as Duarte introduces me as Felicity from Ireland.

"What brings you and your children to Porto?" Carmen asks.

"Just a quick holiday. It's such a beautiful city. Are you here for work?"

"I am," Carmen admits. "There are some very good art galleries here and I have a small sculpture exhibit that opens tomorrow."

"Congratulations," I tell her, and everyone raises a glass to her with well wishes. "I'd love to come by if you don't mind."

She shakes her head. "No, I'd love it. You all, of course, are invited."

In response to more questions from the group, she explains her artistic style and intent. I'm fascinated by the feminism inherent in her work and listening intently when my mobile chirps. Slipping it out of my bag, I try to view the incoming text without seeming too rude. It's Conor, finally responding.

I'm counting the minutes until I see you and the babies again, honey.

The smile that flashes across my face is so wide it hurts, but in the best way possible.

When I look up, I see Boris is watching me.

"Felicity," he says thoughtfully. "That means happiness, doesn't it?"

"Yes, I suppose it does."

"And are you, then?" Johan asks.

I glance over at my beautiful babies and think about the fact that my husband will be here soon. "I am," I say. I haven't always been, and I know I won't always be, but I've found a key to happiness. It's as simple as just giving myself permission to struggle, because, eventually, I know I'll succeed.

Talk flows easily among us, even when Romeo wakes wanting to nurse. They're a smart, cultured group and there's no topic that doesn't have everyone contributing. When Romeo is satisfied, I let Isabel hold him until he falls asleep. Ella soon wants her own late-night snack and the routine is repeated, this time with Geoffrey getting the honors of holding her.

When I later climb into bed, it's with the certainty that all that I went through, as painful as it was, has gotten me to the place I am now: wiser, more appreciative, and, yes, *happy*.

41

Conor

It's been twenty-four hours since Felicity left with the kids. Twenty-four hours of misery. I'm forcing my way through the minutes, spending all my time at the studio and doing what she said I'd do: focusing on the music. What else am I supposed to do? I'm so anxious I'm ready to crawl out of my skin. I feel like Danny Boy always looks, with his perpetually bouncing knee and inability to stop biting at his cuticles.

I was sure to tell Gavin that he doesn't know what the fuck he's talking about and that he should save his relationship advice going forward. He tried to talk with me about it, but I'm not interested in rehashing what could very well be the end of my marriage.

We're just tinkering at this point. The album, *The Point of No Return*, is done. It will not include the song I wrote about my father. Unlike Gavin, I don't invite attention into my personal life, and if that song were to be released, fans and media alike would tear it apart and want to know everything about the subject that drove me to sing and write the first song to appear on a Rogue album.

I did share it with my parents, though. Yesterday, after Felicity left, I had to get out of the house. It was suffocatingly silent without her and the babies. A visit with them was overdue, so I dropped in and got the same delighted reaction I always get from them. My father has been taking a regiment of drugs meant to help with his memory. It's not clear yet whether they'll help stave off the inevitable, but he was in a good way when I saw him.

My mother was pleasantly surprised when I agreed to stay for dinner. I'm ashamed to admit that my visits are never very long. I've always got something else to attend to. Or I did. Before I realized how quickly things slip away when you aren't paying attention. After dinner, we had coffee and biscuits in the sitting room and I mentioned that the album was just about done.

"And? Will it be another chart-topper?" my father asked.

"Who knows, Da. That's never a guarantee."

"I'm sure it will do just as well as the others," my mother said. "You've certainly put your time into it, haven't you?"

"Eh, yeah." I was put off by this comment. There was a tinge of recrimination to it.

"Just, you know," she continued, "every time we see you or hear from you, you've just been in the studio. And Felicity says the same thing about you, that you're very . . . dedicated."

"Ah, leave the boy alone," my father said with a laugh. "He's got to do that thing with the guitar that makes all the girls scream. It's only his job, lovey."

I laugh weakly, thinking of how absent I've been—not just to Felicity but to my parents. "So, I wrote a song that probably won't make it to the album, but would you want to hear it?" I suggested it so they might understand that even when I'm not with them, I'm thinking of them.

They both agreed, and I ran out to my car to grab the acoustic guitar I always keep there. In case of a guitar emergency such as this, of course.

My performance brought them both to tears, though my father did the male thing of trying to cover it up by blaming it on a sudden coughing fit.

"You all right, Da?" I asked, trying to hold back a smile. In what was only a brief moment, he met my eyes and I saw everything I've ever wanted from him: admiration, respect, love.

"I'll get a glass of water," my mother said and jumped up.

"That's no knickers-dropper," Da said when my mother was out of earshot. "But it's the best thing I've ever heard you do, Son."

"I appreciate that. I hope you don't mind that I'm not ready to release it—"

"Oh no, no. You do what you feel is right. I understand entirely."

My father's support for this song, for *me*, is almost enough to convince me to put it on the album. I'm here in the studio, so there's really no excuse not to get the final track recorded. Still, I've been hesitating, getting lost in my head.

"Having second thoughts? Or should I call it millionth thoughts?"

I'm startled from my reverie and turn to see Martin staring at me. He's been hassling me for over a week now about how I keep wanting to change bits here or there on the album. This is the first album where he's had a forceful impact. He's come into his own as a bass player and has ridden the wave of inspiration like the musician he finally realizes he is. After so many years of taking a backseat to Shay's direction, he's found his groove. He's clearly ready to launch this album into the world so he can see if his contribution has made a difference to our fans. I'm certain it will. A confident Martin Whelan is a very good thing for Rogue.

"No, not really," I say. "I mean, we could—"

"Con, it's ready," he says firmly. "You and Gav have done your magic. Shay and I have done ours. We made it all work together. It's done."

I nod and know he's right. But I also don't know what I'll do once we let the album from our grasp because it will be months before the tour starts. In between, we're all supposed to separate to do our own things before returning to Dublin to plan out the videos, media appearances, merchandising, and tour. What will I have during that brief down period? I honestly can't say whether I'll have my family— not the way I want them.

"Besides," Martin says and claps me on the back, "Sophie's been trying to arrange our celebratory dinner for days and days now but keeps having to put it off because you can't quite stop playing with the album. Take pity on her, if nothing else."

I laugh. "Yeah, I'll do it for her."

"And, I've got Lainey here. Wanted her to be part of the dinner. But if we push it off much longer, she'll have to go do her own work."

"Okay, okay. I'm going to do one more listen, then that'll be that."

"You know that Gav left? Shay and Danny Boy left? All the crew is gone, man," he says. "Go home to your wife and kids already."

He doesn't know that my wife and kids are a long way from home. But I put on my best smile and promise that I'll head out soon. I watch him go and then settle in at the soundboard. Just then, my mobile phone sounds and I grab it from my pocket, hoping to see that it's Felicity texting.

Disappointment fills me instead. It's Amelia. She wants to see if we can meet.

Fuck off, I want to write back.

She's the cause of all my problems right now. Why would I want to meet with her?

I shake my head and turn the music louder. The sound of my guitar in the song "Take It Out On Me" comes out of the speakers mounted in the corners of the small space. It's Gavin's song about his brother. It's him finally finding both compassion and a connection with the brother he had never seen eye to eye with until they met at their estranged mother's home late one night. It's brilliant. I try to get lost in it, but I feel compelled to read Amelia's text again. There was something in her wording I need to reexamine.

Can we meet? I'd like to talk. And I have something for Felicity.

What could she possibly have for Felicity? Why can't she give it to her herself? Probably because Felicity no longer wants anything to do with her.

Fuck. I realize I'm in a mood, ready for a fight. I text back.

Tell me where and when.

42

Conor

Thankfully, the café Amelia has chosen is not in one of the trendier areas, meaning I probably won't get overwhelmed by fans. It's quiet at this hour, filled mostly with would-be writers lit by the glow of their laptops and using the free Wi-Fi. They're all nursing a single cup of coffee that has likely long gone cold. Amelia is sitting at a corner table, watching me intently as I make my way toward her.

"I got you a coffee," she says, "but I don't know how you take it."

I take a seat opposite her, ignoring the coffee. "Listen, I'm not here for a social visit. I only came here to tell you you've fucked up my marriage."

She sits back in her chair and examines me. "How so?"

"Felicity. She's *gone*. Took the kids and flew off to fucking Portugal because she couldn't stand to be near me, not after what she knew about our little stunt."

"Is this really a separation? Or is she just taking a moment away, perhaps to get her thoughts in order?"

I squint at her. "You think you're so bloody clever."

It's quiet as she lets that hang in the air between us.

Finally, I admit, "Yes, that's exactly what she said it was. But for all I know, it's the end of us. Maybe she's using this time to convince herself to really walk away."

Taking a deep breath, she releases it with a noncommittal shrug. "I'm not going to try to analyze her—not anymore. I wanted to see you, so I could apologize. I've realized far too late that my willingness to skirt the rules of traditional therapy have created more harm than good. I never should have suggested what I did. I put you in a terrible position. Of course, you agreed to this. You only wanted to help your wife, the wife you told me you were terrified could be a danger to herself or your children. So, really, I understand your anger with me. You have every right to it."

This heartfelt mea culpa has taken the edge off my self-right-eousness. I hadn't expected her to so fully confess to these wrongdoings.

"Well," I say and hesitate. "I, eh, appreciate you saying all that."

She nods and we're quiet.

"But, you weren't alone in this," I admit. "I might have been easily convinced, but I also made sure you didn't bail either. So, as much as I'd like to pretend it isn't the case, I'm fully culpable in this thing."

Silence again settles between us. But it's not uncomfortable. I think we're both sitting with the idea that we've made the wrong choices, no matter our good intentions.

"When does she come back?"

"I'm going to her actually. She asked for two full days, so I'll meet her there day after tomorrow."

"She took the kids, you said?"

"Insisted upon it."

"That's a good sign, I'd think."

My eyebrows go up in surprise.

"Because she had been so overwhelmed by caring for them before, I mean," she says. "I'd think for her to take them and be all on her own is a good thing. I imagine it will very quickly prove to her that she's fully capable."

I nod. Despite everything, it feels odd that she knows so many intimate details about Felicity. It makes me want to level the playing field.

"What is it that's going on with you and Danny Boy?" I ask.

"There's nothing going on."

"No?"

"You know that he leaves me messages now and again?"

"Yes."

"That's all there is."

"I understand why you wouldn't give that guy a chance. I mean, his history? You know it all, I'm sure. He's bound to fuck up again. And when Danny Boy fucks up, it's *spectacular*. No, you're right to steer clear of him. He's a mess."

"He's not," she says in a rush. "He's not and it's unfair of you to judge him based on his past when he's working so very hard to make a different future."

Now I lean back in my chair and smile at her. I was goading her into this very thing, into admitting that she feels for Danny Boy.

Realizing what I've done, she smirks at me. "Now, look who's being clever."

"I can be. And I can fuck up, too. I've been lucky that I've gotten a lot of chances by the people I love. Danny Boy has come a long way in my estimation. He'd be fucking lucky to have you. But I do believe he should have the chance."

My words have a visible impact. She blinks back tears and looks away. "Well, I'm in no shape to attempt a relationship with anyone, let alone a former client."

"We all have our issues, don't we? Doesn't mean we should turn away the chance at love. At happiness."

I watch as she absorbs this for a minute.

"That's very kind of you to say," she says, looking at me. "Thank you, Conor."

I nod. There isn't much else to say.

"Well, I won't take any more of your time. But I hope you'll do me a favor?"

"What's that?" I ask.

She pulls an envelope from her purse. "I apologized to Felicity when I saw her last, but it wasn't everything I needed to say. I hope you'll give her this for me?"

I take the letter from her. "I will."

Standing, she looks down at me and smiles. "I saw a rare Ella concert vinyl on eBay. I can't afford it, but I thought of you. It was a show done in Belgium in the late fifties. I'm sure you can find it if you do a search."

I'm touched by her thoughtfulness. And I already know that I will search for the vinyl. I'll buy it and send it to her. Because even though this all got fucked up, she clearly was helpful to Felicity.

"Thanks, Amelia. You take care."

"And you."

As I watch her go, my mobile buzzes. My wish that it is Felicity reaching out comes true and I'm rewarded with a video she's texted of Romeo crawling. I smile and laugh, in love with how quickly he can move. I watch it five times before replying to the message with the truth. I cannot wait to see them all again.

43

Felicity

The next morning, the kids and I take our breakfast in the back garden with our new friends, chatting easily until we all disperse with our own plans.

Conor is due to arrive late tomorrow morning, so I have the day to myself. I don't do much different than the day before, as we take a long stroll, sit on a bench or in the park on the grass for spells, and explore the neighborhood around us, ducking into art galleries, stopping for lunch with another grand view of the ocean, and window shopping.

In the afternoon, we return to the apartment and I take a quick shower while the kids nap in their cots. I put on a simple short black dress that's open in the back, perfect for the humid weather, and apply a little makeup. We'll head to Carmen's show after a light dinner with Duarte and Isabel. It's funny that I feel so comfortable with this group. Then again, their simple kindness and openness has obviously combined to create the perfect environment to allow me to find the final piece of returning to myself. I already know I'll miss them.

· · ·

CARMEN'S ART show is a wild success, and I'm happy that I helped her sell out her collection by buying two pieces. She works with alabaster, a material usually associated with Greek or Roman classics, but her pieces are modern depictions of women. The ones I purchase resonate with me beyond simply trying to help a new friend. One is of a mother breastfeeding a baby. She looks exhausted but also at peace. When I saw it, I felt like I was looking into a mirror. The other piece is of a little girl holding her mother's hand. The mother is turned away, her face covered by her hair and the girl's expression is one of complete surrender, as if even with her mother not focusing on her, she will follow her anywhere.

I can't stay long, even with Carmen eager to help with the increasingly fussy babies. I congratulate her, and we stroll back to the apartment with our art treasures. The walk settles them and they're asleep by the time I join the group assembled in the back garden by the fire pit. Everyone is there except for Carmen, of course, and Boris who has been at the show since it began. We share a laugh over his obvious crush on her.

"How much longer are you staying, Felicity?" Johan asks.

"Just one more night after this."

I receive a chorus of playful boos for this. "The real world awaits, I'm afraid," I say with a smile.

"What do you do?" Hannah asks.

"I do a mix of media strategies."

"For a company there in Dublin?" Duarte asks.

"Yes, they're based there. But it's really a worldwide organization," I say coyly. "What about you all?" I ask the group. "How long are you staying and where will you go from here?"

I'm engrossed in listening to all their plans until I sense I'm being watched. I look up and realize he's been there, in my peripheral vision for some time. He's in the shadows of the doorway, but I can see his form and there's no mistaking him. He's six feet of calm, cool, and gorgeous. And he's almost a day early. But I don't care about that. I don't care that he's forced the issue and shown up before our agreed upon day. I'm too happy to see him.

I stand and feel the others all look at me with what I imagine is confusion. I don't look at them. My eyes are fixed on Conor as he strides confidently over to me, wraps one arm around my waist, pulls my body to his, slips his hand into the hair at the nape of my neck, and kisses me with a mixture of tenderness and passion that has me going up onto my toes to get more. I hear a couple of wolf whistles and then clapping from the group, and my smile breaks our kiss.

Conor leans his forehead against mine. "I missed you," he whispers.

"I missed you, too," I tell him.

"Forgive me."

It's a plea that comes from deep within him. I know he understands the damage he did. Now, it's my turn to let him know that it's not permanent.

"I forgive you, my love. I do. And I love you."

His whole body relaxes, and he kisses me several times in relief. I nearly dissolve with each kiss, wanting more and more.

Finally, I remember where we are, and I pull away. Looking around, I see the group's not even trying to hide that they're watching us. I laugh. Why should they? We've invaded their space with this public display.

"Everyone, I want you to meet my husband," I say. "This is Conor."

He looks around, as if it just dawned on him that there are others with us. But he quickly puts on his most charming smile and gives a little salute. "Good to meet you all."

"You look a lot like someone," Bryce says.

"It's *him*!" Hannah whispers.

"You're the guitarist from Rogue, yes?" Armand says.

"The *hot* guitarist," Geoffrey whispers.

"Not tonight," Conor says. "Tonight, I'm only Felicity's husband, and father to these babies."

The group reacts well to this subtle way of asking for some

measure of privacy, smiling and segueing into their own conversations.

Conor kneels in front of the stroller and greets Ella, who has woken at the sound of his voice. She greets him with an open-mouthed smile that is so pure and loving it brings tears to my eyes. There isn't an ounce of that old jealousy in me as I watch him pull her from the stroller and press her to his chest. All I think as I watch him is that we are a family. And I've never been happier—even when he wakes Romeo so that he can hold him too.

ONCE THE BABIES are fed and settled again, Duarte and Isabel convince us they're happy to watch them for us so we can go for a walk. They urge us to take all the time we need and I suspect they both see that this isn't an ordinary reunion, that Conor and I have things we need to talk about.

I lead him to the Promenade where the ocean shines under a waning full moon. He holds my hand tightly the whole walk, almost as if he's afraid I'll run away if he doesn't. There are still a lot of people milling about and stationed at the cafés and bars that face the view, but I only see him.

"This is lovely," he says.

"It's a fantastic place. I kept thinking of wanting to share it with you everywhere we went."

Pulling me closer to him, he looks down at me and asks, "Good surprise?"

"*Good* surprise," I tell him with a smile, remembering using that line when I showed up unexpectedly at the studio.

"I couldn't wait, Fee. I just wanted to be with you, to figure this thing out."

"I know. I'm sorry I went away. I realized after I'd gone how drastic that probably felt. But I have to say, it's been really good. I know what I want."

His eyes leave mine and his body tenses in anticipation.

"I want *you*," I tell him.

The look on his face as his eyes meet mine again is full of wonder and love and relief.

"I want our family," I continue. "I want all the messy bits and the hard bits and the bits that make my heart stop because I could just burst from the joy of it all. And I give up on the idea of perfection and what kind of mother I *should* be because whatever I am, it's going to be okay. I won't promise that I'll never fall down again, but I will promise to ask for help when I need it. And I will promise to trust in you. I just hope you can trust in me again."

"Of course, I can, honey. I *do*."

I know he's sincere. I know this is the fresh start I'd hoped for. Tears come to my eyes.

"What's this?" he asks and brushes his thumb over my cheek.

"Happy tears," I say with a laugh.

"God, I love you."

I pull him down to me for a kiss, whispering in return, "I love you, Conor."

"I HAVEN'T STAYED in a room this small in a whole lot of years," Conor says when we return to the apartment.

"It's cozy," I tease.

The room is lit only by the light of the half-opened bathroom door as we check on the kids in their cots. They don't stir. I walk around the bed toward the terrace so I can pull down the privacy shade. Before I can close the sliding door and turn around, I feel the heat of Conor's body behind me.

With one hand, he pulls my hair aside and presses his lips to my neck. With the other hand, he strokes the back of my bare thigh just under my dress. I can hear murmurs of conversation in the back garden, then a burst of laughter. Even though I know they can't see us, I close the door. Conor has a way of making it very hard for me to keep quiet when he touches me.

Instead of touching me, though, he gathers the hem of my dress in his hands and drags it slowly up the length of my body. I raise my arms to help him remove it entirely. Once he's let it fall to the ground, he grabs me firmly around my middle, holding me to him as he kisses me once more on my neck. His possessive embrace is everything I need. His strong arms make me feel like I've returned to my rightful place.

When he takes my breasts into his hands and gently toys with my nipples, I let my head fall back. He's still fully clothed but I can feel the hardness of him as he presses into me. Whereas he's capable of stretching out foreplay until we're both practically panting with need, I'm ready to cut to the chase tonight. I just want to feel the weight of his body on mine, to hold his defined biceps as he thrusts deep inside me, to watch his face go from intense desire to pure bliss as he finds his release.

Turning, I reach for his belt buckle, releasing the catch with ease. He pulls off his shirt and lets his jeans fall to the floor. In the dim light, I smile at the sight of him straining against his boxer briefs. That, combined with his cut abs, pecs, and obliques, has me pushing him down onto the bed and climbing on top of him, ready to flip the vision I had of him on top of me.

I raise myself up so that he can push off his boxer briefs, then pull my panties aside so I can guide him inside me.

"Take this off," he says, pulling at my bra.

I do as he asks while writhing against him.

"You're so fucking beautiful."

His voice is low, full of heat and desire. After months of dismissing such talk, I finally feel the way he sees me. I pull his hand up to my breast and he uses his other one to squeeze my ass, urging me along.

"You're going to make me come," I warn.

Sitting up, he holds me tight against him, kissing me deeply. Then he grabs my hips and tells me, "Come for me, honey."

I wrap my legs around him as the peak of my orgasm washes over me. I try in vain to stop the whimper of pleasure from crossing my lips. Before I can take a breath, he twists us so he's on top of me, pulling my knees up high as he rocks his hips against mine.

"I love you," I whisper and bite his ear. "I love you in me, fucking me, making me yours."

"You are mine," he grunts, getting closer.

"Always," I tell him. I kiss him but then pull away so that when he comes, I can watch his face. It's just the look I was after. He's completely satisfied. And I'm the one responsible for that. I laugh softly in relief.

He looks at me and brushes back my hair. "What?"

"You make me feel like I'm enough," I say softly.

"Oh, honey. You're so much more than that. 'Enough' is not a big enough word for what you are to me. You are absolutely everything."

I don't want to cry anymore. And I especially don't want to cry while he's still inside of me. But the tears threaten once again. "This is all I ever needed."

"What? A good fuck?" he asks with a smile.

I laugh. He's once again done what I needed by making light of things when my emotions threatened to overwhelm me.

"No, dirty boy," I say. "*This* is you. *This* is the babies. It's us."

He kisses me slowly, tenderly. And I know with certainty that whatever comes our way, we'll always figure it out together.

44

Felicity

I marvel at how Sophie has designed the perfect, family-friendly album wrap dinner party. She's engaged an event space that's large enough to have created three distinct areas. A kids play corner has a ball pit and gaming station for Martin's kids, a mini-maze made out of plush cushions that can also serve as a playpen, and individual teepees with each child's name monogrammed on it in case the night goes late enough that they want to lie down for a rest. Then there's a lounge area with comfortable sofas and chairs situated in front of a fully stocked bar. Finally, there's a large round dinner table decorated with dozens of small wooden boxes holding various succulents and chunky candles. As usual, she has thought of everything.

We've only been back home for two days. It was while still in Porto that Conor decided he would get the guys back into the studio upon his return so that he could make a final recording of the song he wrote for his father. He told me how emotionally his father had reacted to it and that the more he thought about it, the more he realized he needed to record it, even if it was only ever for himself.

It's only been a couple hours since he finalized the track. I still can't understand how Sophie pulled all this together so quickly, but I am glad, rather than threatened, by her wondrous abilities.

The rest of our time together in Portugal had been a healing experience. I showed Conor all the things I had wanted him to see with us the first time, and we talked every step of the way. I told him I had decided to tell my father I wouldn't play his game of "half-in" on being a part of my family. But that if he came around and recognized his mistakes, I'd feel compelled to give him the chance to right things. Conor understood and supported the idea. He confessed to having met with Amelia and gave me the letter she'd passed along. It was an honest self-assessment along the lines of what she had told Conor about being in the wrong. She apologized, asked for my forgiveness, said she'd miss my friendship, and also said she was reevaluating her career options, having shuttered her therapy business until she could decide what to do next. It was bittersweet, because while I appreciated her recognition of her errors in judgment, it also made me miss her as a friend. I was left wondering if there could ever be any way back to a friendship. Perhaps, we can start over one day.

The new album has been playing over the speakers positioned near the bar. Conor is by my side on one of the velvet sofas while Lizzy and Sophie's nanny are minding the kids. The title song, "The Point of No Return" starts and I see Conor instinctively look for and find Gavin standing by the dinner table with Sophie along with James and his wife. The two men exchange a look and a slight nod. It reminds me of when I saw them in the studio during the recording of this song.

"Do you remember what Gavin told you that day?" I ask. "When you guys finally got the song the way you wanted it and he hugged you afterward?"

Conor glances at me and I sense he's going to deny his memory of it, just as he did that day. But then he reconsiders, confiding in me. "He said, 'I might not have held on to my own life if it weren't for you. Thank you for saving me.'"

I can tell by the way he's retold this that it is verbatim, and I understand why the words would be burned into his memory. Conor was the first person to truly be there for Gavin, to be the one to absorb his hurt and anger over his mother leaving. He was by his side for so many years after that, up until the thing with Sophie. But it's clear with what Gavin told him after this song that their bond is once more unbreakable. I give Conor's hand a squeeze as thanks for telling me, and he seems grateful that I won't make him say anything more about it.

We're soon called to the dinner table and I find I'm sitting next to Danny Boy. Gavin is on his other side and they're arguing about whether they'd ever chance going up in one of Richard Branson's rockets as a space tourist.

"No fucking way," Gavin says.

"Why not, though? Wouldn't you want to see what it's all about up there?"

"That's what those lovely 4k videos are for. I don't have to be up there to see what it's like. Besides, I got kids here on earth, so that's where I want to be."

"It'd be fascinating, I think. Maybe I'll start saving my earnings for a trip."

"Daniel, listen to yourself."

"What?"

"First, at the rate you make, you'll be eighty before you have the down payment," Gavin says, and Danny Boy laughs. "And second, they'd never let Roscoe go, so what would you do about that?"

"They will if I pay 'em enough."

"Again, remember you may be part of our gang here, but we haven't cut you in on the money side of things."

"Yeah yeah," Danny Boy mutters, but he's grinning.

I can see how much he loves being a part of this group. It's nice that he's not only included, but fully invested in return. I notice how he's changed over the last eighteen months. Being sober has seen him put on some needed weight, but he's still fit. His skin looks smooth and hydrated, a far cry from the blotchiness he used to have. He's quick with a smile, and even his usual jittery nature has dulled.

"Stop staring, already," he tells me.

"Oh, sorry. Was just thinking."

"About what? Finding a toilet to go off to with your man?" He laughs, delighted with bringing up that incident from the studio.

"No. At least not at the moment," I tell him with a laugh in return. "I was wondering why Gavin calls you Daniel?"

"I asked him to."

"Why?"

He shakes his head dismissively and I think he's going to change the subject. But then he says, "I don't mind that everyone calls me Danny Boy. It's just that I got to feeling a long way off from that person. Feels like a lifetime ago that I was him, you know?" He stares off for a minute. "Anyway, a . . . friend suggested I think of myself as Daniel to go along with how I've changed, and I took her advice. Felt right."

I know he's talking about Amelia, but I won't say anything. That's a promise I'll keep to her.

"Sounds like a smart friend," I tell him.

His expression changes as he thinks of her. There's a softening and the corners of his eyes reveal the smile he's trying to hold back. "She's so much more than that."

I let him get lost in his thoughts for her after that, feeling sad that he and Amelia have these feelings for each other, yet they're at an impasse, unable to really connect.

"Reminds me," he continues, "I owe her a phone call."

I try not to smile too broadly at this, but I like being on this side of things.

"Shay says you'll be going out to San Francisco to stay with him for a while?" I ask.

"Yeah, that's the plan. He's promised to take me and Roscoe sailing. My kid brother is a fucking sailor," he says with a shake of his head.

"Well, maybe you could invite your friend to visit you there? It is a great tourist destination. She might like to see the sights."

I just couldn't hold back from the gentle nudge. They'll have to sort the rest out for themselves.

Danny Boy's eyes go wide. "That's a great idea!" he says excitedly.

"I hope it works out."

"What have you done?" Conor asks into my ear from my other side.

I shake my head and look at him with my best innocent face. "Nothing really. It was just a little suggestion."

He wraps his arm around my shoulders and gives me a squeeze. "Have I told you how beautiful you look tonight?"

In fact, he has told me this several times, starting with when I put on the same simple black dress I was wearing when he arrived in Porto. He says he loved how I looked in it the moment he saw me stand in the back garden, lit by the overhead amber string lights and the glow of the fire pit. But I think what he loves is the association he has with it. It was me kissing him back without hesitation when he pulled me to him. After almost two days of imagining the worst, including that our marriage was over and that he'd only rarely get to see his kids, my kiss back to him in that moment, in that dress, soothed his tortured heart and he won't forget it. I'll gladly wear the dress for him any chance I get. But I'll also remind him that I'm not going anywhere without him ever again.

"Conor," I say, suddenly serious.

"Yeah?" There's wariness in his reply.

"The next time you tell me how attractive I am, I just might do something about it," I tell him and lean in to kiss him.

"Please do," he says in between more kisses. "For the rest of our lives."

I pull away enough to look him in the eye. "It's a promise."

And then he gives me that *Conor smile*. The one that is sexy and confident and *all for me*.

EPILOGUE

Amelia

"My dear Ms. Patterson," Daniel says to my voicemail. "I'd love for this call to be a proper conversation. I miss those with you. Anyway, I have news. Roscoe and I are going to San Francisco for a few months. Finally taking Shay up on his offer of having us out that way. So, anyway, I'm thinking I'll put an end to these calls. It's getting a bit pathetic, isn't it? Me blathering on in a recording to you." I can hear him take a deep breath. "You know what I'd love, though? I'd love for you to make your own visit to San Francisco. Make a trip out and we can be tourists together. Wouldn't that be something? I hear they're big on Irish Coffee there. I could take you for a real drink."

He pauses, then adds, "I'll text you Shay's address there, so you can come by anytime, yeah?" He laughs, but I can hear hope in his voice. "Be well, Ms. Patterson."

I've listened to that voicemail countless times since he left it almost a month ago. It brought tears to my eyes the first dozen times I heard it. Because it meant my fantasies that we'd somehow cross paths and then reconnect based on happenstance rather than any active effort on either of our parts would never happen. I've been too afraid to reach out to him. And too afraid that he'd try to reach out with more than phone calls. Afraid, because seeing him again would surely lead me to want to try some kind of relationship. There are far too many reasons why this is a terrible idea. And yet, it has never left the realm of possibilities in my mind.

I got the push I needed to finally take action when a couple weeks after my talk with Conor in that café, I received a package in the mail. I was at my office, packing things up. I'd decided to take a six-month hiatus in order to understand how I'd gotten off-track with my training. The closeness I allowed with Daniel was the first indication that I had allowed my judgment to be compromised. But the way I handled things with Felicity was just beyond the pale. My "good intentions" mattered little when I finally realized that bending the rules without the client's consent is a violation of trust. I wasn't sure what I would do, but I had enough savings to sort it out.

The quick knock on my office's outer door was the telltale sign of a delivery. Those guys never stick around, only drop the package and go. I picked up the box and took it into my inner office and sat in my usual chair. Inside was the Ella Fitzgerald vinyl I'd recommended to Conor. I touched the front of the cover gently and smiled at the unexpected gesture. The note with it was handwritten:

Music has always healed me when I needed it. I hope this does you some good.
Another thing—in us you've found yourself a group of imperfect, but good people.
You're welcome to join our club.
— Conor

The message struck so deeply, that I went straight from packing up the office to buying an airplane ticket to San Francisco.

And now my stomach is in knots as I sit in a taxi being driven from the airport to an area called the Marina District, toward Shay's house. I didn't call ahead. I just did what Daniel suggested and decided to show up. It's what he would do, I realize. Maybe that's why I'm so drawn to him, because he eschews norms and rules and I've long wanted that kind of freedom myself—though I haven't understood that until recently. If I analyzed myself half as well as I do others, I'd see that my lifelong attempt to be the perfect daughter has finally made me reach a breaking point. I've been eager to find a way to slough off the expectations and pressure I've felt for so many years. Closing my business and making a sudden trip to the States is such a crazy thing to do, I think to myself with a laugh.

The taxi driver glances at me in the rearview mirror and I wonder what he sees. I changed out of my comfortable travel clothes and into a red pencil skirt and casual white cotton top, mindful that Daniel always liked to look at my legs. I play with my gold necklaces, unable to stop my nerves.

"This is it," the driver says.

I look out the window and see a gorgeous three-story home that faces an expansive view of the Bay. It's a clear, sunny day and I still can't believe that I'm here. I force myself to go through the motions of paying my fare and retrieving my bag. But then I stand on the sidewalk for more than five minutes, trying to decide what on earth I'll say.

I was just in the neighborhood.

Too cute.

I couldn't stop missing you. This probably won't ever work, but I want to try.

Too much.

I'll take you up on that drink now.

Maybe . . .

Sighing, I turn toward the door and ring the bell, my heart pounding as I hear light footsteps coming toward me. When the door opens, it's a woman who eyes me curiously. She's striking, with a mix of African and Asian heritages. I assume this is Jessica, the woman Daniel had admitted to terrifying when he was strung out. He said he'd always hesitated to be around her after that, uncertain that she'd ever get over that encounter. It's a good sign that she's welcomed him into her home.

"Hi," I say. "My name is Amelia Patterson. I'm a friend of Daniel's."

"Um," she says, hesitating.

"Danny Boy," I clarify, realizing there aren't many people who call him Daniel.

"Oh, yes, of course. He's not in right now, though," she says.

"I see. Well, it was silly of me not to call ahead."

Jessica glances down at my roller bag. "He and Shay should be back soon. Why don't you come in?"

"Eh, only if it's no trouble. I don't want to put you off of whatever you were doing."

Opening the door wider, she gestures for me to come in. "No trouble at all. Oh, I'm Jessica, by the way."

"Good to meet you," I say and follow her upstairs after she closes the door.

The home is stunning, offering even better views from the upper floor, including the iconic Golden Gate Bridge.

Jessica takes my bag and stows it in a hall closet, before suggesting I sit at the kitchen island while she makes me tea.

"Did you just come from the airport? You must be exhausted," she says."I think my nerves are overriding any of that," I admit.

She smiles and it's clear she recognizes my unannounced appearance here for what it is: a grand romantic gesture.

I'm thankful she doesn't press the issue and instead starts setting out milk and sugar for a cup of tea, just the way we Irish like it. She's being a good hostess by automatically offering tea, though I would have preferred coffee. I wouldn't dare be so rude as to say so. When she sits with me, her tee shirt stretches across her belly, showcasing a revealing bump that I can't help but stare at with a smile.

She covers her belly with her hand and returns my smile. "We haven't told anyone yet," she says.

"I won't say a word," I promise. "But congratulations. How wonderful for you."

"It's very exciting, but I can't wait to share the news. My parents are going to be thrilled. And my brothers, too."

She's clearly eager to talk about this momentous life change, and I'm pleased to let her. It takes my mind off the nerves I have.

But then the door downstairs opens, and I can hear Daniel saying something about promising he'll give Roscoe a bath. Then he's getting closer as he ascends the stairs. My heartbeats are loud thuds and I feel my cheeks go red as I wait for him to see me.

When his eyes finally meet mine, he smiles so wide that I have no doubt about how he feels about my unexpected appearance. Then there's a glisten in his eyes as he says, "My dear Ms. Patterson."

"Daniel," I say in return, standing.

He rushes to me, enveloping me in a hug that overwhelms me at first. But just as quickly, I relax into his arms and savor the feel of his body against mine. As odd as it may seem, we just fit together.

Pulling away, he holds my face in his hand and examines me.

"You're really here?" he asks.

"I heard somewhere that they do a good Irish coffee here."

He laughs, his smile lingering as he takes me in. "I never dared to dream this, but in a way, it's all I ever hoped for."

"Hello, Amelia," Shay says.

It takes me a long second to tear my eyes away from Daniel. Shay is watching me. Not just watching me but assessing me. He's someone who can make you feel like he's examining your soul. I wonder what he sees in mine.

And then he leans in to give me a kiss on the cheek as a proper greeting. As he pulls away, he says, "Good to have you here. Stay as long as you like."

"Oh, I was planning on getting a hotel—"

"Whatever suits you is fine," he says. Then he turns and claps Daniel on the back, telling him, "Clean up your dog before you let him in the house." He takes Jessica's hand and they slip away, leaving us alone.

I look up at Daniel, see his unfiltered joy and know that my expression mirrors his. This leap I've taken by coming here is scary and exciting and I'm so glad I did it.

Still, I need him to know what he's getting into with me. "You should know," I say, "that I'm not all that you think I am. I've . . . I've made some mistakes and I'm trying to sort things."

"I've made plenty of mistakes," he says dismissively.

"I'm serious. I should probably never have come here, not when my life and career are so in flux."

"What did you do that was so wrong?"

"Well, for one, I crossed professional boundaries. Definitely with you and with another client."

He watches me for a moment, his face a mask of confusion. "My dear Ms. Patterson," he says, "I knew from the start that we weren't doing traditional therapy. That's why it fucking worked. Don't you ever second-guess what you did with me."

I'm thrown by this. "You . . . knew?"

"Of course, I did. I've seen all kinds of shrinks over the years. I know their game. You're the only one who has ever gotten through to me here." He points to his head. "And here." He points to his heart.

"Oh." I'm still surprised that he understood my process. I wonder if there wasn't a part of Felicity that saw it as well but went along with it anyway, knowing it was helping her. Not that that excuses my actions, however.

"You look beautiful," he says, looking me up and down. "Tell me you wore the skirt just for me."

I laugh. "I did."

"Sorry I'm so grubby. We went for this fantastic walk. I'll have to take you there. There are so many things I want to show you. And I bet Shay will take us out for a sail. That'll be amazing. You won't believe how fast the boat goes. Maybe we'll see dolphins as we go."

"Daniel," I say. "Slow down."

He laughs. "I can't. I can't stop thinking of all we'll do together. There's great neighborhoods we can explore, and some restaurants in Chinatown you'll die for, ridiculous 'Irish pubs', and hikes, and—"

I stop him with a kiss. I don't mind all the ideas he's conjured of what we'll do together. I just want, for now, to be in the moment.

And that moment includes the sudden and very pleasant rush of heat filling my body as he holds me to him and kisses me like I'm the girl he's been waiting for all his life. I surrender to the moment, to him. I feel dizzy when he pulls away.

He shakes his head, smiling. "Better than I even imagined it, Amelia."

Amelia. That's the shift we needed. Him calling me that makes me feel like we can really try this.

"Me too, Daniel," I say and when he laughs it's pure delight.

It makes me feel that, as imperfect as I am, as imperfect as the way this relationship has come about, it's still *good*.

ABOUT THE AUTHOR

Lara Ward Cosio is the author of the Rogue Series - books that feature complex, flawed, and ultimately redeemable rockers, and the women they love. When not writing, Lara can be found chasing her daughters around the house or at the beach, always with music on in the background.

If you enjoyed this novel, please share your thoughts in a review on Amazon or Goodreads

To learn more about the Rogue Series, visit:
LaraWardCosio.com

You can also subscribe to a mailing list to hear about the next installment in the Rogue Series here:
Sign Me Up

ALSO BY LARA WARD COSIO